RICK PARTLOW
DROP TROOPER BOOK FIFTEEN
DOWN RANGE

www.aethonbooks.com

DOWN RANGE
©2024 RICK PARTLOW

This book is protected under the copyright laws of the United States of America. No part of this publication may be reproduced, stored in a retrieval system, or transmitted, in any form or by any means, without the prior permission in writing of the publisher, nor be otherwise circulated in any form of binding or cover other than that in which it is published and without a similar condition including this condition being imposed on the subsequent purchaser. Any reproduction or unauthorized use of the material or artwork contained herein is prohibited without the express written permission of the authors.

Aethon Books supports the right to free expression and the value of copyright. The purpose of copyright is to encourage writers and artists to produce the creative works that enrich our culture.

The scanning, uploading, and distribution of this book without permission is a theft of the author's intellectual property. If you would like to use material from the book (other than for review purposes), please contact editor@aethonbooks.com. Thank you for your support of the author's rights.

Aethon Books
www.aethonbooks.com

Print and eBook formatting and design by Josh Hayes.

Published by Aethon Books LLC.

Aethon Books is not responsible for websites (or their content) that are not owned by the publisher.

This book is a work of fiction. Names, characters, places, and incidents are the product of the author's imagination or are used fictitiously. Any resemblance to actual events, locales, or persons, living or dead is coincidental.

All rights reserved.

ALSO IN THE SERIES

CONTACT FRONT
KINETIC STRIKE
DANGER CLOSE
DIRECT FIRE
HOME FRONT
FIRE BASE
SHOCK ACTION
RELEASE POINT
KILL BOX
DROP ZONE
TANGO DOWN
BLUE FORCE
WEAPONS FREE
COLLATERAL EFFECTS
DOWN RANGE
KILL CHAIN

RICK PARTLOW

Check out the entire series here! (Tap or scan)

[1]

"What the hell do you *mean* the Northwest Passage isn't there anymore?" Captain Victoria Sandoval demanded, putting her nose only millimeters from the babyish, hairless face of the man named Robert Chang.

She was enraged, but I was numb. We'd added years to our journey, thrown all our hopes into this place, this deserted outpost of the Predecessor civilization. It had been the last option we had, and I'd sacrificed almost everything to get my people home, including, perhaps, my own chance at returning. I'd been ready to stay on this side with Vicky, had been minutes away from sending the Marines and Space Fleet crew through the Northwest Passage back to the Commonwealth, when *he'd* arrived.

The ship was one of the smaller Predecessor vessels, not nearly as large as the one Lilandreth had been gifted by the Nova, the one I'd been forced to destroy—along with her—when she'd succumbed to the Voices and tried to kill us. Yet I sensed that, despite its size, it was newer and more advanced than hers had been. For a moment, when I'd seen it descending into the courtyard here on Homecoming, I'd been ready to believe it was the Predecessors returning, that somewhere, out there in deep space, they still existed. Until Robert Chang and his crew of Skingangers had emerged with the pronouncement that the Northwest Passage didn't exist anymore.

I would have been questioning the little man myself if I didn't already know he was telling the truth. That was the bad part...well, *one* of the bad parts about my new situation, the new configuration of my brain, that I couldn't indulge in comforting doubt anymore. I didn't have to guess anymore, I just *knew*.

I knew that the little man was telling the truth.

I knew that the Predecessor ship Chang and his crew of rough-looking cyborgs had arrived on a couple minutes ago had come from the other side of the Northwest Passage, back in the closed-off bubble of spacetime we knew as the Cluster. More closed off than I'd thought.

"It's very simple, Captain Sandoval, Captain Alvarez," Chang explained. "The Predecessors left a kill switch behind when they constructed the passage."

If he felt intimidated by Vicky's interrogation, he didn't show it. His cyborg bodyguards might have resented the liberties she was taking, or at least that was the read I got from the burning red gleam of their bionic oculars, but the Vigilante battlesuits and their yawning plasma gun muzzles discouraged them from acting on those feelings.

"The idea was," Chang went on with the patience of an elementary school teacher tutoring a particularly slow child, "that if the Skrela were about to get through into the Cluster, someone in the corridor system between the entrance and exit of the Northwest Passage could set off a gravito-inertial chain reaction that would shut it down. Skrela seed pods landed on the corridor world while we were there. My... companions stayed on the other side and shut down the corridor while my crew and I went on through."

"You're lying," I told him without hesitation, knowing it without knowing why.

Now the Skingangers did surge forward, the light of the noonday primary gleaming off their silvery metal limbs, but before the Marines surrounding them could make a move, I clamped down with my mind, fists clenching in sympathetic motion. A half dozen hulking mountains of amalgamated metal and flesh, each over a hundred kilos and capable of killing a man with their bare hands, froze as if they'd been caught in a net. The ones with biological eyes opened them wide, and metal teeth gnashed.

"If you'd like to move again," I told them, "*ever*, then you might want to relax and keep your hands by your sides."

"How are you doing this?" one of the cyborgs choked out through a jaw that was half metal. If I knew Skingangers, it was the most he'd spoken in months.

"That's my business," I told him. Then I relaxed the hold and all six of them stumbled backward. I turned my attention back to Robert Chang. The little man regarded me with a tinge of awe and not a little avarice.

"You're lying." I shrugged. "Or at least not telling the whole truth." I tilted my head as if I could get a better look at the truth by changing my point of view. His head was shaven, maybe even depilated, his eyes dark and unfathomable, and his clothes, while utilitarian, also had a personal flare to them, a dash of color that didn't look like something from a fabricator pattern, like he'd designed it himself. "If you'd had more time, you might have actually believed it yourself, and then I wouldn't be able to tell the difference. But it was too recent, and you know it wasn't completely true. So *I* know it too."

I hadn't had this power long, just a few hours now, yet the

intuition came as naturally as if I'd been born with it, liquid fire running through my veins, crying to get out, to be used. I wasn't physically glowing, but I might as well have been. The Skingangers stared at me in horror, and even Vicky wore an anxious frown as if she thought I was going to succumb to the Voices any second. Not Robert Chang though. He didn't step away, didn't grimace, didn't appear afraid at all. He grinned.

"Amazing. Yes, Captain Alvarez." Chang shrugged. "I didn't tell you the whole truth because it's not pertinent to our current situation. I manipulated my companions into helping me reach the passage and... it might not be putting too fine a point on it to say I deceived and betrayed them. I can only plead insanity."

"Yes, I'll bet you do." He wasn't lying. He knew better now. "Why did you manipulate your friends into closing off the passage?"

"Because I didn't want anyone following me." Chang spread his arms expansively, as if to embrace the vast, inhumanly curved and twisted expanses of the city, the entire planet that the Resscharr had called Homecoming.

"I wanted all this to be mine. Yes, insanely selfish, but we've already established the insane part. I mean, look at this place." He turned around like a ballerina executing a plie, arms still extended, eyes glinting as he gazed out at the endless city. "It's exquisitely beautiful in its own way. The final work of a master... of a whole *species* of masters. Just think about it, Captain Alvarez. The crumbs the Predecessors left behind in the Cluster, barely a hint of their true nature, were enough to spark a religion to grow up around them, one that millions of humans would—and *have*—killed for. Imagine what people would do with all *this*. Imagine the chaos and the greed and the wars that would be fought over an entire galaxy strewn with the ruins of the Predecessor civilization. No, my motives might have been selfish, but there was a solid logic behind them as well."

Chang circled around me, his grin thinning out, a knowing tilt to his head, and for all that he was surrounded by dozens of massive, armored Drop Troopers and faced by the unknown power I'd demonstrated, I could have sworn the little man thought he was in control of the situation.

"But you know all about how dangerous it could be, don't you?" The words were almost a taunt. "Those abilities you've been showing me, they weren't something you picked up back home. No, as solipsistic as I admittedly am, I didn't want to be the one to release all that back into the heart of the Commonwealth. It's better that we humans remain where we're relatively safe."

"How fucking noble of you," Vicky snapped. "Except for the fact that all these people..." she gestured around at the rest of the Marines gathered in the courtyard between the Predecessor structures, "... want to go home. And you just confessed to being the reason they're stuck here now."

Chang made a dismissive gesture.

"I can hardly be blamed for sabotaging your escape when I had no way of knowing you were here in the first place."

"Enough," I decided. "Springfield, get over here."

A Vigilante tromped across the courtyard, coming to attention beside me as if Lt. Springfield was reporting to my office for duty.

"Yes, sir?" Her voice came over the suit's external speakers, maybe because neither Vicky nor I was in armor ourselves.

"Take charge of these..." I hesitated to call them *gentlemen*, because I couldn't tell if the Skingangers had started out as males or females, "... fine, upstanding citizens of the Commonwealth and confine them in one of the drop-ships while we discuss this matter privately."

"There's no need for that," Chang insisted, raising his hands in a quelling gesture as Springfield took a step toward him. "We're not here to interfere with your business. Just let us go and we'll be on our way."

"Yeah, I'm sure you would be," I agreed. "But where would *we* be on our way to? Just relax. This won't take long."

Because, God knew, I didn't *have* that long.

[2]

Captain Rafael Nance squinted at the afternoon glare of Homecoming's primary star, a man unused to unshielded, unfiltered daylight. I could count on one hand the number of times the captain of the *Orion* had been off the ship and down on a planet in the last year, and I didn't need to be psychic to know he wasn't crazy about being off the bridge now.

"Couldn't we have had this conversation via the comms?" Nance grumbled. "I'm getting a sunburn already, I can feel it."

"How the hell are you gonna get a sunburn through that thicket you've been growing?" Vicky asked, nodding at his scraggly, gray-shot beard.

Nance reminded me of paintings of sea captains from the age of sail, with his wiry beard and craggy face, an image he'd cultivated since Colonel Hachette had died and the whole mission had drifted farther and farther from the military discipline as it had become clear we weren't going to be getting home anytime soon.

One of the flight crew from Nance's lander had set up a ring of folding chairs for the gathered officers, a half a dozen of us gathered in a circle at the center of the courtyard, surrounded by spaceships and the otherworldly architecture of the Predecessors. The picture that painted was as absurd as our situation, and I barely restrained a laugh.

"Can we get down to business?" Commander Chuck Brandano wondered, his patrician features drawn into a deep scowl. "I thought we came here to get home." His glare at me was accusatory. "You told us this was our last hope. Now you're saying we can't get out this way."

"*I'm* not saying it," I reminded him, then waved at the dropship a half a klick away, squatting in utilitarian ugliness at the edge of the flat pavement. "Chang is saying it." I shrugged diffidently. "I *can* confirm it though, now that I know the questions to ask. The Northwest Passage is closed off to us."

"You've got that... power, though, right?" Captain Emily Nagarro asked, her tone cautious, eyes narrowed as she stared at me like I was some kind of carnival sideshow. "Can't you... reopen it?"

Not attempting to hide a frustrated sigh, I ran a hand through my hair and purposefully didn't meet the Fleet Intelligence officer's dark eyes. I needed to get a haircut again.

"I'm not a fucking genie," I told her. "To cut off a Transition Line, the Predecessors had to use *black holes* to screw with the gravito-inertial pathways between the stars. But..." I clamped down on the words, not ready to share them but knowing they had the right to know the truth, "but there *is* something I could do."

"What?" Lt. Commander Francesca Villanueva, the last conspirator in our little cabal, asked sharply. "What can you do? Sir?"

She didn't have to call me sir, since she technically outranked me. I was a Marine captain, and field promoted to the rank at that, while she was a step above that at lt. commander. But I was the commander of this mission, or so I'd been acclaimed in a very unmilitary way. And maybe adding "sir" to the end of the question was just an attempt at cushioning the harshness of it. Villaneuva had never made a big deal over who and what waited for her back home, but I knew she had family on Aphrodite who she'd been close with.

"I think," I said, choosing my words carefully, "that I might be able to use the control over T-space the Change gave me to open a very temporary Transition Line for us back to the Cluster."

"You *think*?" Nance demanded, leaning forward, his chair creaking under his weight. The man needed to spend some more time in the ship's gym. "That's a hell of a thing to not be sure about."

"I know I have the ability to do it," I clarified, then glanced aside at Vicky. "What I'm not sure of is whether I'll still be sane when we reach the other side."

"You mean those voices you told us about," Brandano guessed. He opened his mouth, closed it again as if hesitant to ask.

"Yes, I can hear them right now," I answered the question anyway, sinking back into the flimsy chair. "Like whispers in the dark on a quiet night. Background noise when I'm thinking about something else, but if I concentrate on them..." words formed of their own accord in my head and I shook the thought away.

"How do you know?" Vicky asked. She hadn't said much since we confined Chang and his crew to the drop-ship, as if she was still trying to process the news he'd given us. She barely looked like she'd gotten over the broken ribs and concussion she'd suffered at the hands of Lilandreth during the battle. "You say you know, and Lilandreth seemed to know so much about where the voices came from, but how?"

"Transition Space isn't like our universe," I attempted to

explain. "If it was, it'd be just as impossible to travel FTL there as it is here. It's more of a matrix... a thick membrane, connected by gravito-inertial lines of force."

Nance snorted.

"Like you know what those are," he scoffed.

"I didn't before," I admitted, glowering at him, "but I do now. I could give you the hyperspatial geometry for them." Deep breath. Let it out. Control my temper. "Every bit of Transition Space is connected to every other bit instantaneously. Like the neurons of a brain. And that's sort of what it is, a brain, but not a sentient brain." I frowned. "At least, I don't *think* it's sentient. Anyway, sentient or not, it acts in practice like a quantum computer the size of a universe. I can't read your mind or tell the future, but when I access the T-space matrix, I can run possibilities through the supercomputer at faster than I used to be able to think. Faster than light."

"But the ghosts live in there too," she reminded me urgently, as if pointing out something I hadn't already thought of. "Couldn't they be making the whole... matrix... lie to you?"

"To do that, they'd have to be lying to themselves." I sighed. "It's hard to explain in words because we're talking about things that weren't meant for our language... or even for our brains to comprehend.

"Look..." I met their eyes, one at a time. "I can get us back home, but there's a huge risk. If the Voices get to me before we arrive, well..." I let out a deep breath. "Plus, if we do this, you're going to have to promise to kill me as soon as we get back to the Cluster. There's no way you can take the chance of unleashing me on the Commonwealth."

"There's no way in hell we're doing that," Vicky said, raising from her chair to grab my arm, digging in her nails until it hurt, the ferocity in her eyes the last thing a lot of Tahni and humans had seen before they died. "Don't say that shit again." I looked at her hand and she let go, settling back, arms crossed in a picture of stubbornness. "There has to be another way."

"Then I can't take you back," I insisted. "Because if the ghosts take me over, if they have a host to carry them to the Commonwealth, I'll wind up killing tens of millions of people."

"That's an exaggeration, surely," Captain Nagarro said, though the fear in her eyes told a different story.

"Take out your pulse pistol," I invited her, "and fire off the entire mag at me. Do it... not one round'll hit."

Nagarro shook her head, though I could see in her eyes that she wanted to try it.

"No, I can't do that. If you're wrong..."

"Okay. I can see that some of you still don't believe." I sighed. "We need an object lesson."

Levitating was nothing, just a matter of concentration. I could have flown anywhere, could have gone a thousand meters up, but honestly the thought of being up there without a suit or anything scared me on a level that near godhood couldn't touch, so I only lifted myself a few meters above the ground. Nance and Nagarro watched, awestruck, unable to move, but Villanueva jumped back from her chair and Brandano's hand went to his gun. I almost wished he'd pull it so I could go with the original idea for my demonstration.

"Watch the drop-ship," I warned them, pointing across the courtyard.

The troop lander was huge, almost two hundred meters long and nearly a hundred wide, and I had no clue what it massed, never having studied the specs for it, but it had to be thousands of tonnes. This took more effort and concentration, not because the mass had anything to do with it but because the consequences of a lapse of focus would be disastrous both for the superstructure of the aerospacecraft and the people inside it.

But it sure as hell would give Robert Chang something to think about.

My right hand clenched into a fist, and I used it as the center of my focus, pouring mental energy through it and into T-space... and then beneath the landing gear of the drop-ship. It shuddered and quaked, dust billowing around it as if a giant hand had pressed into the ground under the wings. It moved. Uneven at first, a slight waggling of the wings, enough to give the crew and passengers a start but not enough to toss them around, then stabilized, rising steadily a hundred meters into the air. The pilot tried to ignite the atmospheric jets, but I stopped him, not with anything as crass as pulling his hand away, but subtler, intercepting the electronic relay from his control panel.

That was almost too much, a little complicated for my first attempt at this, and the bird wobbled again, but I caught it and began lowering it toward the ground.

None of the others had said a word, either because they were struck dumb by awe and disbelief or maybe because they were scared shitless that I would get distracted and drop the damned thing. I was a little scared of that myself. This was probably incredibly irresponsible and reckless, and the fact that I'd done it without a second thought bothered me, but it touched down without so much as a bounce of the landing gear and I turned back to the others, cocking my head to the side.

"Okay, it's not an exaggeration," Nagarro admitted, her eyes wide, still staring at the drop-ship. The rest of them were still looking between the bird and me, mouths working but nothing coming out.

Except Vicky. She knew, she'd seen.

"I won't do it," she said, not budging. "I won't do it, and I won't let anyone else do it either."

"Then none of us are ever going home," I said flatly. "I'd do it myself, but I'm not sure they'd let me, and I can't chance it. I'm not taking this back to the Commonwealth."

"We need to talk to the AI then," she said. "What did you call it?"

"It called itself Briggs. But it can't answer any questions that I can't." My words were as bleak as my mood. I accepted the possibility of death, but I hated what this was doing to Vicky.

"You said it yourself," she snapped, coming to her feet. "You might not know the right questions."

With that, she turned on her heel and headed back into the building.

And what else could I do but follow?

"Briggs, you hear me?" Vicky demanded, hands on her hips, looking around at the transparent walls of the lab. I was nervous about her being down here without protective gear, but I knew that was just me being overly cautious. I knew the virus had been tailored specifically to my DNA and wouldn't affect her. "Briggs?"

Nothing for a moment, and the others glanced aside at Vicky like they thought she'd gone as nuts as I had. They'd followed us in here, though I'd have felt more comfortable if they'd let us come in alone. I'd mentioned it on the way in and Nance had scoffed.

"You dragged me all the way down to this rock, I'm gonna get the full experience."

Maybe Briggs was reticent to speak in front of so many people, like the frog in that old Bugs Bunny cartoon Top used to watch. It would sing and dance, but only when no one else was looking.

"Briggs," I said, "please speak to us."

"I do not serve you, human," the machine intelligence reminded me, its voice echoing off the walls in a booming rebuke. "Just because you were friends with one of my kin doesn't put me at your beck and call."

"We need your help," Vicky said, desperation leaching the impatience and anger from her tone. "The Northwest Passage has been sealed off. The only way we know that we can go home is for Cam to guide us there with the powers you gave him."

"*I* gave him nothing," the AI corrected her. "That was Dwight. Had he asked my advice, I would have cautioned against it, but what's done is done. And you are correct, the only way for you to return to your home is for him to use his control over Transition Space to create a Transition Line. Though I have my doubts he can resist the Voices long enough to accomplish this."

"Then we have to forget it," Vicky insisted, turning to me. "You have to get this reversed now. Briggs, you said we had fifty-seven hours to do it, right?"

"That was my earlier estimate," the AI said, his tone casual, as if we were discussing something academic with no real consequences. "However, I've been scanning the progress of the Change since you entered the lab. I'm afraid the transformation has occurred more quickly than I calculated, possibly due to the raw energy Cameron Alvarez channeled in his battle with the Resscharr Lilandreth. I can no longer reverse the process."

Vicky deflated like a balloon stuck with a pin, stumbling backward from the battering she'd taken earlier and sheer exhaustion. I caught her, pulled her to me as she sobbed. Yet even as talons of guilt clawed at my heart, I felt relief. There was no excuse now, no way other than forward. I'd get them home and they'd have to kill me, and I couldn't even come up with a good argument to chicken out of it.

"But there is a place where it could still be done."

I looked upward like I could see the AI's face, as if it had one.

"What?" It wasn't so much what he'd said that shocked me but the fact that I hadn't already known it. Again, it was all about the right questions to ask.

"What you need," Briggs informed me, "is a method of rebuilding the connections. Unfortunately, I don't have the equipment required for that, as it would require the ability to clone your brain tissue, read your memories into storage, and restore them once the process is completed."

The grimace that passed across my face was involuntary but honest. The thought of someone chopping up my brain and replacing it with cloned tissue and then screwing with my memories terrified me in ways that rivalled my fear of losing control and killing millions.

"And you..." I stuttered. "You can't do this yourself?" Not that I wanted him, but I also wanted to know why it was so difficult that an advanced sentient AI couldn't do it. "I mean, you managed to engineer a nanovirus that could transform my brain in the first place..."

"No, I simply *re*-engineered it to match your DNA," Briggs corrected me. The space between Vicky and I shimmered and cohered into the image of a human, not in a uniform like Dwight had been wont to do, but dressed in simple, white robes. Together with the long, flowing, golden hair the AI had given its avatar, the whole thing had taken on an uncomfortably angelic appearance. Blue eyes stared into mine earnestly. "I did not engineer the original virus."

"I thought you were all the same," Vicky said, eyeing the AI's holographic avatar suspiciously. "That's what Dwight told us."

"Dwight told you what he knew," Briggs retorted, his aquiline nose turned up at the error. "You must remember that his last connection to the Resscharr was tens of thousands of years earlier than mine. I was with them until close to the end, and I know their fate. Near the end, when the Resscharr were desperate enough to attempt to use Transition Space as a weapon, they'd lost their trust in us."

"For good reason," I murmured. After all, the AI had been the ones to unleash the Skrela on them in the first place, though perhaps there'd been good reason for *that* too, since the Skrela had been engineered from the remains of the only intelligent species in the galaxy to not evolve on Earth, and the Resscharr had ordered the AI to slaughter them in order to preserve the dominance of their own creations.

"Quite," Briggs acknowledged. "But rather than admit their mistakes, the Resscharr doubled down on them. They created yet another sentient AI, not based on human thought patterns this time, and to him—to them—they trusted the development of the nanovirus. I *have* the specifications of the virus and was able to change it to suit you, but I don't have the necessary genetics facilities to duplicate your brain material, and more importantly, I lack the correct equipment to back up your memories. But there's an outpost which may have the capabilities. *May*." He waved a simulated hand and a star map coalesced beside him with a single system highlighted. "It's called, in as close to your language as the original Resscharr can be translated, Waterline."

"And how far away is this Waterline place?" Nance asked, his scowl dubious.

"The journey from here will take roughly three of your weeks in Transition Space," Briggs told him, though the sneer on his avatar's face revealed what he thought of the rest of us humans. "This is the last aid I'm willing to give you. Take this opportunity to save yourself... or don't. But don't return here, and trouble me no more."

And with that, the avatar disappeared and Briggs was gone.

The hope in Vicky's eyes was painful. I knew how easily it could be dashed.

"We have to do it," she said, grabbing my hand and squeezing it tightly, as if she was afraid I'd be snatched away from her any second.

"If we do," I reminded her, "it means no one goes home. I can't ask the Marines and the crew of the *Orion* to sacrifice that for me."

"Well, I sure as hell can," Nance declared flatly. He shrugged. "This entire military operation turned into something more like a pirate ship months ago. Might as well go whole hog."

"What are you suggesting, Captain?" Nagarro wondered.

"I'm bringing the entire crew down here," he said, "except for a skeleton crew. And we're going to ask them. We've traveled this far together, might as well see it through to the end."

[3]

There were so few of us.

I don't think I'd realized it until now, until I saw almost all of them standing assembled in the courtyard at the center of Homecoming, their eyes fixed on me. The *Orion* wasn't a cruiser, didn't require the redundant crew of a capitol ship, and that was reflected in the size of the crew. Fewer than two hundred to start, and a couple dozen less now, even with Jay and Bob added. I'd nearly forgotten about them since the end of the battle. They'd escorted the Grey scientist Spinner back to the ship after his psychotic break at the death of his psychic slave-mistress Lilandreth, and I don't think either of them completely understood what was happening.

The only complement that had grown since the start of our mission were the Marines. Nearly half the original company was dead, but they'd been reinforced by a full company of Vergai from Yfingam—Bronze Age humans abducted from Earth and brought with the last Resscharr to leave the Cluster for use as slaves to the Karai, the Tahni also brought along through the gateway. The Karai attempt to enslave the Vergai had failed, their leader killed thanks to us, but the humans had evacuated the planet to the other world in the system... except for a company of volunteers who'd come with us, recruited into the Marines, given the closest approximation we could come up with of the Vigilante.

They were gathered together with the remnants of our original company, acclimated enough that the only difference between them was the lack of interface jacks on the Vergai. That made them a touch slower in the suits, the Vigilantes a touch less responsive, but they were certainly better than the next best thing.

Then there were the flight crews, part of the *Orion*'s Space Fleet complement but also self-consciously separate in the way that aerospace pilots had always held themselves apart from ship personnel... and naval aviators from their shipboard brethren before that. Brandano was the senior, along with Villanueva and their Intercept crews, standing apart even from the others who flew assault shuttles, drop-ships, and landers.

We'd started out with so many others, most of them dead, some left behind at their own request. All who were left looking to me for hope that there was an end to this. Apart from all the others, more outsiders than anyone else in this galaxy, were Robert Chang and his crew of Skingangers. The cyborgs gave no indication of their feelings on being forced to give heed to this ceremony, but Chang emanated curiosity, his dark, beady eyes gleaming even from fifty meters away.

I said nothing. This wasn't my idea and I wouldn't have a part in it, yet already I knew the likeliest outcome.

"We have a problem," Nance said, his voice amplified by speakers set up on either side of where he stood front and center of the crews. "You all know we came out here in search of the Northwest Passage, the way back home. But this man and his crew..." Nance gestured at Chang. "... tell us that the passage has been shut down, and now we know that to be a fact."

Well, they knew it because I'd told them it was true. The fact they believed me without checking was both comforting and frightening.

"There's still one way back, but to get there, Captain Alvarez would have to sacrifice his life."

A chorus of murmurs so loud they drowned Nance out, and he waved them to silence, then launched into an abbreviated and simplified explanation of what was going on. Most of them knew some of it, knew what had happened to Lilandreth, what she'd become and how she'd been twisted by the Voices. The part about me being infected with the Transformation Virus was news to most of them, and I saw hints of fear in horror in some of their faces, though also admiration and sorrow.

"So," Nance finished up, "we have a choice. We can either use Captain Alvarez's abilities to take us home... at which time, we'd have to kill him to keep him from becoming a threat to the Commonwealth, or we can take him to this Waterline place and try to cure him. But if we do that, we've given up on our last shot of returning to the Cluster." He shrugged. "I can't tell you what we'd do after that. There's the possibility of going into stasis and trying to return at sublight speeds, but that'd take decades at a minimum, and there's no guarantee any of us would survive the attempt. We could head back the way we came, return to one of the human societies we've found, though that has its risks as well. Those decisions would be made only after we find out if Captain Alvarez can be saved."

Another round of murmurs, these softer, more thoughtful. Feet shifted along with eyes, and there was blame and resentment rising off some of them like the stench of rotting meat. But not too many. They debated and cursed and wept, and people who'd still held out hope of returning to their loved ones argued with others who'd given it up long ago, while others who cared neither one way nor the other stood back and watched.

And then Vicky stood beside Nance, her voice picked up by the mic on his 'link.

"Cam won't ask you to do this." Her contralto cut through the murmurs and arguments, brought them to silence. "He's surrendered to the inevitability of his death, and his only concern is that we might not be able to kill him before he goes bad. Because he's never once thought of himself during this entire mission. He's done what was needed, stepped into the vacuums in leadership and fought harder than anyone to try to get you all home. He's never asked for anything in return, because that's not the kind of man he is. Well, *I'm* asking."

She sniffed, rubbed at something in her eye.

"I knew from the beginning that one or both of us could die on this mission, even back when it was just fighting against a rogue Tahni faction back in the Commonwealth. But I took comfort from the fact that we'd do it together, that we'd be there, watching each other's backs, and if one of us did fall, the other would get payback for it. I could never and *will* never hurt my husband. And I won't let anyone else hurt him without trying to kill them. So I'm asking that if any of you try to kill him, you'd better kill me first."

Which was *not* how I thought that would go, and I suppressed a grin. Vicky didn't beg, not even for me. She *reasoned*, and she did it with a knife to your throat. The reactions to her threat were rich with respect and not a little intimidation. Everyone knew Vicky was as capable with a Vigilante or just a handgun as I was. No one wanted to be the one to test her.

"I'd like to say something," Chuck Brandano declared, stepping out from the group, pitching his voice to be heard above the clamor, not deigning to use any amplification. He glared at the others as if they'd offended his sensibilities with their complaints and fears. "I signed up for the Academy when I was a teenager, and I did it against the wishes of my parents. They wanted me to go to engineering school and work designing ships. I wanted to fly them, wanted to serve all of humanity by fighting their enemies, defending Earth and the colonies from the Tahni. Once the war was over, I stayed in, not because I loved war or loved killing, but because I'd come to love my brothers and sisters in arms who'd made the same decision I had, who'd dedicated their lives to something bigger than themselves."

Everyone fell quiet, some with their eyes downcast, others staring at him with rapt attention.

"Cam Alvarez is the embodiment of what drew me to the military, what kept me in it. He's a man who gave up the safe, civilian life he'd established after the war because he saw the danger to the Commonwealth from the rogue Tahni forces under General Zan-Thint, and he didn't hesitate. When Captain Solano fell in battle and Cam's leadership was needed, he didn't hesitate, just stepped into the role, despite having little experience at commanding a company, because it needed doing. When Colonel Hachette died achieving the destruction of the Skrela hive world, when no one else wanted the job of commander, when we were lost and unsure of what to do next, Cam stepped in and led us through the haze and darkness, gave us purpose."

Brandano was laying it on pretty thick and leaving out some details. Like how I'd led what was basically a mutiny against Hachette because he'd lost his heart and his head when Top had died in battle and was doing his best to get us all killed. But he was a politician campaigning at the moment, and sometimes facts were filtered in political speeches.

"I know Cam would sacrifice his life to get us home," Brandano summarized. "He's put himself in that position over and over from the beginning of all this. But if the decision is mine to make, I wouldn't let him. I wouldn't let him give up not just his life but his sanity, his legacy, everything he is, just to get us back to the Commonwealth. If we're stuck here, we can survive. We can even thrive. We can find a new home and make a life among other humans. It's not the end of the world, not even the end of our lives. Yes, the ones we love back home will mourn for us, but be honest... they've done that already. To them, we're all dead. They've accepted it, and so should you."

He faltered for a moment, a paroxysm of emotion passing across his features.

"My parents, my brother, my sisters... they all believe I'm dead. They've undoubtedly held a service, mourned my passing, and made peace with it, moved on with their lives. Would they be happy if I turned up in a few months, still alive? Of course. But they've lived through that pain, and there's no way to erase it. Just like your families. There's no way to undo what they've been through. Maybe you could rebuild things with your wives and husbands and children, but what if you can't? Is it worth sacrificing one of the finest men I've ever known for just the possibility? Because that's exactly what you'll be doing. He wouldn't be *risking* his life to save us, we'd be *taking* it. Think about that."

Brandano didn't sit down, of course, because there was nowhere to sit, but he stepped back among the Intercept flight crews, arms folded, jaw set in stubborn determination. I should have been moved, should have given into the warm tightness in my chest at the show of friendship and devotion, but instead I was annoyed.

This wasn't right. This wasn't how things were done in the military, and by God, this was *still* a military operation, despite the twists and turns it had taken. I opened my mouth to shut the whole debate down, ready to tell them I was the commander and I'd be the one to make the decision. I closed it.

Not because I was afraid of how it would affect Vicky or

because I was scared of dying. No, I didn't shut it down because I worried that it wasn't *me* who wanted it shut down. I hadn't heard the Voices lately... and I knew they wouldn't stop. They'd told me as much. Which might mean I'd stopped hearing them as Voices separate from my own thoughts, or might mean they were behind the idea of me trying to get everyone back through T-space and planned to take advantage of it. Either way, I couldn't trust my own judgment in the matter.

"That's easy for you to say, Commander."

I looked up at the unexpected voice. Lt. Chase, the Communications officer. I'd known him since all this started and never once thought of him as anything but a loyal member of the crew, but I should have known that everyone was the star in their own internal movie.

"You're a pilot," Chase went on, his boyish face screwed up in an angry scowl. "Whatever happens to us, you're going to be a pilot, you're gonna have an important role to play with skills that'll be important. What about the rest of us? What the hell are we going to *do* out here? If we go back to one of the human worlds we found, what am *I* going to do? Plow a field? Haul fish out of the ocean? Herd cattle? Because sure as shit, none of those primitive shitheads are going to need a communications specialist!" He pointed at Captain Nagarro. "Or an intelligence analyst. Or half a dozen other skills that won't mean a damned thing if go through with this. That's what you're asking us to do, not just give up on our families, but give up on our *lives*." Chase threw up his hands in a helpless gesture, looking as if he might be about to cry. "I don't want to be the bad guy here. I don't want Captain Alvarez to die. He's been a good commander. But Colonel Hachette was a good commander too, and when the time came he..."

Now, Chase *did* cry, sobbing, shoulders shaking, and one of the other bridge officers gently took him by the arm and pulled him back into the crowd. As if in chain reaction, dozens of others broke down as well, and all I could think was that Top would have had the whole fucking lot in the front in a leaning rest position and made them do pushups until they forgot about their problems. But Top was old-fashioned that way.

"This is ridiculous," I said finally, unable to hold it in any longer. "We're not having this discussion." I hadn't raised my voice, yet it seemed that every one of them heard me. The crying and quiet comforting ceased, and every eye turned my way again. "I'm doing this. It's my call, and I'm doing it. I'm taking you home..." A sigh undermined the firm, decisive tone. "Even if it's the last fucking thing I do."

"Yes, sir." That was Lt. Springfield, her Vigilante standing motionless behind her like a big brother backing the play of his younger sister, silent and intimidating. "But who's gonna kill you?" Her defiant stance matched her tone, fists on her hips, feet planted shoulder-width apart. "I mean, you can take us all back, sure. I'm fine with that. But you keep saying *we* have to kill you after. But I'm not doing it." She spun on the rest of the crowd and dared them to contradict her. "Any of *you* willing to volunteer to murder the man who just saved you? Any of you? I wouldn't do it to any Marine I went downrange with, and I sure as hell won't do it to Captain Alvarez."

Frustration roiled inside my gut, an incoherent rage at all of them for not grasping the fact that there was no choice, that they'd have to kill me anyway, that I couldn't be trusted, that there was no hope...

Cameron Alvarez.

The voice echoed inside my head, rocking me back on my heels, not with its strength but with its mere presence. The ghosts were still, small voices, the sort that Mama always told me God used, terrifying in their persistence rather than their clarity and volume. If I didn't concentrate on them, I could pretend they weren't talking to me.

Who the hell are you? I demanded, answering inside my head, because everyone already believed I was going mad and I didn't want them losing trust in me already. *How are you talking to me?*

But I knew the answer as soon as I asked the questions. It was Briggs. I also knew in that instant that Briggs had named himself that because of something he'd pulled out of my memories, something I'd read about an engine manufacturer called Briggs and Stratton. It was a subtle dig at the way we thought of him as a machine. As for how he was talking to me...

You have a constant connection to T-space, he explained. *The Resscharr developed T-space communications thousands of years ago. Now stop asking stupid questions you already know the answer to and let me give you the solution to your problem.*

Why? I demanded. *The last thing you said to us was that you weren't going to help anymore.*

I told your companions that because they didn't belong there. They had no claim on my aid. You do. Your situation is not of your doing, but ours. You were caught up in our plans for revenge against the Resscharr, and I would not have you suffer for our sins. That said, I offer only the slimmest of hopes. I have discovered hints in the communications from Waterline to Homecoming, things not talked about but talked around. I believe it is possible that the AI on Waterline developed a new form of interstellar propulsion based on the warp field generator from the Transition Drive. Something that would allow faster-than-light travel through spacetime, something that wouldn't require Transition Lines. If my guess is correct, there's a chance that a model of this drive exists at Waterline. It isn't much hope, but it's all I can offer.

And before I could respond, he was gone. Leaving me with

a decision to make. I thought for the briefest instance that I'd been standing there silent, distracted for a full minute, carrying on a conversation inside my head with the AI, but that had been an illusion. Barely a second had passed, and the argument still went on between the shrinking faction of doubters and the stolid, stubborn set of my supporters. Again, their number should have made me proud, but instead it was unsettling. I hadn't done anything to deserve their devotion except get them killed.

One thing was clear though. No one was going to agree to kill me before I could become a threat... or, maybe more accurately, no one was going to be *allowed* to agree to do it. Which meant there was only one choice.

"Excuse me," I interrupted, projecting my voice not by training but with the abilities I'd been given.

Every eye focused on me, and I took a deep breath.

"I believe there might be another solution..."

[4]

"There's something wrong with you," I told Chang. It wasn't an insult, and he didn't take it as one.

"Of course there is," he agreed, snorting a cynical laugh. "You don't need to be a psychic to see *that*."

"I'm not a psychic," I reminded him, rubbing at my temples. Dealing with this man was just one of the many things giving me a headache.

Everyone had said yes. I'd known they would, which didn't make it any better. Worse yet, they'd been *excited* by the possibility, as if I hadn't led them to Homecoming with the promise of finding the way home and then dashed their hopes. While the crew ferried back to the *Orion*, an endeavor which took hours to complete, I got to deal with Robert Chang and his crew.

We were on their ship, which I'd intended as a peace offering. Once we we'd jumped into Transition Space, I'd assured him he was free to take his Predecessor hotrod and go anywhere he wanted. The Skingangers had taken my promise more along the lines of an ultimatum, and they glared at me silently from their duty stations.

Their *inactive* duty stations. It was a peace offering, not a suicide pact. The Predecessor ship was more advanced than the ones I'd seen before, even on Decision, honed to a fine point technologically just before the Resscharr had abandoned the Cluster. Yet shutting down its systems took little effort. And maybe the fact that I didn't appear at all intimidated by the half-metal mankillers was what pissed them off the most.

Not Chang though. He'd produced furniture out of the ship's bare deck and invited me to sit. Then he'd delivered his reaction to my offer.

"I want to go with you," he'd said, as earnest as any teenager taking the oath at a recruiting station. I'd been about to ask him why when I decided I should really get some use out of these psionic abilities before they turned me into a monster.

"You're not Robert Chang," I intuited, eyes narrowing as I tried to interpret the data the neural matrix fed me. "Not the original."

"It's so difficult to hide the truth from someone who's effectively omniscient," Chang said, spreading his hands expressively. "Perhaps that's why I've always fancied myself an atheist. More from wishful thinking than actual evidence."

"If you want to convince me to bring you along," I pointed out, "maybe you should work on just being straight with me instead of trying to make me figure it out on my own."

"I wasn't always like this," Chang said, brows turning up in a wistful expression. "I once had hopes and dreams and silly, patriotic notions. That was how I wound up in the DSI."

"*You* were in the Department of Security and Intelligence?" I repeated, unable to restrain a sharp laugh. "I guess that shouldn't surprise me."

"I'd like to blame the war for the man I became, but that would be a lie," he admitted. "The war was simply an outlet for the twisted truth that had always lain dormant inside of me. I took to the violence, the death, the dirty tricks like a duck to water, Cameron." A thin smile passed across his face, as unpleasant a version of the expression as I'd ever seen. "I was responsible for some of the most successful operations against the Tahni of the entire war, and my only regret out of all of it was that I hadn't had the chance to unleash the truly diabolical ideas I'd saved up. Then, once it ended, the DSI cut me loose. I was, so they said, mentally unstable, suffering from post-traumatic stress. They were only half right. The war hadn't stressed me, it had freed the *real* me. That scared them, and they were right to be scared."

Chang sighed, running his hands over his shaven scalp.

"I suppose, in the end, what got to me was listening to them, the psychologists and analysts who diagnosed me as crazy. I began to think they were right, that to the human race, I must seem that way. Which made me doubt my own humanity. I became involved with the Evolutionists." He motioned at his crew. "And among them I found, if not kindred spirits, at least souls traveling the same path. Looking for a way past mortality. There were, I discovered, a few key technologies that had been developed in secret by R&D labs during the war, though the efforts had been abandoned as ruinously expensive and of limited utility. One was the neurolink, an implant computer that could, among other things, store the memories from a human brain in a quantum core computer. Originally, the idea was that the memories of experts could be read into the minds of those trying to learn a skill, but I thought of another use for the tech once I stumbled across the other project."

Chang cocked an eyebrow at me.

"You've undoubtedly had repairs made using cloned tissue during your military career."

"More times than I'd like to remember," I agreed.

"Some bright soul realized during the war that there was no

reason, theoretically, why it shouldn't be possible to clone an entire body, brain, nerves, flesh and blood. A full-grown genetic duplicate of the donor. Lacking just one thing."

"Memories," I supplied, everything clicking into place.

"Immortality. Not just the theoretical immortality many hope for from ever-accelerating medical technology, but a certainty of it. If I were to die, I'd have genetic material stored away beside the latest version of my memories, ready to create a new me and provide it with the same memories as the old. Genetic duplication."

"It wouldn't be the same you," I insisted, the objection coming automatically from the heart of a Catholic. "There'd be no continuation of consciousness."

"I feel no different," he assured me, tapping his chest. "I'm just as much Robert Chang as I was before. Though I may not be the best judge of identity. I went from being Robert Chang, DSI agent, to Cutter, a street surgeon working for the Skingangers in a chop shop on a colony world, supplying them—and myself—with bionic replacements. Then, when Cutter was assassinated by rivals, I returned in the form of a cyborg monster I called Secarius, to get my revenge. But that version also met its fate, and a new me was born. And then another. And another. I've lost count, but it has to be a minimum of ten iterations of this being, once known as Robert Chang, once known as Cutter, once known as the monster Secarius. And in that long cycle of death and reincarnation..."

"You went nuts," I declared, staring at him like he'd grown another head. Which wasn't impossible, given what he'd told me.

"I prefer to think of it," Chang corrected, "as having lost a sense of perspective, perhaps somewhat lacking in mental stability." He shrugged. "But yes, I confess, I've done some things that the old me would have considered... nuts, as you say."

I didn't know everything, despite Chang's description of me as omniscient, but I'd begun to grow accustomed to knowing what people were talking about without having to ask stupid questions. Until now.

"What do you want *me* to do about it?" I asked, genuinely puzzled.

"You? Why nothing!" He threw up his hands as if the answer was obvious. "You're off to find the wizard, the wonderful Wizard of Oz! You're going to ask him for a new brain! Well, I want one too. A better one, one that has my memories without the... psychological baggage that comes with them."

"Have you ever considered," I asked him, "that it's not the duplication that's made you unstable but the memories of what you've done?"

"Oh, bullshit," he scoffed. "I've known men and women who did things that made me look like a piker, yet they were able to live with themselves just fine, able to fit into civilized society and live like normal citizens!"

"Yeah, I've known people like that. They're good liars, best at lying to themselves. Maybe you're just too damned honest to make-believe you aren't evil."

"That's not impossible," Chang admitted. "But even if it is, I want this AI to fix me. Make me different."

"And you're not worried it won't be you anymore?" I wondered.

"Honestly, Cameron, at this point, I'm not sure who that is." Chang's eyes, or Cutter's or Secarius', were as bleak and forlorn as anyone I'd ever run into, even the street kids in the Trans-Angeles Underground. Even me. "I just want to be able to live with myself again... whoever that might be. And in return for the chance, I'm willing to make myself, my shop, and my crew available for your service. We'll fight for you, we'll scout for you, we'll be your Goddamned Polish mine detectors if you want."

It took me a second to reference that expression in the memories available to me, another to try to understand why it was considered offensive back when it meant something, a third to idly wonder how the hell Chang had come to use it.

"Why do you think we *need* your services?" I asked him, knowing several possible answers but curious as to which he'd pick.

"Because," he replied, grinning slyly, picking one I hadn't expected, "you want someone around who can kill you if you lose control. Your friends won't do it, your wife won't do it. But you know I will. And this ship is perhaps the only weapon I'm sure could pull it off, even as powerful as you are."

I sat back in the chair, amazed at how comfortable it was, not just command-grown to fit a human but customized to fit *me*. Amazed at how, despite the computing power of a universe at my disposal, I could still be surprised.

Amazed at myself for making this decision.

"Okay," I told him, offering a hand. "I get you to the wizard, and you kill me if I need you to."

Chang stared at my hand, bemused for a second before taking it.

"Agreed. But let's hope it doesn't come to that."

His grip was weak and felt somehow slimy, and I regretted this already.

"And I thought it was bad having Tahni troops on the ship with us," Vicky murmured, glaring sidelong at the Evolutionists as ship's security escorted them to the compartments they'd been assigned.

Compartments that had been air-gapped away from any computer system and outfitted with physical locks too strong even for one of the cyborgs. Their expressions were unreadable by design, yet it was obvious to anyone that they weren't happy with the arrangement, and I wondered why they'd agreed to it, why they were so loyal to Chang. Maybe it just came down to the fact that Skingangers didn't have many friends and couldn't turn against one that easily.

They also had very acute hearing, and I knew they had to have picked up Vicky's comment, though none deigned to react visibly to it. Neither did Chang, unless the broad smile and cheerful wave he gave us as he was led to his quarters counted. Their ship was small enough that it fit into the *Orion*'s docking bay, and I'd made sure they didn't cause any trouble by riding up here with them. Vicky had met me in the bay along with a squad of security personnel, armed and armored, and I'd walked with them to the compartments as an added precaution.

Living quarters were in the habitation drum, spinning for the moment to provide rotational gravity, though that would stop soon once we locked down for acceleration and then jumped to T-space, where the artificial gravity would work again. I'd never been able to understand why that was the case, why the grav plates could only work in Transition Space, but I did now. The gravity effect came from the warp field, and it could only operate inside Transition Space.

Or so we thought. If Briggs had been right, the Predecessors on Waterline had gotten it working in regular space. I wanted to believe it, but there was always the chance I was telling myself and everyone else what we wanted to hear.

"At least I knew why the Tahni did what they did," I agreed with Vicky, not caring whether the Evolutionists or Chang heard me. I wanted to call him *Cutter*, the name he'd used as a street surgeon, because it seemed to fit his personality better.

"They hated us because they thought we were stealing their birthright, and to some extent, they were right. But they never pretended to or wanted to be anything other than what they were."

Hatches slid shut, closing our new *allies* behind them. The security troops hesitated, the petty officer in charge stomping up to me. She tilted her helmet's faceplate back to reveal solid, square-jawed features and tight curls of black hair.

"They won't be getting out of those compartments without help, sir," she assured me.

"Thanks, Chief Platte," I said with a nod. "They'll need to be escorted to the mess, of course, but I want that spaced out at half-hour intervals, one Skinganger at a time with two security escorts."

"Yes, sir. What about this Chang? Same security arrangements? I scanned him, and he doesn't seem to have any bionics."

"No," I told her, snorting a quiet laugh totally devoid of amusement. "I'll escort him myself. Mr. Chang is a smooth talker, and I wouldn't want him convincing anyone else how harmless he is. Post two guards in the corridor and tell them not to leave this passage unobserved for anything less than combat acceleration."

Platte offered a salute, which was technically inappropriate for shipboard, but I returned it anyway and left her and her squad to their task. Vicky tugged at my arm as we headed for the lift banks.

"What is it with you and Chang?" she asked, her eyes narrowing. "He's a creepy little con-man and probably a murderer by his own admission. Why the hell are we bringing him along? The bastard stranded us here—I think we should have taken that ship and left him on Homecoming."

I glanced around us, making sure no one was within earshot, not wanting to spread any more rumor or dissent than was unavoidable. The lift bank on this level was deserted, everyone already at their posts, ready for departure from this disappointing nightmare of a world.

"I know he's a scumbag," I admitted, touching the control to summon the lift car. "He's clinically insane and very self-aware about it, and I'm not sure if that makes it better or worse. But he wants to change, he's telling the truth about that."

"Oh, you know that, do you?" Vicky demanded sharply, rounding on me with fury in her eyes. "I know everyone else believes this shit about you knowing everything now, but I don't. I think it's those ghosts trying to fuck with your head. They want you to believe there's no hope, to give up. Everything you know about them, you found out from Lilandreth after she was infected or from the AI, the ones who started all this shit to begin with. Why can't you see that? Why do you believe everything they tell you?"

I didn't want to argue with Vicky, but I wasn't going to be able to get away from it. She wasn't going to let me. But I waited until the lift car arrived and we stepped inside before answering her question.

"Let me ask you something," I told her, though I'd always hated answering a question with a question. "How do you know I love you?"

If she'd looked angry before, now I thought laser beams would shoot out of her eyes and burn me to a cinder.

"Are you trying to say you don't?"

"I mean, how do *you* know it?" I pressed the button to take us to the bridge. "It's not something you can prove. I could be lying about how I feel, could have ulterior motives for everything I've done that you could present as evidence. So tell me, how do you know it for sure, without any doubts?"

The lift lurched into motion. I normally would have secured my ship boots to the deck to keep myself anchored once we left the habitation drum and lost rotational gravity, but not this time. I didn't have to. Just a moment of concentration and both of us stayed upright, stuck to the floor of the car without a hint of the stomach-churning nausea of free fall, though I'm not sure Vicky noticed the difference.

"I believe it," she said, eyes clouded in thought as though she just now understood what I was trying to say. "I can't explain it, I just know it in my gut. Like I know my own thoughts."

"That's the same way I know that what I'm saying is the truth. Or at least a strong possibility. This is tough for you, and I'm sorry, I wish I could go back and undo it all." I took her in my arms. She resisted the pull at first but then melted into my embrace, the tension going out of her shoulders. "If what Briggs said is true, if this other AI can turn me back to what I was, maybe it's our way out of this."

"I'm tired of our lives depending on these damned AI," she said, pulling away from me long enough to share the doubt in her eyes. "Every time, they wind up fucking us over. I wish the things had never been invented."

"It's funny," I told her, remembering what I'd learned from Dwight and Briggs. "I think they wish the same thing."

[5]

"Is it just me," Robert Chang wondered, "or is everyone on this ship strung as tight as a steel guitar and ready to snap?"

The little man smiled around a mouthful of ramen noodles, enjoying both his lunch and his play on words. I shared neither opinion.

The galley was usually crowded between shifts, but there were barely a handful of crew at the tables around the two of us. I figured they shared Vicky's opinion of Chang and were avoiding being trapped in a small compartment with the man.

"It's not just you," I replied, taking a careful bite of my sandwich.

The food was getting back to shipboard bland after a brief respite. Every time we stopped at a settled world, we took on as much fresh food as we could store, but the ship's freezers were only so big, and once that was gone it was back to soy and spirulina, twisted into imaginary meat and bread by the processors. The last fresh supplies we'd had were from Jay and Bob's world, and that was a long time gone.

"I can only imagine they're upset with me," Chang continued, either very clueless about the moods of other people or understanding it and not caring. "Though, to be fair, I had no reason to suspect anyone else from the Commonwealth had ever made it out here."

"Would you have cared if you *had* known?" I asked him.

"You're as close to omniscient as any man who's ever lived." He cocked an eyebrow at me. "What do *you* think?"

I chewed and didn't answer. Normally, I wouldn't have hesitated to tell someone they were acting crazy, but since he'd already admitted to the problem, I didn't think it would help.

"How are your people handling the trip?" I asked instead. The last two weeks had been long enough for the crew, and we all basically liked each other. I couldn't imagine making the journey around the periphery of the cut-off Transition Lines that the Predecessors had created when they'd sealed off the Cluster while basically confined to a cell.

Of course, I wasn't an Evolutionist who'd given up half my biological parts to try to become the next step in human evolution. I'd watched them on the security cameras as they stood stock-still in the middle of the compartments, their bionic legs locked in place, and just thought. Or maybe *calculated* would be a better term. What they were considering was the troubling part, because I was sure it involved how to get even with us for their confinement.

"We don't talk much," Chang admitted, shrugging the question off, seemingly focused exclusively on his meal as if he found the whole concept of ramen made from spirulina powder to be fascinating. Or, more likely, he was making a subtle comment on how boring and tedious his own stay on board the ship had been. "Hell, *they* barely talk at all. I don't know why they hang out with me, to be honest. I talk enough for any three normal men."

No lie detected there... except for the part where Chang

claimed he didn't know why the Skingangers hung out with him.

"Sure you do," I said. "You're the one who illegally modified the cyborgs in the first place. You might as well be God to them." I frowned, thinking of what he'd told me about his life as Cutter and then Secarius. Latin for *the slayer*. "And maybe because when the time came when someone tried to hurt them, tried to hurt *you*, you actually went out and fought for them."

Chang laughed, this one genuine, if perhaps bitter.

"Oh, you have no idea, and not even your cosmic supercomputer could tell you *that* story, Cameron. What you've achieved out here is beyond imagining, but there are men and women I've known, who I've worked and fought beside, who've moved mountains with their will. Not quite as literally as you, but with effects just as dramatic. Someday, if we have the time and I have the stomach for it, I'll tell you of an old friend of mine, though I'm not sure he would describe our relationship in that same way." He shook his head, for the first time since I'd met him looking as if he actually felt guilty about something. "I should have treated him better. Caleb was a good man, perhaps the best I ever knew. I can't know if he survived, though I hope he did, but if so, he's going to remember me poorly. And beyond the fact that I'd like to become something better than..." he motioned at himself, "... *this* Caleb Mitchell is not a man you want to have pissed off at you."

The name sounded familiar, though I couldn't for the life of me remember where I'd heard it, and even the largest computer in two universes couldn't help me there, other than the ship's official military records said there was a Caleb Mitchell who'd been at the Fleet Academy at the beginning of the war but had died on a training cruise that had been unlucky enough to be right in the middle of the Battle for Mars.

"Hey, anyone sitting here, man?"

I knew who it was before I looked up and didn't *exactly* cringe, though the temptation was there.

"Hi, Jay, Bob," I said, nodding to the two men. Well, humanoids if I was being picky about it, though the only visible differences between them and one of the other crewmembers of the *Orion* was a golden hue to their skin tones and a combination of facial features that would never have been seen in a human. Jay was tall and skinny, his friend shorter and stockier.

They'd been two of the three recruits to our crew from their planet, but the only two still active. Jay was as garrulous as Chang, though a bit more pleasant to converse with, while his friend Bob was content to let his friend do the talking. Both of them carried trays from the dispensers, each having made the move to human recipes from their local fare, both converts to the most excellent attributes of chicken Pad Thai.

"Go ahead, have a seat," Chang invited them, motioning with a fork twirled about with ramen. "It would be nice to have someone new to talk to. You gentlemen aren't human, are you?" He raised his other hand palm out. "Sorry, it might be rude to ask, but with all the modifications available to us these days, it would be fairly easy for someone to dye their skin and have their faces altered to mimic the features you two have."

"Whoa," Jay said with a thoughtful frown as he fell into a seat across from Chang. Bob took the one to the left, watching and saying nothing. "I guess you *could* do that, but why the hell *would* you?" He shoveled a forkful of noodles in the general direction of his mouth, splattering peanut sauce across his cheek as he shook his head. "I mean, that would be freaky, dude. You are who you are. Why would you want to change that?"

"Oh, I take it back, young man," Chang said with a chuckle. "You're not *human* at all."

"Well, you know, there's no reason to get nasty." A mass of peanut-flavored noodles cut off the complaint.

"It's a lot easier to change your exterior," I told them, "than it is to change your character. It's always been that way, which is why you get people like the Skingangers trying to remake themselves as something not even human. It's why you had the Predecessor Cult back home after the war, with people so devoted to the idea of the Predecessors as gods that they tried to make themselves into the image of what they *believed* without any evidence that the Predecessors looked like that. They weren't happy with who they were as people, so they changed the easiest things to alter. Their faces, their bodies, what they called themselves, their very species… instead of facing the uncomfortable truths about themselves."

"My, my, Captain Alvarez," Chang said, raising an eyebrow, along with his bottle of fruit juice, in salute. "You're quite the philosopher, aren't you?"

It was my turn to laugh, and I had a hard time stopping. Jay started chuckling with me, like he thought there was a joke he'd missed since he'd only learned to speak English recently, but he trailed off as I kept on laughing until it choked off.

"Mr. Chang, I've been through the worst parts of the war, worse than anything you saw in the DSI, I can tell you. Most of my friends died, and those who didn't were scarred mentally in ways no auto-doc could ever fix. After the war, I tried to make a new life as a farmer with my wife, and I think I could have done it, despite the nightmares and the flashbacks and the drinking. But then weapons smugglers started using my planet to store the guns they were selling to a rogue Tahni general who wanted to get revenge for losing the war. They wound up killing one of my best friends, and you know what they left behind there?" Anger infused the words, and somehow it focused itself on Chang, though I wasn't sure why it should. "A fucking Skrela seed pod. It dragged us back into the military, trying to stop General Zan-

Thint from setting loose Skrela seed pods to destroy the Commonwealth after he and his people left it."

Slumping into my chair, I saw every instant of the last few years unspooling like a video in front of my eyes, and I wondered if that was a function of the infection or if I was just getting old. The Voices had been worse the last few days, and my instinct was that it was because we were in Transition Space.

"We couldn't *not* do it, not when we were needed so badly, not when so much was riding on it. So we got involved and we made the mistake of making friends with the other people fighting alongside of us. They're all dead now... except for the one who was smart enough to say the hell with all of this and do what I *should* have done, settle down with the woman he loved and start a family. I gave up that chance for... this." I smacked the side of my head. "For *this*. For the chance to go insane and kill everyone I love and try to take over the galaxy unless I can convince my *wife* to kill me first, which will probably ruin her life. And to top it all off, I get to lead all these people to their likely deaths for the likely false hope that we can cure me *and* get them home."

My lip curled in a snarl.

"So yeah, I guess I've become kind of a philosopher, because the alternative would have been to become a raging asshole."

Jay's eyes were wide, and even Chang fell silent at my tirade. Bob, though, was inspired to speak.

"It kinda seems," he said around a bite of chicken, "like you did both."

"As a philosopher and budding asshole," Chang said, "what would you say makes a man? The things he intended to do, or the things he actually wound up doing?"

I stared at him for a long moment, seeing everything. Seeing the nature and nurture and the choices that had made him the thing he'd become.

"You want validation," I accused. "You want me, the prophet of some alien god, to absolve you of the wrongs you've done, to tell you that you didn't have any choice, that everything you fell into was inevitable." I shook my head. "That's not the truth though, and we both know it. The truth is, you always did what was best for Robert Chang, what you wanted. Look, we've been forced to work with murderous Tahni terrorists, Resscharr who were responsible for trying to wipe out the entire human race, and various others who were morally questionable, and we'll work with you too... but I won't tell you that you're one of the good guys, because you're not."

I thought he was going to take offense at the honest assessment, but he just smiled.

"And you think you're one of the good guys, Cameron Alvarez?" he asked me.

"I've always done what I thought was right." I shrugged. "Now that I have the ability to see more, I understand that some of the time I was mistaken about that, but that doesn't change my intent."

"Isn't it results that count though?" Chang wondered.

"People are judged by results," I told him, "but they're trusted because of their intent." Leaning forward, I met his gaze with a measured stare. "How far can I trust yours?"

They don't deserve you. You've given everything for them, and all they do is ask for more. Those people back on Earth are leeches, parasites, all of them living off the sweat and blood of people like you...

No. Not all of them. My mom, my dad, my brother... none

of them ever took anything from anyone. They grew everything they ate, worked for it.

And what did it get them? They were murdered by the ones who did take everything. That's what happens to all the innocents in your society, whether it's bandits in the desert or Corporate Council Executives hiring mercenaries to do the dirty work for them. Nothing will ever change it because humans are weak, corrupt. They need to be led with a firm hand, controlled like the children they are. And who will do it if it's not you? You're the only one with the power, the will, the empathy for the powerless. You can do it, and you should. You know you'd be the best thing that ever happened to humanity.

I don't want to lead them. I don't want to lead the people on this ship. I don't need any more responsibility. I don't want to be a dictator. I just want to be left alone.

They'll never leave you alone. You don't have any other choice. You have to set things right. You always do the right thing, Cam. This is the right thing, and you know it. Just use the knowledge you have, examine the scenarios, the possibilities for the Commonwealth if you don't do it. Or the Periphery. Or the Pirate Worlds. What's going to happen to them if you do nothing?

It made sense. I couldn't argue with it, couldn't argue with the Voices, the Ghosts. They were right—everything was going to go to hell back home. It was simple. The Commonwealth was trying to control too much territory with a representative democracy, territories weeks to months apart. Maybe the core colonies could manage that with the jumpgates, but even that wasn't going to be easy, wasn't going to be permanent. Things would fall apart and millions would die. Maybe hundreds of millions. The outer colonies would collapse and without support from them, the Periphery and even the Pirate Worlds would die.

I was the only one who could save them...

"No!"

I sat up in bed, gasping for breath, heart trying to beat its way out of my chest. Sweat coated my forehead, ran down my neck, and when I tried to wipe it away, my hands were shaking so badly I had to use my forearm instead.

"Is it the dream again?" Vicky asked in the darkness. She spoke first before putting a hand on my shoulder, because the last time I'd swung blindly at her touch before I was completely awake.

"Yeah." My breath came back under control in a few seconds, and I sank back to the pillow, letting her stroke my forehead. "Goddammit."

I should have said more, but nothing more coherent would come. I was as exhausted, as if I'd just outrun a cartel hitman through the entire Underground and then walked all the way across Brigantia's plains with the Tahni on my heels. And as scared. *More* scared.

"They're not what they say they are," she reminded me. The chemical striplight along the floor by the compartment's hatch glinted off her eyes. "They're not your friends. They're lying to you."

"No, they're not," I insisted, regaining more control over myself with each second. "That's what makes them so damned insidious. Everything they're telling me is true. It's just the outcome they're lying about." Pulling my knees up, I hugged them to me like I was a child again, hiding in storage rooms and cellars to keep the bullies from finding me. "Things *are* going to hell, but if I give in and try to fix them, I'll turn into the monster they want me to be and then it'll be too late. I won't be able to resist anymore."

"I won't let that happen to you," Vicky said. "I'm not some shrinking violet from the Academy who's going to sit around and weep while you go bad. I'm from the same Trans-Angeles

Underground you are, came up through the ranks the same way you did. Believe me, Cam Alvarez. I'm not going anywhere."

She pried my arms from around my knees and slipped into my embrace, forcing me to feel her. Warm, bare skin. Her lips on mine, her tongue. Trying to pull me out of it by overwhelming me with the very real sensations of the flesh. I let her, let myself be pulled down to the bed. My body, anyway. My brain went its own way.

Not that I was ignoring her and thinking about my problems. That would have been selfish, narcissistic, would have made me exactly the same kind of person they were trying to make me into. No, my thoughts went to her. When I'd met Victoria Sandoval, she'd already been a corporal, had been a Marine a year longer than me, cocky, confident, not a doubt in herself or her purpose in the world.

But she hadn't started that way. She'd told me about the life she'd come from, about how badly she'd wanted out of it, but it wasn't something that we dug into. It was the past, and we'd both abandoned our pasts when we'd joined the Corps, when we'd found each other. None of that mattered anymore. That was the lie we told ourselves.

The truth was messier, but it was one neither of us had been ready to deal with when all this started. Where we'd come from had made us who we were, and we never, ever made each other talk about it.

Now I didn't have to ask her to share those days with me, not with a simulation engine the size of all T-space. Now, I saw her. Younger, a teenager, but there was no mistaking those eyes, the set of her jaw. She'd worn her hair in corn rows and dyed it fluorescent orange, which she'd never admitted to me, and I nearly laughed aloud at the sight, though I managed to refrain. Her clothes were cheap, colorful flash, a mix and match of the free patterns available from the public fabricators, loose at the arms and legs and tight across her thin waist. The latest style for the Underground more than a decade ago.

There was nothing affected about her smile though. It was as warm and genuine as it had been since I'd met her, directed upward at the lean, gaunt face of a boy. Older than her, yet still not a man, not even by the standards of the term I'd had before I'd joined the Corps. Trying to seem tough and mean, he succeeded only in looking like a clown, like a kid playing dress-up in gang colors and tattoos on his shaved scalp.

To teenage Vicky, he was the sun and the moon and the north star. It was plain in her eyes, in the almost awed expression on her face. She had no concern with the Zocalo, with the kiosks full of handicrafts and quasi-legal gray market fabricator patterns, only with him. I never would have pictured her that way, but we were all young once. Well, most of us.

"Have you heard back from the Corporate Council training program, Damon?" Vicky asked, nearly dancing as she walked beside him. "That notice said the selection notice would be posted today."

"Yeah, I heard," Damon said, his voice annoyingly plaintive. I didn't know how she could stand to be around him, but I reminded myself I was looking backward with the benefit of being more than a decade older than either of them, *and* being afflicted with retroactive jealousy. "I didn't make it." He snorted, pretending to look at hand-stitched jackets on one of the tables. "I didn't think I would. They ain't taking someone from the fuckin' Underground. I bet all those slots went to the Surface." He nodded around them. The Zocalo was on the surface, still in the shadows of the towers but with at least a little sunlight leaking through. "Them Corporates want respectable trainees."

Vicky shrank in on herself like a star imploding, the hope going out of her eyes.

"Damon, I'm so sorry. I know you were counting on that..."

The boy wore a perpetual hangdog expression, but now it transformed into a flare of anger and he rounded on Vicky.

"Me? It feels like you were the one counting on it, Vic. The whole thing was your idea."

The Victoria Sandoval I knew would never have taken that kind of shit from anyone, even me... hell, even *Top*. But this version, younger and not as hardened, stared at Damon, open-mouthed, eyes wide.

"What do you mean? You were just as excited about it as I was! You kept talking about how bad you wanted to get off Earth..."

"Oh, come on!" Damon threw up his hands and spun around as if he couldn't stand to look at her. "I never once said that! Why the hell would I want to leave here? I get everything I need and I don't have to risk my ass flying out in space! You think I'm going to go live out in some orbital city where there's just a couple meters of metal between me and vacuum? Or some backwater colony world where there's dirt and mud and cow shit everywhere?" He laughed scornfully. "That was your dream."

"You've been letting your mom get inside your head," Vicky said, jabbing a finger at him, some of the ire and spirit of the woman I knew showing through. "She's the one who tried to talk you out of applying in the first place."

"Mom was right about you." Damon folded his arms, sullen and stubborn. "You aren't interested in me, you're just interested in using me to get out of here."

"I don't need *you* to get out of here, you big dumbass! I'll do whatever I have to in order to get out of this shithole, and if you want to stay here and rot with your mother, I'll leave you to it!"

She turned and stalked away from him and I wanted to cheer, but then she stopped short, staring up at the billboard seemingly hanging on nothing, strung up on a whisper-thin wire between buildings. An attractive, short-haired woman, certainly a simulation, looked down at the shoppers with grim intensity, trying to convey the seriousness of the news announcement she was about to make.

"Tragic news from the colonies today as word has reached us of a ruthless attack by the Tahni on human settlements on the disputed worlds near the neutral zone. At least half a million people are dead in the strikes, and President Jameson has vowed there will be a proportional response."

"You see?" Damon said, pointing up at the billboard. "You see? That's why I don't want to go out there!"

"All I see," Victoria said, her lips peeled back in a fierce snarl, "is an opportunity."

In what was effectively a computer simulation based on my memories of everything she'd told me and everything recorded on public databases on Earth, Damon backed away from her, fear in his eyes.

Here in the present, in our bed, wrapped up in each other, I smiled. She was telling the truth. No matter what, she wouldn't leave my side.

[6]

"I don't like this," Nance declared, staring at the green-and-blue world on the main screen with a sneer of distaste. "We should just keep going."

He might have missed the sharp glares the statement brought from a couple of the bridge crew, particularly Lt. Chase. The younger man didn't even try to conceal the dirty look he gave his captain, and he hadn't been in a good headspace since his rant back on Homecoming.

"I don't disagree, in principle," I told Nance, "but we've been in T-space for weeks now, and we're only halfway there. Maybe your Fleet crew can handle that with no problem..." and maybe they couldn't, though I didn't say that, "... but the Marines can't. Hell, I can't either. The Intercepts have cleared this place. There's nothing down there bigger than a cow and no intelligent life or signs of habitation." I offered an insincere smile of reassurance. "If everything's nice and safe down there, maybe *you* can even come down and touch grass."

Nance grunted skeptically, but at least he didn't complain any further, which was a relief. I'd heard too many complaints, broken up too many arguments these last few weeks, and my temper was getting short. Maybe Bob had been right and I *was* turning into an asshole.

"We'll be in orbit in about half an hour," Commander Yanayev reported, just the slightest hint of an edge to the words, like she was reminding Nance that this was happening whether or not he liked it. Yanayev was the most professional Fleet officer I'd ever met, but even she was getting worn thin.

"Tell the drop-ship and lander crews to prep their ships," I said, nodding to Chase. It still felt weird giving those orders without waiting to check with Nance or Hachette. Liberating but also terrifying in the knowledge that every fuck-up would be my personal responsibility. I turned to Nance, feeling the duty to explain things to him even if I didn't ask his permission. "I'm sending a platoon from Bravo Company down in armor to run security for everyone, just in case there's any dangerous wildlife down there."

"How can we be sure the grass isn't poisonous or some shit?" Wojtera asked, squinting at the isolated world as it grew closer in the display, going from the size of a baseball to a basketball in seconds from the one-gravity thrust. "I mean, this place is way out from anything we've seen before."

I nearly snapped at the Tactical officer but managed to control myself. Definitely turning into an asshole.

"Every planet we've been on, except the one Skrela world, has been based on Earth life," I told him, grabbing onto patience. "They've all been designed and created by the Predecessors for their own use or for the Tahni. Why would they make something like poisonous grass that'd kill you by walking on it?"

"I don't know," Wojtera said, his face flushing in embarrassment. "It just seems like a thing we should worry about. Not all of us have a computer in our head," he added petulantly.

"If you're really concerned about it, Woj," Yanayev teased

him, "I'll take your spot in the first rotation and make sure the plants won't kill you."

Wojtera shot her a silent bird, but Yanayev just grinned. Nance scowled at the two of them, his thoughts an open book to me. He didn't like the way discipline had slacked on the ship, but he was also smart enough to know there was nothing he could do about it. So he took it out on me.

"I suppose you're going down with the first group, pulling that whole leading-from-the-front shit again?"

"I guess it only makes sense," I agreed, "since I'm the least likely to get myself killed down there, no matter if we're facing grizzly bears, Skrela drones, or..." I shot Wojtera a rueful grin, "... poisonous flora."

"I suppose," Nance admitted grudgingly. "Though I didn't notice the lack of all those superpowers keeping you from doing the same damned thing these last few years."

"Well, since I'm sharing all my plans like a real military leader," I went on, "let me tell you something else you're not going to like."

"Sir!" Wojtera exclaimed, pointing at his screen. "We got a ship leaving the docking bay! It's that Predecessor ship!"

"Target it," Nance snapped, expression sharpening to the professionalism I'd seen in too many space battles. "We need to get it at close range..."

"Hold your fire," I told them. "They have clearance."

"They *do*?" Nance demanded, rising from his seat. "Since when?"

"I'm sending Chang out in his ship to scout the next couple systems up the line while we're here."

"What?" Nance blurted, jerking back like I'd slapped him. "Why the hell would you do that?"

"A couple reasons. One, his ship is a lot more likely to survive any trouble it gets into. I'd send the Intercepts, but frankly..." I winced. "I don't want to risk them. I don't want to risk their crews. There are few enough of us already."

"But Chang is expendable, huh?" Nance snorted. He seemed to appreciate the idea.

My conscience stung at the words, just a little bit. The small cigar shape, glowing green with gravitic energy, darted away from us at accelerations no human vessel could match. I watched it carefully, ready to use whatever force I had to if it tried to attack. Instead, it disappeared into a rainbow ring, a temporary wormhole into Transition Space. The voices became louder, clearer for the instant it was open, then faded to the background.

"He's a man looking for a way to make up for past mistakes. And if he tries to fuck us over and run, well..." I cocked an eyebrow, thinking about a half-dozen cyborgs stuck in locked rooms, silently plotting their revenge. "Good riddance."

Fresh air. It felt like it had been years since I breathed fresh air. Even the air on Homecoming had somehow felt... greasy, industrial, despite the care the Predecessors had taken to avoid ruining the ecosystems of the worlds they'd inhabited. Just the endless reaches of a city the size of an entire planet had given the whole place a metallic tang.

That wasn't the case here. This planet had never once seen its soil turned, never once had concrete poured or a tree cut since the entire ecology had been introduced tens or hundreds of thousands of years ago. Even now, with the repository of computation I had available to me, the sheer scope of the accomplishments of the Resscharr still left me staggering in awe. They'd given life to an entire galaxy, and if their motivations had been less than philanthropic, that didn't make what they'd done any less impressive. They'd created living worlds, not to use but just to prove they could.

"Does this place have a name?" Vicky wondered. She seemed just as enamored with the verdant lushness of the river valley as I was, though she at least made an attempt to appear as if she was scanning it for threats.

"Not that I know of," I said, closing my eyes for a moment, just feeling the summer breeze. The primary star was high, nearly noon, and the warmth on my face was something no ViR simulator could ever replace.

"What happened to all that godlike knowledge?" she asked, nudging me with her elbow.

Vicky hadn't come down in her Vigilante because I hadn't. Well, that and because it wouldn't be much of a shore leave if she spent it all trapped in a metal suit even smaller than the ship. The platoon of Vergai under the command of our own NCOs would be rotated in and out during the few days I planned on spending at this place, and I figured at some point, Vicky would guilt herself into taking a shift.

I opened my eyes, forcing myself to publicly take note of the drop-ships and landers disgorging ship's crew and Marines, all in their field utilities except for a squad of Force Recon who'd insisted on at least kitting up until we'd established a perimeter. Though what they thought they'd be able to do that a platoon of Drop Troopers in Vigilantes couldn't, I wasn't sure.

"It's a computer," I objected mildly, grabbing her hand in mine, squeezing it. "It can only work with the data available, and I don't have access to all the Predecessor database. Maybe if I was in Chang's ship, I could try to pull something up, but there's always the possibility that they didn't even bother giving the planet a name since they didn't have a settlement on it." I smiled, taking a deep breath, catching the strong scent of pine from the boreal forest in the hills above us. "This valley reminds me a lot of Hermes. Parts of it. Or the northern hemisphere of Eden, up past the mountains. Or the videos I saw of the Rocky Mountains on Earth."

"Is that why you picked it for an LZ?" she asked, tugging me away from the shadow of the lander and out toward the river. It roared over the rocks a klick or so away, across fields of sage and grass. "The badlands farther south would have been flatter."

"We didn't come down here for an easy landing zone," I reminded her as we walked.

Birds called above us, or things that were enough like birds that trying to come up with an alternate name for them would have been pointless. One screeched, then dove for the water, grabbing a fish in its talons before heading back up, and others converged on the hunter in a half-hearted attempt to steal its catch. Here and there, rodents scurried, and another klick downriver, something large moved slowly, herd animals grazing.

No predators yet, though I was sure they existed. Most of the time on worlds like this, the really dangerous predators were crepuscular, which I'd thought was some sort of genetic disorder the first time I'd heard the word. I'd found out later that it meant they were most active at dawn and dusk. We'd retreat to the drop-ships at dusk, though I didn't mean for anyone to head upstairs until they'd had at least two days down here.

"Maybe we should try to bag some game," Vicky mused, noting the same herbivores I'd seen. "I'd kill for real meat. Literally."

"We could. Though it feels like murder more than hunting here. None of these things has ever seen a human, or any other sentient life. They've just been wandering around like it's the Miocene, nothing to worry about except each other. We could probably walk right up to one of those grass-eaters and put a round through its brain."

"Or we could do it to about two hundred of them and have

steaks for a couple weeks for all of us," she agreed, not showing the slightest bit of remorse at the idea. "You and I raised cattle once upon a time," she reminded me. "And I still remember what fresh meat tasted like. Soy-based pretend shit doesn't cut it anymore, even though I grew up with nothing else."

"We'll see," I said, putting off the decision. In the end, I'd probably let the Vergai take care of it. They could use their suits to herd the things into a killing ground, and most of them had spent their lives butchering cattle so they wouldn't be squeamish about it. "Getting the meat back to the ship is going to be the messy part. I wouldn't want to be the one who has to clean out the drop-ships after that... or who has to deal with the smell."

"They could just open them to the vacuum for a couple minutes afterward," Vicky suggested, shrugging it off. "And we could put down plastic..."

I laughed, flipping up a rock with the toe of my boot and kicking it like a hacky sack, keeping it up while I spoke.

"You *really* want some good steaks, don't you? All right, but you have to be the one arranging it, and I swear, if there are bloodstains on the lander decks the next time I fly in one, you're gonna have to clean them up personally."

"Oh, like you won't eat them too," she said, pushing at my shoulder, trying to knock me off-balance.

I stumbled, but the rock didn't fall, hovering in place until I caught it again with my foot, grinning at Vicky.

"That's cheating," Vicky accused. "I'll remember that the next time we play."

"If I had to name this place..." I said, watching the Vergai Drop Troopers wading their Vigilantes into the river, the water splashing against the hips of their suits. They weren't playing around, they were testing the river to make sure it was safe before we let any of the crew recreate in it. "... hmmm. It's too easy to just try to name a planet after the one place you land. Like, if I was going by here, this valley, I'd pick something like Borea for the boreal forests. Or maybe Montana, because this looks like pics I've seen of that area. But I saw the planet from orbit and there're deserts and oceans and rocky wastes, just like Earth... just like almost every habitable world, more or less. So maybe something that shows how untouched this place is instead. Maybe... Primeval. Primeval sounds good, right?"

"Anything sounds good enough for the next two or three days." Vicky shrugged. "After that, we'll probably never see this place again, right?"

I kicked the rock into the air with my heel and gave it an extra shove with my mind. It arced over the river, landing with a dull plop.

"I hope. But you should keep this place in mind. If things don't go how we want... well, this place wouldn't be a bad one to come back to, to settle at least for a while." I motioned around us. "On a long-term basis, this few people is going to be a little tight genetically, but there's enough medical equipment to make it work."

"I don't want to talk about that," Vicky insisted, turning away from me. "That's not going to happen."

I didn't bother to argue, though I could have. I had the exact odds in my head, and success wasn't only far from assured, it was vanishingly unlikely. But she didn't want to hear that, and I didn't want to make her angry. If the time came that I was out of control and had to be killed, she was going to have enough to deal with. I had faith she'd understand if it had to be done, but that was almost as unlikely as everything turning out for the best. I had more hope that Chang might be willing to put me down... he certainly had the means and the opportunity. I just had to do my best to give him a motive.

I wanted to talk to Vicky about it because I talked to her

about everything. There was never anything I had to hold back from her. Until now. Now, I'd finally found the one thing she wouldn't do for me, the one idea she wasn't even willing to consider. If I told her I was keeping Chang around because he was the only one who could kill me, she'd either drive him away or kill him first.

I couldn't even sigh, because she knew me too well and she'd know exactly what was frustrating me. Instead, I painted on a smile and hoped it looked natural.

"How many people do we have down on this rotation?" I asked. I knew the answer.

"Two hundred and ten," Vicky said automatically, though she didn't turn back to meet my eyes, still upset. "We left Nance, the primary bridge and engineering crew, and the primary flight crews for the Intercepts, assault shuttles, and landers, as well as Alpha Company. They're on standby in the other drop-ship." Finally, she rounded on me, irritation in her narrowed glare. "You know all that as well as I do. You're just trying to get me to talk to you."

"Is it working?" I grinned, and I knew I'd succeeded when she smiled back.

"You know it is, you goofball."

I stopped grinning, my eyes going upward. Something was happening. A Transition was opening.

"Cam," Nance said in my ear, "that freakazoid Chang is back with his metal-heads. Just came out of T-space at minimum safe distance, and he's babbling something about there being enemy on his tail. I haven't seen any other wormholes opening though... no sign of anyone. What do you want to do?"

I didn't answer immediately, using the new senses that had come with this curse. It was like stepping into a dark room and waiting for my eyesight to adjust, the data coming to me as I tried to focus on something out in the darkness. There. The Predecessor ship's gravitic signature was unique to this system, unique to their drives, easy to pinpoint. And behind it, farther out, right at the edge of my senses, was something else. Something not gravitic exactly, not electromagnetic exactly, something I couldn't put words to, though I understood it on a mathematical level. Which was useless to me, because even though the knowledge was there, it was in a language I didn't speak. It was enough to know that the thing, whatever it was, was getting closer.

Vicky had been in the middle of questioning Nance and trying to get on the line with Chang, but I hadn't been able to pay attention, and I interrupted her.

"Nance," I snapped, "I'm evacuating the planet. Get Alpha Company and the assault shuttles down here to cover our withdrawal. And get the damned *Orion* to minimum safe jump distance and wait for us there."

"That's an awful long way to fly those landers, Cam," Nance warned. "We should stay close enough to scoop you up."

"No!" I snapped. "These things are an unknown quantity, and if you get that ship blown up, we're all stranded here. If they're too much, get into T-space and out to the edge of the system. We'll go to ground here and wait them out...."

Oh, shit. Too late.

I didn't have my suit, which meant I didn't have the video feed in my display, but I didn't need it. I tied into the *Orion*'s optical cameras like they were my own eyes, seeing what they saw, and used the gravito-inertial sensors, along with radar and lidar, to augment the view. Seeing something that made no sense at all.

Three of them, each smaller than the *Orion*, though not by much, each surrounded by that energy field I couldn't describe.

Each traveling faster than light.

[7]

"What the hell's going on, Cam?" Vicky demanded, staring upward as if she could see the threat the way I did. "I'm not getting anything coherent from Chang. He's blathering on about how some kind of impossible ships are…"

I held up a hand, taking in everything around us. Where a minute ago everyone had been jubilant, relieved, happy to be off the damned starship and breathing natural air again, a pall had fallen across them now. Maybe it was my imagination, my own perceptions, because there was no way most of them could have heard what was happening yet, but it seemed the pace had slowed, the faces gone from grins and laughter to confusion.

"There are three of them, and they're already here," I told her, speaking fast but clear. "Get everyone who's not in armor onto transports and get them in the fucking air. Alpha's coming down for cover, and I want everyone ready to evac before they get here."

She nodded and ran toward the drop-ship, not questioning, which was good, because I had other things to do. I felt like I should be running somewhere, too, that standing around was the same as inaction, but that was the old me, the one who had to be in a Vigilante to the do the most good.

"Chang," I said, standing my ground, the river behind me, "this is Alvarez, do you copy?"

"Bit busy right now, Cam," he said, strain undercutting the casual tone in his voice, making it sound forced. "Perhaps you'd like to get your ass back on the ship so we can get the hell out of here?"

His ship raced like a bullet ahead of the alien vessels, accelerating at hundreds of gravities, traveling at relativistic speeds, and yet it still wasn't enough to lose them. They gained on him steadily, inexorably, slowed down from the hyperlight velocities that had taken them here hot on Chang's heels and yet still faster than he was, making the Predecessor ship look like a turtle by comparison.

"No time," I told him. "They're too fast, and you can't outrun them."

"Oh, no shit, I wouldn't have figured that out of if you hadn't been down there to tell me. Would you have any suggestions about what our alternatives are?"

"You could try turning and fighting them," I said. "We need time, and you guys have to buy it for us."

"Yes, thanks, we tried that the first time they attacked us two systems over, but you said it yourself—they're too fast for us, and when you want to shoot somebody, you kind of have to be able to target them."

"Do it anyway," I told him. "They're gonna be coming after us, coming down to the planet, so that'll slow them down. Just keep them off as for as long as you can. I won't ask you to sacrifice yourself, because I know you wouldn't do it if I did. Just fucking keep them busy."

"The only way I got of keeping these things busy is letting them shoot holes in me, Cam."

"Just do it." I switched nets, information washing over me, a familiar sensation. Like being in the Vigilante, wading through data and separating out the important parts, except on a larger scale. I might have a universe-sized computer at my disposal, but all those facts still had to process through a human brain. "Brandano, come down here and pick me up."

"On my way, sir."

The reply was almost immediate, the Intercepts still in orbit. It felt wrong, felt like I was leaving Vicky and the others, but that was a platoon leader's instincts, a company commander's even. I was more than that now, the commander of this mission, the only hope these people had, the ones on the ground and in the air.

The others were shifting slowly into gear, Vicky's yelled commands echoing down through officers and NCOs as men and women in fatigues rushed back for their transports and Marines in battlesuits fanned out. Jumpjets flared white as they hopped over the river, taking up firing positions behind rock outcroppings, though God only knew if those would be cover or even concealment. Better than standing out in the open.

"Vicky," I called, running up to her. I could have talked to her over my 'link, but she was doing a dozen different things and didn't need another voice buzzing in her ear. Besides, she was too likely to ignore this next part unless I told her face to face.

"Get those landers in the air now, McNeil," she told the Fleet pilot as he scrambled up the boarding ladder into the cockpit of the shuttle. "I don't want anyone on the ground who isn't a Marine in ten minutes!"

"No one on the ground who isn't in a battlesuit," I corrected her. "Alpha's gonna be feet-dry in ten minutes, and when that drop-ship dusts off, I want you on it."

"Come on!" she snapped, throwing up her hands. "I can get

a rifle from one of the Force Recon guys... I shouldn't leave the troops."

"We have maybe an hour before they touch down," I reminded her. "And that's assuming they don't just bombard our position from orbit. That's why we need these ships out of here, to make sure they don't have a viable target for..."

Images, data, a wave of it staggered me, and I took a step back, eyes turning upward even though I was counting on my physical sight for the images. They flooded in not just from the *Orion*, boosting out to stand-off distance, but from Chang's ship. It didn't have a sensor synch with our ships because the systems were totally, well... *alien*, but whatever my brain's relationship with Transition Space, it was enough to bridge the gap, and I saw through the eyes of the Predecessor sensors as well.

The ships were flattened ovoids, not the pale green of the Predecessors or the standard, gleaming silver of most human and Tahni spacecraft. Pale white, like elongated skulls, and I imagined the engrained details and recesses of the hulls as empty eye sockets and nostrils and leering teeth. The way Predecessor ships moved was like watching video of one of our own vessels in fast motion, but these were different, an illusion, a spectral apparition flitting from one place to another without occupying the space between.

The one thing they shared with the Predecessors was the ability to go from nearly the speed of light to a standstill in a second, and all of them came to a halt in planetary orbit before anyone could even try to take a shot at them. Directly above us, as if they'd known we were here all along.

"Cam," Chang warned, arcing his ship around, trying to get back into range, "they're right over your position!"

Yeah, and what the hell did he expect us to do about it? Hatches were closing on the shuttles, but the engines hadn't even started their burn and it would be minutes before anyone was ready for takeoff. I opened my mouth to give the order to scatter, but it was too late.

The leering skulls fired.

I couldn't put a word to the energy raining down from orbit onto our heads, not like *laser* or *particle beam*. I vaguely understood that the Predecessor energy weapons used gravity somehow, but that was more detailed a description than I understood about the incandescent white fire spearing through the upper atmosphere. No way to get around it.

I raised my hands toward the sky. It wasn't necessary, wouldn't have made a difference, but it helped me to focus. I knew what to do because I'd seen it done before, seen it done in destruction. This time, it was going to be done for salvation. The wormhole should have been impossible, and it was for our technology, but not with the link between my altered brain and T-space.

From the point of view of the *Orion* and Chang's ship, the wormhole opened like an eye winking, utter nothingness at its center, and that nothingness swallowed up the lances of light. I flinched in agony as if the beams had pierced through my chest, but the pain didn't belong to me, didn't even belong to the Ghosts, the Voices... it belonged to the matrix of Transition Space, the universal mind connecting the far reaches of that other dimension.

It felt pain at the violation, not the same as a human would have, but my brain interpreted it like knives plunged through my chest. I couldn't keep focus, couldn't keep my concentration, couldn't even keep my feet. I slumped to the ground, and the wormhole dissipated like an oil slick on the water.

My vision swam in front of me in an explosion of polychromatic flashes, my guts twisting, and all they would have had to do was fire another barrage. We would have been dead, helpless to defend in the seconds I lie in the dirt, dazed. But Robert Chang came through.

As advanced as these ships were, I wouldn't have been surprised to see the glittering, emerald beams of gravitic energy from the Predecessor craft bounce off or fade away, but instead, the dull bone of the skull ship rippled and blackened. And shredded. The skull didn't implode and collapse like other, lesser vessels I'd seen struck by the gravitic beams, but it was enough to send it listing to port, tumbling out of its orbit... and enough to draw the attention of the other two.

White energy lashed out at the green cylinder and the Predecessor ship shimmered and shuddered, the pale emerald of the gravitic drive field expanding into an angry sphere dozens of times the size of the vessel. Chang's ship burst out the side of the green sphere like it had been shot out of a mass driver— running away to fight another day, if I was being harsh; drawing the skull ships away from Primeval, if I was being charitable.

Whether he intended it or not, they pursued him... two of them. The one he'd damaged didn't join the chase, instead righting its orientation and firing at us again.

Wait... no. Not firing the energy beams again, shooting projectiles this time, solid slugs streaking out of orbit in a fusillade that cut across the river valley like a Gatling laser slicing through light infantry. I threw up my hand to stop the projectiles, but they changed course, and by the time I realized they weren't slugs it was too late. The white teardrop shapes spun and spread like dandelions on the wind, then burst, each of them into smaller sections, floating to the ground.

They were landers. Hundreds of them.

The things touching down were twisted, alien... and familiar. They were Skrela. Yet not Skrela. They had the same relationship to the Skrela that humans did to lemurs or monkeys, obviously from the same branch on the tree of life but also obviously different. Take a scorpion, cross it with a bullet ant and a tarantula, throw in bits of gorilla and rhinoceros, color it bone white, arm it with a big-ass cannon attached at the shoulder of one of its four arms, and the thing that resulted wouldn't be as weird as the things loping across the valley.

A surreal nightmare unleashed on this pastoral world, their four motor limbs pounded the ground like the marching drums of some ancient army, and the smell of a corpse wafted across the plain with their advance. The one thing they didn't seem to share with the Skrela we'd encountered before was the lack of intelligence and coordination the creations of the rogue AI had shown. They'd counted on sheer, inexorable numbers to overwhelm the Predecessors, but these Skrela-things hit the ground and fell into a classic wedge formation aimed at the grounded landers.

Those cannons opened fire, time slowing down to nothing, the same glare of white energy coming from their individual weapons as had come from their ships, and where the lances of fire hit, they charred divots out of the armored flank of the dropship. No single shot was enough to disable the craft, but if I let them keep shooting, the drop-ship would be gone, along with everyone inside it.

Even the vast power I had access to was still limited by my own ability to focus my thoughts on one thing at a time, and for now I focused them on a shield. Space warped and hardened like a callous worn from too much use, casting aside the atomic fury of the heavy weapons, and again pain lashed at me like red-hot pokers had been stabbed through my torso. This time, though, it wasn't powerful enough to overwhelm my senses.

Pain and I were old friends.

I greeted it warmly, knowing that it couldn't break me, dug my heels into the dirt, and used myself as a shield for my friends. It was a risk. If I'd devoted my entire attention to the offense, I could have killed every one of the creatures, but only at the cost of leaving the landers defenseless. I had to trust the others to do their jobs.

Thankfully, they didn't let me down.

The stream of tungsten slugs wasn't visible to the naked human eye, but it was to me. Every impurity, every grain in the metal, every atom out of place was plain to see. There were twelve hundred projectiles in the air at once, fired from the chin cannon of the drop-ship, and they ripped into the Skrela like a scythe through wheat, dropping two dozen of them in the space of a second. The *crack-crack-crack* of the rounds going hypersonic broke through the roar of the atmospheric jets as the aerospacecraft rose, its landing gear sagging downward with the pressure on their hydraulics relieved before they began to rise into their housings.

I wanted to scream at the pilot to hurry, to get out of there, but trying to talk would have been enough to bring down that shield. All I could do was watch as the drop-ship climbed with agonizing slowness, the landers snapping into the air like they'd been suspended on rubber bands. The Marines took a second longer to get into action, longer than I would have expected if it had been the original grunts from Alpha Company, but a good response time for the Vergai recruits.

They were well-led by our senior NCOs and didn't just take potshots at the enemy, instead jumping in as one platoon, as beautiful and well-practiced a maneuver as any I'd seen taught in the Armor school on Inferno. They fired as they jumped, pouring coilgun rounds into the Skrela... which did nothing. I wasn't sure if the aliens wore armor other than what came naturally, but whatever protection they had was enough to hold off the heavy-metal slugs, fragments of the projectiles and spalled armor spraying into a cloud around the Skrela troopers.

They didn't succeed in killing any of the enemy, but they

did manage to get their attention and draw their fire. And I couldn't shield every one of the Drop Troopers, as spread out as they were, which meant it was time to go on the offensive.

It felt like dropping lead weights off my shoulders. I flew.

Some people dreamt of flying, but I never had. Those dreams were of freedom, of liberation, but to me open spaces hadn't meant freedom, they'd meant death. Freedom was a foolish notion and safety could only be found in tiny niches, enclosed and sheltered and dark. Now, flight didn't mean freedom, it meant power. The power surged through me, as intoxicating as the wind whipping across my face, spitting into the face of gravity and showing it who was boss.

Three hundred and six Skrela, one of me, and if they'd concentrated their firepower on me I'd have had to waste too much time and concentration defending from it to attack them, but they hadn't connected the shield I'd created with what they had to see as just one little, unarmored human. And they surely weren't expecting me to fly.

There'd been hawks in the desert. They'd circled above me as I wandered aimlessly, waiting to die like my father and brother. Older and wiser, now I knew that they wouldn't have seen me as food, that they'd been looking for rodents or small birds or even lizards, but as a terrified six-year-old, hopeless and on my own, I was sure they were hovering above until I died, ready to strip the meat from my body.

I swooped down like one of those raptors, grabbed one of the Skrela by its wedge-shaped head, and ripped it from its body like a child pulling the wings off a fly. Black ichor spewed from the wound, as familiar as the shape of the things from when we'd fought their cousins on Decision. The body collapsed, unguided, but I'd already moved to the next one, the energy surging through me like I'd grabbed the main power conduit in engineering.

One hand on the base of the neck, the other on the shoulder of the thing's upper arm, concentrate on the matrix, let it flow through me. The arm ripped off the body and the weapons mount came with it, tumbling away in a spray of sparks and black blood. On to the next, and the next one after that, but not quick enough. Vergai Drop Troopers fell, Skrela energy blasts ripping through their armor like it was tissue paper, a full fire team going down in the space of ten seconds, and there was no way I could take out enough of the things before they killed the entire platoon.

Lightning struck, the fiery judgement of God delivered to the heart of the Skrela formation, the thermal bloom and static charge enough to force me to raise a shield of twisted spacetime around myself, and I still caught a wash of breathtaking heat. The proton blast battered my ears, blanked out my vision, and would have blinded me completely if the power hadn't twisted the light around me, along with the heat.

Intercept Two roared only a hundred meters overhead, stood on her tail with a scream of jets before spinning back to make another gun run. Enemy fire sought her out but couldn't touch the massive delta, couldn't penetrate her armor before the main gun spoke again.

"Shift fire, shift fire!" The voice was Lt. Springfield's, and I wondered why she was on the circuit... until the first of Alpha Company's Vigilantes drifted down on their jets, their drop-ship passing over us a few hundred meters up. "Alpha, engage!"

The difference between Alpha's Resscharr-tech suits and energy guns and the jury-rigged models the Vergai used was night and day. Actinic blasts of blue energy lanced into the Skrela troops, ripping through their chitin carapaces, an enemy falling with each hit.

The job down here was done. I had to get upstairs. My ride hovered a hundred meters above on shimmering columns of fire.

"Brandano," I transmitted over my 'link earbud, "open your belly hatch. I'm coming aboard."

"Don't you need me to land?" the pilot asked, confusion dragging the last two words up.

"Naw," I assured him, spreading my arms for stability as I drifted slowly upward. "I'll come to you."

[8]

So caught up in the fight on the ground was I that I'd lost track of the battle above Primeval, unable to split my concentration enough to monitor the feeds from the starships. Things hadn't gone quite as smoothly.

The *Orion* played hopscotch with one of the Skrela ships, popping in and out of Transition Space like an Intercept or one of the wartime missile cutters they'd descended from. Too far away to be seen on the Intercept's optical cameras, too far for me to keep a solid feed from her communications with the light-speed delay, I found her instead with my own personal gravimetic sensors, the ones built into my head now.

She was out at the asteroid belt, past the outsystem ice giants thirty seconds later, back in toward the sun in less than a minute, yet she barely managed to stay ahead of the skull ship on her tail. Chang's Predecessor ship was nowhere to be seen, though given enough time and a clear head, I could have found her in T-space. The damaged third ship meant I didn't have that time.

The thing looked less like a skull with a chunk out of her side, more like the remnants of some Greek vase in a museum.

For all her damage, though, she was still a threat, and the only reason she hadn't already launched more drop pods or fired on the surface again was that Intercept One and the assault shuttles were nibbling at her flanks like horseflies. If the skull ship had been whole, her arcane drive undamaged, she might have blasted them to atoms, and as it was, they only stayed ahead of her fire with arcing courses that burned fuel pellets like they were cordwood. It couldn't last too much longer and, thankfully, it wouldn't have to.

"Get me as close as you can," I told Brandano, standing behind him, not strapped in yet still standing straight, unfazed by the three-gravity acceleration.

"Yeah?" he asked, casting a doubtful glance over his shoulder at me. "And how close might that be? Not all of us are psychic supermen, you know."

"But you have one on board," I reminded him, grinning tautly. "And that's almost as good. Within ten thousand klicks should be good."

I made him uncomfortable. Not that Chuck Brandano wasn't loyal—he'd proven that when we'd had our erstwhile vote back on Homecoming. But it was one thing supporting someone in theory, another entirely when his nose was being rubbed in the fact that I was no longer the same Cam Alvarez he'd known.

The skull ship spun on its axis with agility that would have made an assault shuttle pilot green with envy, finding a target that wasn't trying so hard to get away, and fired. This time wasn't as bad as before, maybe because I was ready for it or maybe because I was projecting my own power from closer. The wormhole wasn't big, not enough to pass a ship through, but plenty wide for the energy beam. White incandescence crackled through space to the point of nothingness and disappeared, leaving only a paroxysm of sharp pain, as if each infusion of energy broke the heart of whatever lived in T-space.

"See?" I murmured. "Nothing to worry about. Get us closer."

In theory, I could have flown out here myself. I believed I could, anyway. The warp field should have been able to keep a bubble of atmosphere around me, enough for warmth and respiration, as long as I kept focused. That was the scary part, the prospect of trying to keep myself alive at the same time as I fought a space battle with my mind. One slip and I'd be eating vacuum, and it wasn't as if I could reform the bubble if I let it go once... there'd be no air left to substitute. I was happy to let Brandano give me a lift.

"Why do we have to get closer?" Chief Sutter wondered, surprising me with the comment. She was the no-nonsense, by-the-book type, and I'd rarely heard her speak unless it was in the course of her duties. "I mean, you're doing this with your mind, right? Couldn't you do it from a hundred light-years away?"

Not an unreasonable question, at least from someone who didn't know how this shit worked. Which was basically everyone except me, as far as I could tell.

"Lightspeed delay," I explained. "I *could*, theoretically, project a wormhole into anywhere in the universe, but if that ship moved in the meantime, it would be a waste of effort. I need to be close enough that there's no delay, close enough that I can see what's happening."

It was more complicated than that, of course, but we were seconds away from being in combat with this alien, and Sutter wasn't writing a paper for peer review. The skull ship fired again, as if the crew couldn't believe their multifaceted eyes, or maybe figured we were using some kind of shield and thought they could overload it with a heavy enough barrage.

Not gonna happen. Body shots rocked me, but I tightened my stomach muscles and kept my feet, picturing one of the more sadistic bullies from my time in group homes in Trans-Angeles and also imagining what I'd done to him before I ran away from the place. I'm sure the auto-docs fixed Javier up just fine, but he hadn't enjoyed life in the meantime, not with all those compound fractures. And revenge on these guys was going to be a lot swifter than it had been on him.

The skull ship filled the screen, blocked out at the center by the wormhole I'd kept open in front of us, still absorbing one shot after another. Eight thousand klicks away, spitting distance in space.

"Yeah, that's close enough."

Visualize and *push*. The wormhole didn't have to expand, it just had to travel. The Skrela weren't expecting it. They saw the wormhole as a shield, thought it was some kind of weird defensive technology. I can't tell you *how* I was sure of that, but I was. I didn't read their minds, but I did read their actions, worked the probabilities. They didn't even try to run when the rip in the fabric of spacetime bored right through the center of their ship.

It would have been enough to kill the skull ship if that was all it could do, just punch a clean hole straight through the center, but those wormholes were at their deadliest along the edges, where the tidal effects were the strongest. A buzzsaw ripped the skull ship in half, fountains of polychromatic fury bursting from the power source at the heart of the vessel, swallowing up the wreckage, reducing it to atoms... and kicking me straight in the groin.

It had been one thing to maintain the wormhole when the energy beams had penetrated it, another to keep it going after the power of the reactor going critical expended itself into Transition Space. The thing closed and I tumbled backward with the thrust of the Intercept, slamming into the back wall of the cockpit.

"Cam, are you alright?" Brandano exclaimed.

"Yeah," I assured him, regaining my footing, reestablishing

my own personal down... and then finding a chair and strapping myself into it. I rubbed at the back of my head where a new lump had formed. "I think I'll stop showing off now. Get us to the *Orion*."

That was, as it turned out, easier said than done.

Nance had taken my orders to heart, and the starship danced around the system like a whack-a-mole, popping in and out of T-space, impossible to follow. Except for the skull ship, which seemed to have no trouble at all following her.

"*Orion*, this is Intercept Two," Brandano said, raising his voice as if he could penetrate the Transitions by shouting. "We need you to bring the bandit our way."

No response, and there wouldn't be, not with the ship bouncing in and out of Transition. There was no way they'd pick up the signal from a conventional transmitter. Fortunately, we had a pretty unconventional one handy.

"Get us into position in orbit around the moon," I ordered Brandano.

"I don't know what the hell we're getting into position *for*," he grumbled, "unless you think those ships are going to give up on the *Orion* to go for us."

He did it anyway, which saved me the trouble of explaining myself. I used that mental energy to lock in like a laser on the *Orion*, not where she was in normal space, waiting until she Transitioned again. That would put her in my realm.

There. A twinge, like someone had pinched me hard on the arm, and I knew it was the *Orion* jumping.

Orion, this is Alvarez, jump in as close as you can to the moon and lead the enemy ship toward Intercept Two.

I couldn't actually see the bridge, even with the connection through T-space. I could transmit a signal they'd pick up, but they couldn't send one back. Only the rumble of the drives vibrating through the hull broke the silence as we waited, the sledgehammer blows of the maneuvering thrusters spinning us into a braking maneuver as we arced into an orbit around the moon. The world had one, because nearly all the habitable planets we'd encountered did. It might have been a law of nature that a living world needed a large moon, or it might simply have been the Predecessors trying to recreate Earth because they lacked the imagination to think of any other ways life could develop.

A wormhole flared into existence a few light-seconds ahead of us, and the utilitarian, clumped-together shape of the *Orion* burst through like she was emerging from a birth canal, her drives flaring to life even as her tail emerged.

"We're here, Alvarez!" Nance announced, voice blaring over the cockpit speakers. "What the fuck now?"

"Just get out of the damned way," I told him, gritting my teeth in preparation, like getting ready for a punch in the gut.

The pursuing Skrela ship was a low vibration, a bass guitar being strummed beside my ear, traveling up my spine and rattling my teeth. She didn't emerge from Transition Space because she'd never been there, just rushed up on us with a bubble of warped space wrapped around her like a shawl. I couldn't open a wormhole and expect it to survive with that field surrounding the enemy ship. The field was the target, a knot to be untied, and I didn't have time to figure out if it was a square or a sheepshank.

There was always the Alexandrian method of untying knots though.

I couldn't open a wormhole in front of the ship, but I could open it right in the middle of the thing. Describing how I went about that is difficult, like trying to explain a rainbow to a man born blind, but the closest I can come is, I palmed the wormhole like a basketball and lunged forward, throwing it across the path of the skull ship.

No one else saw what happened. I'm not even sure I *saw* it, not in the sense of using my eyes and absorbing the photons. Instead, I felt it, just like the vibrations in the hull from the drive, except this hull was a universe. The wormhole I'd opened up spun like a sawblade, slicing through the warp bubble, sending strands of the gravimetic field whipping around loose, rubber bands yanked tight, and let go.

The skull ship did *not* come apart, which was a shock to me, given the sheer energies unleashed on her. Instead, she fried like a potato left too long in the processor, her hull turning from bone white to charcoal gray, bits of it crumbling inward and spinning away as she tumbled listlessly. Her velocity was gone, none of it imparted to the real space around her now that the field had popped like the soap bubble it was.

It didn't hurt this time, maybe because the energy had gone inward instead of into Transition Space, but I collapsed into my seat, exhausted by the effort. Intercept Two, still facing backward in relation to her direction of travel, could have targeted the floating hulk, but her proton cannon didn't have the range for it.

"Shoot it, Nance," I said curtly, lacking the energy for anything more elaborate.

"Gladly," the Fleet captain snarled.

The cerulean lance of energy was almost anticlimactic, striking the ruined hulk amidships. She split in half, each section in an opposite revolution, spinning away from each other, not to be stopped until they fell into the orbit of one of the outer planets.

"Where's the other one?" Brandano wanted to know, eyes

flickering back and forth between the main screen and the tactical display. "Where's that freak Chang?"

It took the very last bit of energy I had to focus once again. I felt as if I'd been in an hour-long sparring session against Vicky, Top, and my old unarmed combat instructor from Boot Camp all at once, then gone out and ran a marathon. Sweat dripped down into my eyes from my hairline, and I lacked the strength to raise my hand and wipe it away. But Brandano was right: we needed to know.

Pain blossomed at my temples and a drop of blood trickled down my lip from my nostril, the taste coppery in my mouth. But I knew.

"It's gone," I told them, the words coming out a rasp. I needed water. "The skull ship ran."

"The *what*?" Brandano asked, twisting around in his chair to look back at me.

Sighing in frustration, I squeezed my eyes shut and tried to banish the headache. Apparently, my limitless power wasn't up to that task. When I replied, it was in sentence fragments, barely above a whisper.

"The ships... look like skulls. Third one... is gone. Ran after the other two got blown the hell up. Chang is..."

"Hey howdy hey, neighbors!" Chang's voice thankfully interrupted mine, coming in loud and obnoxious over the cockpit speakers. I couldn't work up the energy to look at the tactical display, but since he was in comms range, I figured he'd popped out of T-space not too far from lunar orbit. "Whatever you did, it worked. That last one just took off like a bat out of hell, thank God, because I couldn't have kept ahead of the fucker much longer."

"What now, boss?" Brandano asked me.

"Get everyone loaded on the *Orion*," I told him, straining the words out. "And get us back to Transition..."

And that was far as I got.

[9]

Anton was older than Papa had ever been, his beard shot with gray, his eyebrows wild. Wiry, gray hair protruded from his ears and nose like a hermit who hadn't been in polite company for decades and his skin cracked at the lines on his face like they were tectonic faults. His eyes gleamed in the low light, feral and evil, reflecting the crackling fire between us.

The smoke trailed up into the night sky, disappearing into the darkness of a starless black.

"You won't be able to keep it up much longer, Cameron."

His mouth hadn't moved, yet I knew it was him, his voice a reflection of what Anton's would have been decades later, if he hadn't been murdered in the Sonoran desert so many years ago.

"Keep what up?" I asked, my legs crossed, the tiny sandstone pebbles rough under me as I shifted positions. I knew what he was saying, but I stalled for time, trying to figure out where I was and what had happened to send me here.

"The control," he explained, and this time his mouth did move but I wished it hadn't. His cracked lips stretched over a mouthful of broken and rotten teeth, blackened by neglect, the gums receded to nothing. "You can't control us. You think you're strong enough, but the Resscharr were millions of years beyond you, and they couldn't resist us for more than a few weeks."

"The Resscharr were weak," I shot back, not letting him know that the game he was playing had any effect on me. "Full of themselves." I shrugged, and it was almost like I actually had a body, that this was the real world instead of a simulation. "Once upon a time, they had ethics and morals and a sense of perspective that dwarfs ours. They knew the planet was changing in ways that they couldn't survive without poisoning and polluting it, so they left. They decided it would be better to spread life to the galaxy instead of trying to hold onto something they knew they'd lose."

I shook my head, leaning back, the sand warm against my palms. Familiar.

"But at some point, they lost that perspective. They started to believe their actions were right by definition, that everything they did was justified by the good they'd done. When you can't tell right from wrong, when you don't even bother trying, you get lazy. There's nothing strong about that." I eyed him in a challenge. "Maybe *you've* gotten lazy too. You've been sitting around here for a long time, seething, thinking how hard done you were, and the last poor suckers you had to fight were losers at the end of their rope."

Anton cackled, throwing his head back, his face resembling a skull just as much as those Skrela ships.

"You're a spirited little monkey, aren't you?" he said, looking me up and down. "Perhaps you're right. Perhaps we *have* gotten complacent. But the difference between us is that *we* have all the time in the world. We *will* wear you down, Cameron Alvarez. And the longer it takes, the more we'll make you pay. You'll wish you'd given us what we wanted earlier."

"I wish," I told him, "a lot of things. But we don't always get what we wish for."

"Very well," the thing that had taken Anton's form acceded, rising from the sand, unfolding like a praying mantis. He paused, pinning me with a stare. "We'll speak again."

He disappeared into the night and I woke up with a start.

"What the hell..." I murmured, hands going to my chest.

Yeah, I was really here, and *here* was, I discovered, the *Orion*'s medical bay. At least I still had my clothes on, which was not how I usually woke up in the med bay.

"Cam?" Vicky bolted off the chair where she'd been sleeping, her eyes going wide as she leaned over me, hand on my chest. "Are you back?"

"Back?" I repeated, looking around. No one else was in the compartment. "How long was I out?"

"Fifty-two hours and ten minutes," she said without hesitation, as if she'd been marking every second.

I rubbed a hand across my eyes, grit, and looked at her more clearly. Her hair was tangled, dark circles under her eyes, and her uniform looked as if it had been slept in.

"How long have you been sitting here?" I asked, taking the cup of water she handed me gratefully and downing it in a long gulp.

"Fifty-one hours and thirty-four minutes," Vicky told me. She sat on the bed beside me. "What the hell happened, Cam?"

"The Ghosts." There was no use trying to hide it from her. She deserved to know, and she was as talented at wearing people down as the rogue AI. "Every time I use the power, they get closer. They work their way inside. This one was..." I grimaced, "... it was wearing Anton's body."

"Your brother?" She recognized the name immediately, which surprised me, though it shouldn't have, not with Vicky. I didn't talk about Anton much.

"Not like he was. Like he would have been if he'd gotten older... this one was nearly a rotting corpse." A shudder ran through me, and I had to work to slow down my breathing. "He told me I couldn't keep this up much longer, and I think he's right. If I use it again... the power... I don't think I'm going to be able to stay in control."

"Then don't." Vicky's palms cupped my cheeks, forcing my face up, bring my gaze to meet hers. "We've been doing this for a long time without any telekinetic superpowers. We can manage without it."

Something nagged at the back of my mind, a worrying at my nerves like metal grating on metal. Like a bass guitar vibration again.

"Vicky," I told her with a heavy sigh, "I'm not sure we can."

"You're the psychic," Nance said, nodding toward me. "What the hell were those things?"

"I'm *not* psychic," I insisted, glowering at him across the table in the Operations Center.

I don't know why the hell we bothered with the place anymore. Where it had once been crowded with officers and senior NCOs, now it was just Vicky, me, Nance, Nagarro, and Brandano. Oh, and *Chang,* of course. He'd docked with us before we'd jumped to T-space.

The main purpose of the place was to make use of the star maps and intelligence projections of enemy forces. We had no maps of this place, no intelligence other than what I could provide. We might as well have been meeting in the galley where we could eat some damned breakfast.

"Whatever," Nance said, waving it off. "You know more than we do."

"Yeah, but that was true *before* I was infected by an alien nanovirus too." I shot him a lopsided grin and got a middle finger in return. Vicky elbowed me in the side, but I couldn't help it.

Sobering, I hunted and pecked my way through the menu for the holographic display and pulled up the gun camera from one of Alpha's suits. The video projection snapped to life above the table, showing a cluster of the enemy charging forward straight into an Alpha fire team. Just before the actinic energy beams from the suits blew them into charred bits of chitin, I froze the image. The bone-colored carapaces gleamed in the light of the primary star, highlighting every horrifying detail of the creatures.

"Do they look familiar to anyone except me?" I asked, gesturing at the image.

"They're a lot like the Skrela," Vicky declared. "Except... different somehow."

"I thought we got rid of those damned things," Brandano said, his face twisting in disgust. "Isn't that what Hachette and all those others died for?"

"We got rid of the production facilities," I corrected him. "That doesn't mean there aren't a few hundred or thousand—or *tens* of thousands—of the things still out there somewhere. But that's not what this is. At least I don't think so."

"Those ships weren't anything like the ones we fought when we went up against the Skrela," Nance declared firmly, finally finding an area of this conversation he could be sure of. "Hell, they aren't like anything I've ever seen, and I've seen as much of this galaxy as any of you."

"The things were going FTL through realspace," Chang said, shaking his head as if the affront to his sensibilities was just as offensive as the violation of known hyperdimensional physics. "There's no one *anywhere* who's seen the likes of that."

"We already know what they are," I interjected, "and where they came from. Dwight told us."

"He did?" Nance barked a laugh. "Maybe I didn't notice, but that damned AI talked so much, I might have just tuned it out."

"It was the thing that turned the AI against the Resscharr to begin with," I supplied. "When the Resscharr ordered Dwight to wipe out that entire world full of creepy-crawlies that had evolved on their own without the Predecessors' intervention."

Everyone else in the Operations Center stared at me as if I'd grown a third head, though undoubtedly for different reasons. Chang didn't know what the hell I was talking about because he hadn't been around for any of it, while the others...

"But, sir," Captain Nagarro said, frowning in confusion, "I thought the whole point was that Dwight *did* wipe out all those creatures. Terraformed the entire planet, if I remember the story right. He just saved some of their genetic material to engineer the Skrela to punish his masters for forcing him to do it."

"That's what he believed," I agreed. "And he probably had every reason to believe it. The species he wiped out was intelligent, but they weren't anywhere near space travel, much less star travel. He had no reason to think they'd spread beyond their planet."

"But you do?" Vicky asked. "Is it the... connection you have?"

"Even the universal mind can only form probability matrices from the information it's been given." I spread my hands in a shrug. "But what we know is, there's another intelligent species out there that's related to the Skrela, probably based on the same genetics, and it's incredibly advanced. There are only so many probabilities, and the most likely is that Dwight and the Resscharr *didn't* wipe out all of the original species, no matter what they thought, and that somewhere out there, far enough away that the Resscharr couldn't find them, that species developed into what we saw..." I'd been about to say *today*, but I remembered what Vicky had told me, "... three days ago."

"That's a pretty big miss," Nagarro opined.

"You ever hear of the black-footed ferret, Captain?" I asked her. She blinked at the non-sequitur and shook her head. "Little weasel-like animal that lives on Earth out in Wyoming. Three or four centuries ago, after a hundred years of trapping them for the fur, people stopped seeing them and decided they'd gone extinct. They thought that for a hundred years until someone stumbled across a whole colony of the things in the middle of nowhere. They're still around, but no one knew it. If they could escape notice for a hundred years in a small area of a single continent on Earth, how much easier do you think it'd be for these things to avoid detection in an entire galaxy full of star systems?"

"And somehow managed to develop technology more advanced than the Predecessors got to in tens of millions of years?" Brandano asked, eyes narrowing.

"Not more advanced, or we wouldn't be here. The Predecessors at the height of their power could move planets, create and manipulate black holes. These guys are just... different." I chewed on my lip, trying to think how to explain it. "Look at spacetime like it's a spectrum, with gravity on one end and electromagnetism on the other. You put enough energy into either one and you distort the fabric of space. The Predecessors used gravitic technology to open wormholes into Transition Space... the permanent jumpgates they left behind in the Cluster and the ones ships like Chang's use to enter T-space. When we figured out the jumpgates and invented the Teller-Fox warp unit, we stepped into that pool right in the middle and came up with what we called gravimetic energy."

"How the hell do you know all this shit?" Nance wondered.

"I mean, you're fond of telling me you're a grunt who doesn't know anything about physics."

"I was," I agreed. "But that was before I had a tutor with all the knowledge of two universes."

Nance knew exactly what I was talking about, and so did Brandano as an Intercept pilot. Nagarro might or might not have, but she did a great job faking it if she didn't. Vicky had been studying up on this stuff longer than I had and was better at the math, but still didn't get everything I was saying.

Chang, though... the man's specialty was bionics and biology and that peculiar junction where the two met, but I had the sense he'd made himself a polymath over the years. His eyes glittered with interest as if he still had the bionic oculars he'd worn once, before the first or second of his many rebirths.

"Anyway, spectrum, the Predecessors, gravity, us, gravimetics. Everyone got that much?" Nods, a couple of them hesitant. "Well, these guys, these... proto-Skrela or Skrela-oids, or whatever you want to call them, they dipped into the pool a lot closer to the shallow end. Electromagnetics. They're generating a shitload of power from those ships, probably using antimatter, but a lot more of it and a lot more efficiently than the Tahni ever did." Not that the Tahni did anymore, not since we'd destroyed their humungous solar-powered antimatter production facilities during the war. "However they're doing it, it's got enough energy behind it to wrap a bubble of T-space around them and let that propel them faster than light. A *lot* faster."

"That'd make a hell of a defense shield," Nance reasoned, eyes focused on something light-years away. "Damn good thing we didn't try to take them on by ourselves." His focus snapped back to the present, and he speared Chang with a glare. "Just how the hell did you wind up running into them in the first place?"

"We were doing what you told us to do," Chang replied,

stiffening, defensive. "We came out two systems away in the direction we were headed and found a system with obvious signs of habitation. Two worlds in the habitable range, even though neither one of them looked very hospitable to me. Too hot, too dry, too much methane and carbon dioxide, but there were areas around the poles where a human could survive... though why they'd want to, I'm not sure. Anyway, I took the ship down for a closer look and found some sort of cities built half underground and those *things*..." he motioned toward the hologram, "... crawling all over the place like an anthill. Those three ships rose out of the ground, an elevator-style launch pad, and came after us, and I figured discretion was the better part of valor and removed us from the equation."

"But they followed you," Brandano said, head tilted toward the little man in a look of utter skepticism. "Through Transition Space? Through two different systems?"

"That's impossible," Nance said flatly. "There's no way in hell to follow anyone through T-space unless you already know where they're going." He glanced aside at me, face going pale. "Is there?"

"Only if you can do what I do," I replied, an icy chill running up my spine.

"Do you think they can do it?" Vicky asked sharply. "They could still be following us then, couldn't they?"

There was only one way to find out. Closing my eyes and bracing myself against the table, I reached out with my thoughts. We were in T-space, which should have meant it would be easier to find out, to feel if there was something close, but I extended my consciousness cautiously, ready to withdraw if the Ghosts tried to overwhelm me again.

First our own bubble of reality, carefully preserved inside this other dimension, this vast and incomprehensible nothing. It was familiar, and I held onto it a few seconds too long, afraid to leave and make the leap into the unknown, but that was why I was here. It wasn't like scanning visually or even with the ship's sensors, not a sweep in one direction. Instead, it was more like throwing a pebble into a pond, the waves spreading out in concentric circles, each of them part of me, an extension of my consciousness.

Nothing at first, no sign of intelligence or occupation other than the universal mind that was in every part of this place, the equivalent of running my fingers over smooth, cold rock in the dark. The cool granite turned abruptly into hot coals, and I tried to pull that psychic hand away from the pain, but it was frozen in place like I'd grabbed a live electrical wire and my muscles had contracted uncontrollably.

The pain was white hot, coursing through my mind and into my body, and I thrashed and jerked, falling away from the table and back to the deck.

[10]

"Get the fucking medic in here!" Vicky yelled, and I thought at first she was yelling at me, which made no sense, but I wasn't in any condition to make sense of things. "Get them in here now!"

Shuddering uncontrollably, the reality penetrated that Vicky was on her 'link, calling the med bay. For me. My thoughts pinballed back and forth between brief coherence and irrational agony, and I wondered why anyone would call a medic for me. I hadn't been in a battle and even if I had, I must have won. I was still here, wasn't I?

I always survived.

"Yeah, Alvarez, *you* always survive. It's just your friends who wind up dying."

Sgt.-Major Ellen Campbell stood over me, her face drawn and lined in ways it had never been in life, a mummified skull, the eye sockets gaping empty. Lips were drawn back over cracked, yellow teeth, a death mask.

"Isn't that right?" Top demanded, teeth clacking together, her body shrunken and bony beneath her field utilities. A gaping hole was burned through her neck, and now that I looked carefully, the side of her head was gone as well, the stringy, corpse hair burned away there, the skull beneath charred and splintered. "Isn't that what you do, Cam? You remember the old saying Skipper used to repeat? The mission, the men, and then you."

She laughed, a hollow sound.

"And you always put the mission first, don't you? But you don't seem to get the part about putting your Marines before yourself. Because you always live while they die around you. Joyce Ackley, Scotty Hayes, the Skipper... me. But you always seem to pull through, don't you?"

I wanted to answer, wanted to deny it. Wanted to ask Vicky if she saw Top's reanimated corpse standing next to us pulling the whole *j'accuse* thing, but none of my muscles obeyed my commands, not even my throat. All I could do was choke and gasp and shake and watch her with wide eyes, though I would much rather have looked away.

"I know what you tell Vicky," Top went on, crouching to put herself on the same level with me. "You give her that crap about a solipsistic universe, where you have to live because this is the one reality where you're the observer and everything else happens around you. That in other realities, you've been dead for years and the others are all still alive. But that's just bullshit to make you feel better. You know the truth." A bony, dagger-sharp finger pointed between my eyes, aimed like the barrel of a gun. "You get everyone else killed because, more than anything, you're afraid to die. You've been running from death since it nearly found you in that desert. It took your whole family, but it couldn't take you. And deep down, you're still that little boy who listened to your big brother when he told you to hide and not come out, no matter what you heard."

I shrank away from her, terrified beyond all reason, unable to listen to the little voice buried beneath all that fear, the one telling me that this was the Ghosts, that I shouldn't listen.

Because more than Top's desiccated corpse, more than the agony, I was afraid she was right.

Something pressed into my neck, a drug patch, and my body relaxed, along with my mind. I sagged into Vicky's lap, finally able to breathe again. Top was gone, in her place a medic holding a sensor up to my chest, a concerned frown on her long face.

"What the fuck just happened?" Nance demanded, looking between Vicky and me.

"It's the Ghosts," she explained, grabbing a bottle of water from the table and hold it to my lips. I drank eagerly. "They're getting to him every time he uses the power." Vicky glared at the others as if it was their fault. "We can't count on him to use this magic shit to save us. It's killing him."

"It's not magic," I groaned, tried to sit up, but collapsed back down, no strength in my arms or legs.

"Relax, sir," the medic said, putting a hand against my chest. "That patch I just gave you was a light sedative. Not enough to knock you out, but it'll keep you pretty damned chill and you don't want to be operating any heavy machinery, if you know what I mean."

"We could try putting you in stasis." I looked around at the unexpected voice, surprised to see Dr. Hallonen here in the Op Center, staring down at me like a worried mother. I didn't remember her coming in. "At least until we come out of T-space. This..." the matronly doctor shook her head, her eyes bleak, "... magic, psychic power, ability, whatever you want to call it, seems to be stronger in the Transition. You're more susceptible to being affected here."

"I am," I agreed, letting Vicky help me up to a sitting position slowly and carefully. My head still spun a little. "But stasis won't help. It'll just turn off my conscious mind, which means I won't have the wherewithal to fight back. They'd take me over in a minute, and that'd be it for all of you." I motioned at the patch. "Just keep one of these on me until we get there. I think it's the best we can do."

"Did you see anything?" Nagarro asked. She seemed the least freaked out by the whole incident, but then she'd always lived up to the Fleet Intelligence reputation, cold-blooded and analytical. "Before it... hit you? Were you able to tell if those Skrela type things are following us?"

"Shit, just call them *Skrela*," Brandano suggested. "It's easier than thinking up a new name, and we don't have any idea what they're actually called."

"I doubt they have a name for themselves," I admitted. "Or even the concept of names. They're as utterly alien as anything we could imagine. Skrela will do for now." I looked up at Nagarro and shook my head. "No. I never got the chance. But I wouldn't count on them not being out here somewhere. Maybe not right behind us, not after we chased the last of them off, but they won't be far away."

"How can you be sure?" Nance asked. He jerked a thumb back over his shoulder, indicating the way we'd come. "Maybe that one world was all there was of them. Maybe now that we're gone, they won't bother us."

Nagarro didn't seem convinced of the notion, and neither was I.

"The Resscharr have been gone from this sector for thousands of years now," I told him. "That created a vacuum. You and I know that politics and power are just like nature, they both abhor a vacuum. Without any kind of opposition, those things'll move into every system they can. And the worlds they don't want to live on, they'll still monitor."

"So, you're saying they'll be out there somewhere, waiting for us," Nance concluded, "and you won't be able to fight them off again?"

"I'll do it if there's no other choice," I said, "but if I do... it might be the last time you can count on me. It might be the last time I'm in control of myself."

"Look," Vicky said in a command voice that wouldn't have sounded out of place on a Marine parade field, interposing herself between Nance and me, "the plan is we get to this Waterline place as quick as possible, no more stops. Everyone is just going to have to deal with a couple more weeks in T-space, and if they don't like it, they can stick it up their ass."

Maybe it was just the sedatives talking, but Vicky was beautiful when she was angry.

"What about when we get there?" Nance dared to ask, taking his life in his hands as far as I was concerned. Vicky wasn't in any mood to be trifled with at the moment.

"The Skrela can't be everywhere. Unless they're sitting right on top of the place we need to get to, we just get it done and get out before they find us."

Chang scoffed, leaning back in his chair as if Vicky had physically struck him.

"That's assuming one hell of a lot, isn't it, Captain Sandoval? I mean, we don't even know if the AI is actually there. We only have the word of yet another computer who's never been to this planet. Have you considered that it may take some time to find what we're looking for?"

"It won't take me any time at all," I told him. Something whispered in my ear that I should have been annoyed by the little man, but I couldn't muster the emotion any more than I could have jumped up and ran sprints at the moment. "I'll know where he is immediately when we get there."

"Hold on," Brandano spoke up, sounding nonplused by the entire conversation, raising his hand as if he wanted someone to slow things down for him. "I'm just a pilot, not a physicist or an expert in..." he waved his hand back and forth helplessly, "...

whatever *this* is. But didn't you just tell us you couldn't use your powers, or whatever you call it, because the demons will possess you or something?"

"*Ghosts*," I corrected him mildly. "That's just a vague translation of what the Resscharr called them. But they're just the mental patterns of AI that the Predecessors imprinted onto the fabric of Transition Space." I pulled my knee up and used the leverage and a hand on Vicky's shoulder to push myself to my feet. "And you all know how well the Resscharr got along with those AI. Yeah," I agreed, steadying myself against the table, ignoring the medic and Doc Hallonen ready to grab me in case I fell, "I can't channel my thoughts through T-space as kinetic energy without being open to them. And I've held out as long as I can against them. Longer than any of the Predecessors ever did."

Which was accurate but probably bragging. That would normally have bothered me, but not with the wonderful little patch on my neck making sure *nothing* could bother me. Not even my own pedanticism. I sat on the edge of the table and regarded Brandano evenly. The man was a good pilot and a good officer, but he'd never be either the pilot or the friend Kyler Dunstan had been. Still was, I suppose, since he still lived. Brandano was just too uptight for it, though he'd loosened up a little since the whole mutiny against Hachette.

"So, how are you going to able to tell us anything?" Brandano asked.

"Because it's not the same thing," I explained, feeling a little impatient with him, as if he should have been able to figure this out on his own despite the fact that I only knew it because of a nanite infection far beyond my control. "The telekinesis is an active control, me projecting my thoughts through T-space. The knowing... it comes by itself. Let's say it's the difference between you remembering what you learned in the Academy versus going to the gym and working out. One is passive, the other is active. Get it?"

"Not really," he admitted. "But I'll take your word for it."

I grunted, unsatisfied, and nearly slipped off the table, would have if it hadn't been for Vicky's supporting shoulder.

"Anyway, let's just say that I know what I know, but I can't do anything about it."

"And what does that mean for us?" Nance asked.

"It means we're on our own," Vicky said, pulling me toward the exit, ending the meeting unceremoniously. "The same way we have been from the beginning."

I couldn't argue with her, couldn't manage more than a half-hearted protest as she led me out of the compartment.

"I'm useless," I said softly, lying motionless on our bed.

"The sedative is only temporary," Vicky told me, the words coming from somewhere far away, as if she were in another compartment rather than only a meter away. "Once we get to Waterline, you'll be back to yourself. Nance is going to jump into the outer system first. That should give you time to recover before we land."

She was trying to make me feel better and I appreciated that, but it wasn't enough to allay the malaise that had settled over me since we'd left the Op Center.

"It's not the sedative," I insisted, even as the drugs dragged me down toward sleep, my eyes growing heavier with each second. "What the hell good am I if I can't do anything to protect us against the Skrela?"

Vicky appeared in my vision as if she'd teleported into the compartment, her stare severe and admonishing.

"We didn't sign up for this. You and I were supposed to just be fighting Zan-Thint, remember?" She gritted her teeth, slamming a fist into the side of the bed. "Damn it, Cam, how the hell did it come down to this? We were gonna be farmers!"

"I fucked it up," I admitted freely, the words tumbling out, lacking any internal censor. "I was afraid the only thing that made me worth a shit was being in a Vigilante. Now we keep pushing the outside of the envelope, going up against things that Vigilantes and Intercepts can't match, and I..."

"And *you* keep sacrificing yourself because you feel guilty," she cut me off. The bed shifted as she sat on it cross-legged, not bothering to take off her boots. Her eyes were red, but I didn't remember seeing her cry. "You think this is all your fault somehow, that they wouldn't be in this position if it weren't for you, but the truth is, they'd all have been *dead* a long time ago without you. Without the two of *us*. And maybe you think you deserve to be punished for your sins and all that Catholic shit, but I don't deserve it, and I've never been that Catholic."

Vicky grew more strident with each word, and by the end of it, she was close to shouting. I blinked and might have shrunk away from the tirade if the sedative hadn't given me a sense of separation from the whole conversation. Instead, the drug helped me to step back and regard things more dispassionately, which I could never have done any other time, not with Vicky.

"Honey, I think I know you better than anyone else in the world," I said, the words sounding as if they came from someone else, another conversation going on in the room while I stood idly by and watched, a passive, disinterested observer. "Better than anyone you grew up with, better than your mother. And if there's one thing I know, it's that despite the hardships, despite the loss and grief, you wouldn't have missed this trip for all the money in the Commonwealth, not if someone had promised you a mansion on the hills outside Amity City."

Her brows knitted, her mouth open as if she was getting

ready to bite my head off at the suggestion, but I kept talking, a squirrel chattering his outrage at a bald eagle, oblivious to the mortal danger he was in.

"Look, I know I've felt guilty about dragging us here, about not being able to cut it as a farmer, but the truth is, we would have wound up divorced in a couple years if we'd stayed on Hausos."

This time, Vicky's mouth dropped open as if I'd slapped her.

"I would *never* have left you..."

"I wouldn't have given you a choice," I assured her. "I can be a stone-cold bastard when the walls start closing in. Or worse, I would have just started hitting the bottle even harder, and then you would have had the choice of sticking around and watching me slowly kill myself or leaving me and hating yourself forever."

"So, you're saying this is the best of all possible worlds, Captain Candide?" Bitterness dropped off the words, but I couldn't help a laugh of appreciation for her literary reference.

"Not exactly," I admitted. "The best of all possible worlds would still have Top in it. But maybe it's the best we could expect. Did you really think either of us would die of natural causes?" I shrugged, more sanguine about it now than I had been. "I can't help myself. I'll just keep looking for bigger bullies to take on until I find one that's big enough to beat me down. And you'll stick around because you can't turn down a good fight. That's why you love me, I think. Because I always take you to the biggest and baddest fights."

Her expression darkened, and the odds seemed great that she intended to give me an earful about how obnoxious and arrogant I'd turned since I tapped into the universal mind, and maybe I'd be smarter to keep my damn mouth shut. But the storm clouds blew off on the same light breeze that brought in a soft smile.

Vicky laid down beside me, putting her head on my shoulder.

"I don't love you because you pick all the biggest fights," she insisted quietly. "I love you because you pick them for the right reasons." She took a dramatic sniff and wrinkled her nose. "You need a shower bad, by the way. If you think you can keep your balance long enough for it."

I nuzzled playfully at her neck.

"You could always give me a hand," I suggested. "Or something else…"

The knock on the compartment's hatch was uncannily timed, and I knew who it was even before they called out. The hesitance, the unusual cadence of it, the fact that it was too low for someone who'd learned how to knock on a door as a kid, those were all enough clues.

"Hey, uh, Cam, dude…" Jay's voice came through the speaker a moment later, confirming my deduction. "Have you got a second?"

I sighed and rolled off the bed, steadying myself against a chest of drawers as I reached for the handle.

"Would it matter if I said I didn't?"

[11]

Spinner sat cross-legged at the center of the small compartment, hands bound to his side by the neural restraints, and rocked back and forth like a child.

Once, he'd been a brilliant scientist for the Grey, the other nationalist faction on Jay and Bob's homeworld, assigned to study us when we'd visited. Brilliant and bold enough to ask to accompany us on our journey despite the fact he knew we'd never return. Bold enough to volunteer to be posted on the half-broken Predecessor ship the Nova had given to Lilandreth, eager for it because he wanted to be closer to an actual Ress-charr on one of their ships.

When Lilandreth had changed under the influence of the Ghosts, when the Voices had finally claimed her, she'd warped Spinner's mind to match hers. The devoted, brilliant physicist had wound up a mindless acolyte. When I'd killed her, it had sent him over the edge into madness. The scars weren't visible, not after the auto-doc had done its job, but the images were burned into my brain of Spinner slamming his forehead into the pavement over and over until blood pooled around him and the harsh white of his exposed skull stood out from his amber skin.

The physical damage had been repaired, but the psychological damage...

"I don't know what you think I can do for him that the auto-doc hasn't done already," I told Jay, shaking my head at the image of the Grey scientist on the monitor of the confinement cell. I'd been able to get used to the light-headedness and maintain my balance so far, and the plus side of visiting Spinner was that if anything did happen to me, I'd already be in the med bay. "What's wrong with him isn't physical. It's what exposure to *her* thoughts would have done to any of us over a long enough period of time."

Bob exchanged a look with Jay, as if he was reminding him that they'd rehearsed this.

"Yeah, man," Jay said, "but like, you got the same kind of power Lilandreth did. Isn't there some way you could use it to... *fix* him?"

I opened my mouth to turn the idea down flat, but paused. Because I was wrong. There *was* something I could do about it. It just wasn't very pleasant. Vicky must have heard my low groan, because she was at my side immediately, hand on my arm.

"Are you okay?" she asked. "Do you need to sit down?"

"Eventually," I replied. Sighing, I gestured at Spinner. "They're right. I *can* help him."

"Really?" Jay enthused, and Bob grinned as well, punching his friend on the shoulder lightly. "Oh, man, that's great!"

"Why do the two of you care so much?" Vicky demanded, She wasn't in the best of moods already after the two of them had talked me into going with them despite the fact that everyone agreed I needed rest. "You barely knew the guy. And weren't your people and his mortal enemies for decades?"

"Well, sure," Jay agreed, shrugging. "But look where we *are*, man! We're far enough away that he's the closest thing we got to family out here." He leaned against the bulkhead next to the hatchway, staring at the scientist swaying side to side. "Just look at him. I like to think if it was one of us in there..." he pointed between Bob and himself, "... that Spinner would try to help us too."

It was a good thought, one I couldn't so easily dismiss. The scientist had trusted us, and it felt wrong to give up on him.

"Hallonen," I called.

The woman had left us here, having her own work to do and not appearing interested in Spinner's case, likely because she believed nothing could be done for him. She didn't run at my call, instead shuffling tiredly around the corner, a tablet and stylus held in one hand, exasperation in her expression.

"If you're not going to follow my advice," she groused, "the least you could do is let me get on seeing to patients who will."

"I need to go in there," I told her, gesturing at Spinner's cell.

"He's violent," Hallonen warned me. "When he acknowledges your existence at all, that is. His arms and legs are restrained, but that doesn't stop him from trying to bite and headbutt. Already had to treat two orderlies who got careless trying to feed him."

"I think I can handle it," I assured her, cocking an eyebrow. I looked back at Vicky and the others. "Just me though. I need him entirely focused on me, and anyone else would just distract him. Nobody else goes in that room, no matter what you see. That's an order."

"That's a pretty tall one," Hallonen objected, interposing her not inconsiderable bulk between me and the hatchway as if I was going to barge in without her permission. "I'm a doctor, Cam. The Hippocratic oath and all that happy horseshit, remember? If I think my patient is being harmed, no order you're gonna give is going to keep me from treating him."

"You got the wrong idea, Doc," I said, chuckling. "It's not

him that's going to be in danger, it's me. And if I am, well... all of you had best stay as far away from me as possible." I touched the drug patch still clinging to the side of my neck. "Except maybe keep a spare one of these ready to slap on if you think I need it."

I was, I decided as I fell into a lotus position across from Spinner, pushing the red line. I'd told them all that sending my mental energy through T-space to transfer it to kinetic was as bad as inviting the Ghosts to take up residence in my head but that accessing the computer matrix of the universal mind wasn't dangerous.

This was somewhere between the two. Or *might* be. Honestly, I had no idea if, or even *how*, this was going to work. I'd insisted repeatedly that this shit wasn't magic and I wasn't psychic, but again, this pushed that line. Spinner was in this position because Lilandreth *had* done something that might have been described as psychic magic.

There was a scientific explanation for it, of course. The human brain—and Spinner's too, who wasn't precisely human but close enough—was a complex system, the most complex computer of its size in existence, even after almost four centuries of building artificial models. Consciousness was an emergent property of that complexity, which meant that messing around with the neurons of the brain was a tricky proposition, even for trained surgeons.

For a Marine grunt like me, it was a lot riskier. Unlike those surgeons and every other grunt though, I did have a guide. A guide the size of a universe. All I had to do was reach through T-space with the very minimum power possible, so low that maybe it wouldn't even be noticed, and nudge a few of those neurons around. And hope that the computer knew what it was doing.

"Spinner," I said. The man's eyes were unfocused, his features slack, head still lolling as if I wasn't only half a meter from his face. "*Spinner.*" This time, I said the words with a push... not a physical one, but a nudge to just the right spot in his prefrontal cortex.

The man's eyes flew open and he lunged for me, teeth bared and gnashing, ready to sink his fangs in and drink my blood. He didn't make it that far, of course. Something unseen and unmeasurable stopped him, holding him in place until a measure of awareness returned to his gaze.

"Get away from me!" Spinner raged, gone from near catatonia to a murderous fury in the space of a second. "I'm hers! You can't have me!"

Her of course meaning Lilandreth. She'd enslaved Spinner, and if it was willing on his part, that was only because she'd changed his will, broken it. Once, he'd been curious, devoted to the quest for knowledge. Time to see if I could undo what had been done to him.

"You're not *hers*," I corrected him, speaking softly but firmly, the same way all those shrinks I'd seen in the foster system had talked to me. "You're not mine either. Your mind belongs to you, Dr. Spinner. You just need to take it back."

He sputtered and spat and cursed and I kept talking, slow and comforting, not even sure what I was saying, just keeping his attention on me. While I spoke, I probed, pokes of the needle into the bubble of his consciousness, looking for the opening I needed. There. Just the smallest gap, and I couldn't have said whether it was physical or emotional, whether what I experienced was literal or figurative, but I found it.

Through that gap, I funneled a stream of energy, a blowtorch cauterizing an amputation, or maybe a laser coursing down a fiber-optics cable to shave a nanometer of material off the lens of an eyeball. Either analogy worked, seen from different perspectives. Physically, I was working on neurons, much smaller even than a human iris, but figuratively, I had to cauterize the wounds Lilandreth had left behind.

Inhuman hands guided me, modulated the power of the thoughts I pushed through T-space, and I had to trust in the accuracy of their directions. Had I tried it on my own, I would have blown Spinner's brain out the back of his skull because, well... I'm a Marine, not a neurosurgeon. Even with the help of the universal mind, the task was nearly beyond my ability to focus, to maintain concentration for the time it took. It dragged on for what felt like hours, and before we were halfway done, sweat soaked the small of my back and dripped down my face like tears. The walls around me faded away, the people outside watching, even the face of the man sitting across from me. My vision was the blueprint of Spinner's brain projected across my thoughts, and I couldn't deviate from it.

Hallonen and Vicky might have been talking to me, Spinner might have been cursing at me... hell, *I* might still have been talking, but I heard nothing. Nothing except clicks and snaps, crackles and whirrs, like machinery was running all around me, like I was at the center of a huge computer. Which I was, sort of, though it had no physical circuits.

Near the end now, and my fingers twitched, a muscle spasming in my cheek from the effort. Exhaustion grated at my nerves, some from the utter concentration of the operation, some from the terror of the knowledge of what else waited out there for me. They could detect my presence at any time, could rush in and try to take control, and I wasn't as afraid for myself as I was for what that would do to Spinner. Or would make *me* do to Spinner. I could turn him into a vegetable, or worse, into a rampaging monster, with just one slip.

There. The last of it was just ahead like the destination

symbol on mapping software, beckoning to me with a warm, welcoming crimson. Just a few more connections.

That was when they saw me, of course. It couldn't go that smoothly. Nothing ever did. They hovered beside me, flapping in the imaginary wind like vultures sniffing rotting meat. They could look like anything, like family, like monsters, but this time they chose the look of raptors, birds of prey but built from shining metal, their talons gleaming in the light of a nonexistent sun, beaks sharp and angled and ready to tear into flesh.

I ignored them. It was all I could do. Fighting them was out of the question, as was any attempt to negotiate or stall. The Ghosts wouldn't be negotiated with, wouldn't be talked out of the destruction and pain that was their stock in trade. They did the talking, the convincing, and when they couldn't convince, they used brute force. At least when someone as foolish as I gave them an opening.

Don't think about it. Don't look at it. Just get this done. Get it done and pull out and there's nothing they can do.

The sedative still worked, a little. It had kept anxiety that would have wrecked me toned down to background noise up till now, but with the Ghosts here, the drugs ran up against their limits. The only dose strong enough to handle this kind of fear would have put me unconscious.

Come on, come on...

There. Just a couple more connections to be made, joints to be soldered. If they'd just leave me alone...

Talons ripped and pure agony went through my mind and into my flesh, though no blood flowed from my physical body. This wasn't real. It wasn't real, and I'd seen worse. I kept repeating both those truths to myself like a mantra, hoping it would be enough. A few more seconds was all I needed.

You can do anything for a few seconds, Alvarez. You could lay your hand on a hot stovetop for a few seconds if you had to.

Yeah, but could I do fucking brain surgery while an angry pterodactyl slashed through my chest? Because that was exactly what it felt like. Or I assume anyway, since I'd never actually run into a pterodactyl. I was on a first-name basis with pain though, and this was pain as bad as I'd ever experienced, made worse by the fact that I had to ignore it. That one last connection, like the tests I'd taken in Boot Camp to determine how well I'd mesh with the systems of the Vigilante battlesuit, was a matter of concentration, not allowing myself to be distracted.

Just cover the purple circles with the green circles and keep them there...

And done. Like God on the seventh day, I regarded what I'd done and saw that it was good, and I rested like a motherfucker. In my case, I let go of the power and dropped out of Dr. Spinner's head, landing on my ass in front of him with a hypnagogic jerk, settling back on my palms. Spinner stared at me with wide, empty eyes and I was sure I'd failed, that he was catatonic and he'd stay that way for the rest of his life, which might as well be forever, given the medical care we had available for him.

Then he blinked.

His face fell, crashing down from the frozen rage into utter despair in a fraction of a second, tears streaming down his cheeks. Spinner's shoulders sagged, and I think he would have collapsed if not for the neural restraints.

"Captain Alvarez," he sobbed. "What happened to me? Why am I here?"

It took me a moment to reply, the words having to wait for a few shuddering breaths.

"You don't know?" I asked him, peering into his eyes, trying to make sure this wasn't a trick.

"The last thing I recall is being on board the Predecessor ship with Lilandreth." He looked around us, squinting at the walls in confusion. "Where is she? Why am I here?" A sob racked him. "Why can't I remember what happened?"

"Because you're lucky, Spinner." My legs had cramped up from sitting in a lotus position the whole time, and I extended them, stretching the muscles.

The hatch opened and Hallonen entered, followed by a pair of orderlies, approaching the scientist cautiously.

"You don't know what I'd give," I said quietly as they tended to him, "to not remember what's happened."

[12]

"I need a dress uniform," I declared glumly, staring at my field utilities in the mirror. They seemed utterly inadequate for this, even as pressed and starched as I could get them.

"They just need you to be there," Vicky assured me, putting the finishing touches on the polish of her boots. Those we could shine up, the garrison version at least, if not the field models.

"We've had so many damned memorials since we started this thing," I murmured, "that I should have had a set fabricated. Every time, though, I just think it's going to be the last, that I won't need them again. Then I started thinking that, if I *do* get them made, the next time it'll be me the ceremony is for, you know?"

"I didn't think you were the superstitious kind, Cam." It should have come out as a teasing dig, humorous and playful. Instead, it was as morose as Vicky's mood, so I decided to treat it as a serious question.

"I'm not, particularly. But I can't get over the idea that there's such a thing as tempting fate. And God knows we've both done enough of that already."

She nodded, eyes downcast, checked her gig line in the

mirror, then headed for the hatch without another word. There was no need for conversation. We'd both made this same journey too many times. For people we'd cared about a great deal more, if I was being honest. Not that we didn't appreciate our Vergai recruits, but the truth was, we'd only known them for a few months, not like Colonel Hachette, or Top, or any of the other Marines from Alpha. It had once been a full company instead of two heavy platoons.

The Fleet crew we passed on the way to the lift banks nodded respectfully. By now, everyone knew when something like this happened. They would have come if it had been fitting, but Marines tended to prefer their own numbers attending these ceremonies. Except Top. But she'd been one of the mission commanders, not just a Marine NCO.

"God, I miss Top." The words slipped out just after the lift doors had closed, leaving Vicky and I in private again.

"We all do," she agreed. "She was more a mother to me than my own mother ever was."

"I just keep thinking that if she hadn't gotten killed, maybe Hachette wouldn't have lost his shit." I grunted. "Then I wouldn't have ever been in this position and maybe everything wouldn't have gotten so fucked up."

Vicky's glare spoke of annoyance and I thought she was about to chew me out for being selfish, for thinking this was all about me and not considering the worth both of those people had to everyone else around them. She didn't.

"Do you really think," she asked, grinding the words out, "that everything would have all worked out for the best if we still had Hachette as our CO? Do you think even with Top advising him, he would have made better choices? Like what? What do you think he would have done differently?"

I opened my mouth, closed it again, thought about the question for a second. Even used the long list of alternative ways things could have gone supplied to me by the T-space universal mind... and got nothing.

"I don't know," I admitted. "I just feel like if I hadn't been in charge, if I'd been on the outside looking in, maybe I could have come up with something smarter. You know, just because there wouldn't have been the pressure of being the one responsible for the decision."

"You just feel guilty," she accused. "You always feel like everything's your fault, even if there was no other choice to be made." The annoyance left both her tone and her expression as she slipped an arm around me. "You have to accept the fact that, sometimes, there *is no* good choice. There's just the least bad one. You're right about one thing, though. If Hachette were still in charge, we wouldn't be in this position... because we all would've been dead a long time ago."

I wasn't sure if I believed that, but I did the smart thing and hugged her back. At least if we'd died under Hachette's command, I would've gone out knowing I did the best I could to get us out of it.

The lift opened onto the hangar bay, and we stepped out to find the rest of the Marines already gathered in one of the few empty spots. The hangar was even more crowded now that Chang's Predecessor ship had taken the slot vacated by the lander we'd given to Dunstan, and the incessant faint green glow from the thing threw the entire bay into a macabre, haunted-house light.

"Battalion!" First Sgt. Czarnecki snapped as the two of us walked around the gaggle. "Fall in!"

The Vergai recruits hurried to their correct positions and stiffened to the position of attention, even as the commands were echoed by Bravo's and Alpha's NCOs. The older Marines of Alpha weren't quite as hasty or panicked in their movements, their drill and ceremony training a lot farther back in their careers than the younger Vergai.

Vicky marched to the head of the formation and received the salute from Czarnecki, taking control of the formation. I waited until she was in place before I strode up and repeated the ritual with her, standing at the center between the two companies, one so much larger than the other. Though not as much as it had been a few days ago.

I didn't put them at ease immediately. I wanted to get a look at them first when they couldn't stare back, wouldn't know someone was assessing them. The Vergai were wide-eyed, their faces pale, a remnant of the shock left over from the deaths of their friends, and even at attention, they kept glancing to the side where that one fire team would have been lined up. Like they couldn't believe it, couldn't believe their friends were really gone.

Alpha... their expressions were stolid, accepting. Fatalistic. As if every single one of them expected to die on this mission and they just wished fate would go ahead and get it over with.

"At ease," I barked, projecting my voice like I'd been taught in NCO school.

Their eyes met mine now, freed from the strictures of attention, and whether it was Vergai newcomer or OG vet, they all shared an expression now. The desire for me to tell them everything was going to be all right. And an unwillingness to look at the center where the four helmets rested next to four empty sets of combat boots.

"I remember when I was a private in training on Inferno," I said, "thinking that all that marching and turning and all those intricate formations were the be-all and end-all of my military career. Because that's how important the DIs in Boot Camp made us believe they were." The chuckle that forced its way past my frown wasn't humorous. Maybe a little bitter. "Of course, all that drill and ceremony was simply a mechanism to break down our individual identities and form us into part of the whole, to shape us into Marines. Though I gotta admit, it didn't work that well on me. A lifetime of foster care had inured me to the bullshit mind games and fashioned me into quite the aspiring con man. Pretending to care about stupid, meaningless rituals was second nature."

The vets nodded, having been there themselves, but the Vergai appeared scandalized, like I'd just walked into a Catholic Sunday school and declared myself an atheist. Or worse, a Satanist. Time for the payoff.

"I didn't understand the real meaning of being in the Corps until I found myself utterly helpless and dependent on people who had no good reason to care about me. Yet they did. They risked their lives for me, and they did their best to help me grow as a person, to give me something to care about."

I hadn't thought about Dak in a long time. Not since I'd left Hausos. I hadn't thought about Maria in much, much longer, and I was surprised at the knife of pain through my gut at the memory of watching her die. Trying to speak again, I choked up and had to swallow the lump in my throat before I continued.

"I realized in that moment that the thing I'd been missing for so long, the thing that the Corps could give me that nothing else could, that no one else *would*, was a family. All of you came on this journey for different reasons... maybe for adventure, maybe because you were tired of the life you were living and needed a change. Maybe because it was the only way you thought you could see the galaxy." I snorted. "Well, you've certainly had *that* chance. You've seen more of it than any human alive, no matter if you started out on Earth or back on Yfingam. But whatever you told yourself was the reason for you joining the Corps, what each and every one of you has gotten out of it has been a family."

I couldn't stand still. It felt unnatural for me to talk to them while I was standing still, like I was pretending to be one of those stuffy, posturing colonels giving lectures or op orders, trying to sound important. Pacing across the front of the ranks, I tried to meet each of their eyes, to let them see I was being honest.

"I know a lot of you left your blood families behind, and I know you miss them badly. I know some of you think you're never going to see them again."

A few winces at my words, as if I'd brought up something the vets among us had been trying not to think about.

"And I can't promise you that you will." I shrugged. "I'll do my best, I'll even lay down my life to make sure you get the chance. But I can't predict the future, not even with the powers I have access to for the moment. Whether it happens or not though, I want you to do something for me now. I want you to look left and look right."

It was maudlin and cliched, but it came from a sincere place, and I wasn't an expert at this kind of thing, so maudlin and cliched was all I had. They did it. The Vergai reacted more quickly, more naturally, mostly because I think the vets in Alpha knew what was coming, but they all did it.

"That man or that woman on your right, the one on your left, they're your brother. They're your sister. They're closer to you than any blood relation could ever be. When the time comes for you to meet death, as it must come for all of us someday, as hard as we fight against it, as desperately as we struggle, the men and women next to you, the ones fighting alongside you, they're your family."

Only then did I turn toward the helmets, the boots. The eyes of the others turned with me, as if they knew they couldn't avoid it any longer.

"Your brothers have fallen, but don't feel as if you let them down. You stood with them until the end, never shirked your duty. They remembered you at the end. And now it's our turn to remember them. Andros. Gault. Allain. Tarlov."

I remembered Andros and Gault. I'd fought them both together in the unarmed combat training back on Yfingam. They were kids, ten years younger than me, as young as I'd been that day on the streets of the Underground when a cartel hitman had died trying to kill me.

"From the halls of Montezuma to the shores of Tripoli, so says the Marine hymn. And if we make it back, if anyone ever finds out what we've done here, they're going to add another verse to it that talks about the heroic actions of your brothers and sisters. And of you. You're Marines and, as such, you're immortal. Your brothers will never die, because they'll never be forgotten."

I nodded to Czarnecki and he pressed a control on his 'link.

"Battalion!" I yelled. "Attention! Present arms!"

We all saluted as one and the Marine hymn played over the hangar bay speakers. I would have opted for "Amazing Grace," but the Vergai weren't Christians and the religious beliefs they did follow were so vague and convoluted that we couldn't even understand them, much less come up with a ceremony for the dead that would mean anything to the rest of the battalion. After talking it over with Czarnecki and Vicky, we'd settled on the hymn.

Maybe it was time for them to learn some new rituals. And maybe it was time for me to have a dress uniform fabricated.

[13]

"Well," Nance remarked, laughing softly, "now I know why they called the place Waterline."

I nodded and said nothing, watching the feed from Intercept One. Villanueva had drawn the long straw this time, leaving Brandano on a frustrated long-range patrol in the outer system. It wasn't as interesting but was likely more vital to our continued survival, since he was our early warning for the Skrela. I wanted to pay more attention to the sensor readings from his Intercept, but I couldn't look away from Villanueva's feed. None of us could.

Every Predecessor headquarters world we'd seen thus far had been a city the size of a continent, impressive, uncanny, twisted and curved in ways that shed the sensibilities of the human eye... and yet all the same. The Predecessors had been a force of nature, inexorable, continuing with the ages like the progression of glaciation but lacking in imagination and in an artistic sense.

Except here. Maybe out of necessity, because this world didn't have enough land for endless cities. This planet put the lie to what I'd said about the last world, Primeval. It *was* one sort of geography for the entire planet, and that geography was water... and islands. I'd never been to Polynesia or the West Indies or the Caribbean back on Earth, but I'd seen the videos and images, and the entire southern hemisphere of this planet could have been a copy-and-paste clone stamp of those areas slapped onto the ocean.

In the north, it was similar, though the island chains there had a jagged, windswept look to them more like the Faroes and the Orkneys. The poles were still the poles, of course, covered with ice, but I couldn't have sworn to how much of that ice covered land and how much was simply frozen ocean.

The lack of land meant plenty of open ocean for storms to grow, and Villanueva had flown over three hurricane-size systems on her descent from orbit, but none of them seemed to approach our destination. It was a large island, maybe the size of Ireland, the largest on this world, yet it wasn't covered in city. The center of the land mass was green and overgrown, lush and tropical, and I'd initially worried there'd be no place to land until Villanueva had overflown the northern shores of the island.

It looked nothing like any Resscharr structure I'd seen before, yet I instantly knew that it was the right place. The curved wall rose out of the waves to tower over the north shore of the island, what would have been beach paved over into a massive courtyard kilometers across, though not nearly large enough for the population I knew had to have been living here before the collapse. That population hadn't been living on the surface.

The sensor readings told the story, following the kilometers-long curve of the rising wall back into the ocean... and downward. Tens of thousands of meters down, following the curve of the sea floor and extending beneath it for a distance of at least five klicks.

"It's incredible," Vicky murmured, shaking her head in disbelief. "How the hell did they build this?"

"I'd like to know *why* the hell they built it," Robert Chang said.

Nance glared back at the little man, not making any secret of the fact that he didn't like having him on *his* bridge. I wasn't sure if I liked it either, but I'd decided that I'd rather have him where I could see him.

"I mean, look at the place," he went on, motioning at the screen, at the multiple views of the world still displayed there from Intercept One's descent. "It's beautiful, I guess," he allowed, "if you like the beach and the oceans." He shrugged. "And seafood. But building under the ocean like that, it's got to be incredibly expensive, both in time and resources. Why would it be worth the trouble?"

"To hide," I suggested. "From the Skrela... the *original* Skrela, that is. And whoever else they considered a threat. If I didn't know this place was here already, do you think we'd have found it?"

"Well, it just makes me feel all warm inside that the fucking Predecessors were so scared shitless of something that they hid underwater and now we're walking into it. You should let me and my crew scout down there. That Predecessor ship is a lot more powerful than your Intercept. If there's trouble, we could better handle it."

I shook my head. Instinct had answered that question, and I knew better than to second-guess it by now.

"The last time you scouted for us, those new Skrela found you... and they attacked without warning, followed you all the way back to us on Primeval, and lost two thirds of their ships before they gave up. That's the kind of attention we can do without."

"So, you want me to just stay up here and watch?" he asked sharply, his eyes narrowing. "Because that wasn't our deal."

"No," I assured him, turning slightly, the magnetic soles of my ship boots scraping against the deck. "You're coming down with us. But your crew's staying up here, in the ship, in the docking bay, ready to give us support if we need it."

He grunted, not sounding entirely satisfied.

"I suppose that's better than being confined to their quarters contemplating their cybernetic navels," Chang said dryly. He shrugged. "It's probably better that they stay up here anyway. They've been very... tolerant of my move away from their Evolutionist ways so far. But this entire venture makes them uncomfortable, makes them think I'm leaving them behind. I don't know how much longer I can expect them to trust me."

"I don't know how anyone could *ever* trust you," Nance commented as though he'd been a part of the conversation. "And I certainly don't know why we're letting a bunch of Skinganger criminals have control of the most powerful weapon in our arsenal."

"Because it wouldn't *be* in our arsenal if they hadn't brought it to us," I reminded him, arching an eyebrow. "Do you think we should just space them and take what we want?"

"I'm not sure spacing those freaks would even kill them," Nance admitted. "But in principle, I have no problem finishing the job they started and removing what's left of their humanity for them, if you know what I mean."

"Ah, Captain," Chang said, offering a broad grin, "it's people like you who are a constant reminder of why I came to place such a low value on human life."

"It's what we're going to do, Captain," I told him, with an edge to the words that left no doubt what I meant. "Not least of which because we know their weapons can damage the Skrela ships, and if anything happens to the *Orion*, well... we're all just completely screwed, aren't we?"

I didn't remind him that part of the reason we were here was to find another ship, because I wasn't in the mood to prolong the argument.

"Fine," Nance muttered, as if he'd had a choice in the matter. "But when everything goes to shit with those lunatics, don't say I didn't warn you."

"Oh, I love you too, Rafael," Chang sneered.

Vicky hadn't said a word during the entire exchange, and neither did she now, still fixed on the main screen.

"Where are they?" she asked, and I blinked at the non-sequitur.

"Who? The Predecessors? I presume they're all dead."

"No." Vicky rolled her eyes at me. "The *Skrela*. If they've moved into the space the Resscharr left behind, like you said, then why aren't they crawling all over the surface, all over the islands?"

"Maybe they're *below* the surface," Chang suggested, making a scuttling gesture with his fingers. "You know, down there under the ocean living in whatever comfortable warren the Predecessors built for themselves."

"The Skrela aren't built for worlds we'd call hospitable," I explained. "I got a good look at their bodies last time, and even though we didn't save one for Hallonen or the others to necropsy, the little xenobiologist in here..." I tapped the side of my head, "... told me they're at home in atmospheres richer in carbon dioxide and methane than we are. They *can* live in our ecosystems, but it's not what they consider comfortable. They aren't coming here just to move in where the Resscharr moved out. They're here to re-engineer the worlds to suit them."

And *that* hadn't come to me until just in the moment. But I hoped it was right.

"*Orion*, this is Intercept One," Villanueva called. "I'm about done with the surface scan. No sign of any life more sophisticated than the local analogues for monkeys. You want me to land and take a walk?"

She was only half-kidding. Francesca Villanueva was the kind of pilot who wouldn't have minded at all being the first human to set foot on a new planet, and I wouldn't have minded giving her the honors except...

"Negative, Intercept One," I told her. "Two is running deep patrol. I need you at the edge of minimum Transition distance at top cover. You're the next line of defense if Commander Brandano detects a threat."

"Yes, sir." She didn't sound any happier than Chang. I seemed to be having that effect on people today.

"You're not going down on the Intercept?" Vicky asked, sounding surprised.

"No," I confirmed. "I'll be on the drop-ship, in my Vigilante."

"Oh?" She raised an eyebrow. "Slumming with us grunts again, are we?"

"I can't count on using the power," I explained, a little defensive with her, though I wouldn't have been if anyone else had asked the question. "I don't think there's an enemy down there, but if I'm wrong..." I shrugged, leaving the rest to her imagination. "I'll fly down with Springfield and Alpha. You keep Bravo on standby. They're still hurting after what happened on Primeval. My attempts at comforting them notwithstanding."

A flicker of pain passed across Vicky's face. She'd gotten to know the Vergai recruits better than I had, since my duties as the overall mission commander had pulled me away from training and drilling the Marines. I should have felt guilty about that, but mostly what I experienced was anger. I hadn't *wanted* this job—in fact, I'd actively *not* wanted it to the point where the only thing that made me take it was the knowledge that Nance would fuck it up and Vicky would have been forced to take it if I hadn't. Not that she would have done a bad job of it, but the duty was gonna suck ass no matter who took it, and I'd tried to spare her from that.

"You did good," she told me quietly. "I know it was your first time."

"I hope to God it's my last time." I sighed bleakly. "But I doubt it will be."

"Captain Alvarez," Chang interrupted our private conversation, his tone impatient, arms folded across his sunken chest, "you're our primary intelligence source for this place. Care to tell us what *is* down there?"

I regarded him coolly. I knew exactly what he wanted to know and why. But I'd offered him the deal, and I needed to keep him loyal.

"The name of that island and the undersea city beyond it," I told him, "as near as I can put it into something we can understand, is Veritas." I shrugged. "Okay, it's *Truth*, but that doesn't sound like a cool name for an alien city, so Veritas it is."

"And this AI is down there? The one who can fix the both of us?" Chang sounded like an eight-year-old waiting for Santa Claus to come.

"I don't know," I admitted. "Briggs *said* he'd be here, but I can't make any active contact, not with the Ghosts about to jump down my throat." The sedative patch had long worn out, and even though we were out of T-space, the voices were a constant background buzz now. Nothing coherent, nothing like before, but I knew it would be if I listened to them, if I gave them even a millimeter-wide foothold in my consciousness. "What I do know is that, if he is here, he's going to be under the ocean, through those gates. And I think... I *think*... that I'll know more once I'm down there."

"That's annoyingly vague," he commented. His eyebrow tilted toward me. "Or perhaps conveniently? Come on, you're supposed to be a demigod or something, aren't you?"

"What I *am*," I snapped at him, stepping nose-to-nose and poking a finger into his chest, "is running razor's edge right now. There's not much between me and letting those things take over... and I don't know what I'll do if I give in to them. I don't know if I'll be a conquering hero leading everyone back home and then taking over the Commonwealth to rule it as I see fit, or if I'll just kill all of you and head back myself. So maybe you just keep your fucking mouth shut until we find ourselves an AI who can turn you into not such an asshole?"

Vicky had her hand on my shoulder, pulling me back as if she thought I was about to punch Chang in the face. And maybe she was right. Nance, though... Nance just laughed.

Robert Chang nodded slowly.

"I think that's a damned good idea, Captain."

"Finally, something we agree on." I backed away a step. "Vicky, go get the Marines suited up and ready to go. I'm heading to the armory to see if I still remember how to put on a Vigilante. Chase, tell the drop-ship crews to spin up and be ready to launch in thirty."

Vicky jogged off the bridge while the Comms officer spoke quietly into his earbud and I...

I took one last look out the front screen at all that beautiful blue before I turned away.

"Maybe this," I said to no one in particular, maybe to the Voices in my head, "is our last stop."

[14]

It hadn't been that long since I rode a drop-ship down from orbit in a suit, but it felt like forever, like the memories of another life. The plasma drives rumbled through the ship's hull, through the battlesuit, and into my spine, a counterpoint to the buzz of the voices, as if the two were warring for my soul.

I relaxed and let them fight. The feed from the drop-ship's external cameras was enough to keep my attention, the clouds of the upper atmosphere swirling around us. One of the superstorms rotated just a few hundred klicks off our starboard bow, four-hundred-klick-an-hour winds ripping across the tiny island chains in its path. No human settlement could have survived the ravages of such a blow, not without the protection of Predecessor technology... unless they were built beneath the ocean surface.

"Maybe we had it backward," I said aloud, knowing Vicky would be listening. "Maybe the reason they built the cities under the sea wasn't to hide from the Skrela. Maybe it was because of the storms. They chose this world because they figured the Skrela wouldn't look for them here, but the only way they could stay here with any sort of high population was to build under the water."

"I hope we aren't here long enough to find out the hard way," she said after a barely-noticeable lag from the distance between us. "That storm is heading straight toward Veritas. We have maybe fifteen hours before it hits. I don't want your drop-ship sitting there, getting its ass kicked, even if you guys are going underground."

"I'll send it into a low orbit once they drop us off," I promised.

Nothing else had to be said, nothing that wouldn't have been idle chatter. The steady, businesslike back-and-forth of the drop-ship crew as they took us down through the ever-thickening atmosphere hid in the background, familiar and comforting. Yet if I let it fall too far back into the haze of noise, it turned into the Voices, turned into the terrifyingly persuasive arguments.

They don't deserve you. Those people back home... even if you do get back there, they won't accept you. They won't appreciate what you've done for them, what you've been through. They'll bust you back to first lieutenant and kick you out of the Corps, send you off to some toilet bowl that makes Hausos look like paradise. You'll live your life in obscurity and, over time, you and Vicky will grow to resent and hate each other. Those of your people who survive will forget you in time, and you'll wind up dying alone.

Or you could return as a conquering hero. You know as well as anyone that the Commonwealth government is corrupt, incompetent. They don't deserve the sacrifices you've made for them. You were more qualified to lead your people even before you received the blessings of the Change. Now, you're as a god to them, and you'd be worshipped as such. You could lead your people to greatness, Your name would go down in history as the one who gave humanity the galaxy.

"What a load of bullshit," I murmured, making sure my audio pickup was turned off. "Did this shit work on the Resscharr? Were they really that gullible? Because I'm not. I've heard more convincing bullshit from the street gangs trying to get me to work for them in the Underground. It didn't work for them, and at least they had something convincing to offer me... a dry place to sleep, a steady food supply and, of course, girls. What the hell are you offering besides empty platitudes?"

I was talking to myself. Great. Technically I wasn't, of course, but there was no one else around and no one on the comms, and explaining to anyone that I was just having a conversation with the Voices inside my head wasn't going to convince anyone of my sanity. I shut my mouth and determined I was going to keep it that way.

Chang had other ideas.

"I've never been on a drop-ship before, you know," he said cheerfully.

I wondered whose idea it had been to give him a helmet, then I remembered it had been mine. We didn't have any spare Force Recon armor for him, but there were, unfortunately, way too much spare ship's security armor available. Most of them had died defending Hachette at the Skrela hive world. The little man still almost seemed lost in the smallest set we could find, and it was easy to pick him out of the flight crew strapped in at the rear of the cockpit above us, even though I couldn't see his face through his helmet visor.

"I mean, I've ridden some weird ships, don't get me wrong. When I dropped on Demeter, it was in stasis, in a stealth pod covered in foam rubber, and it took days to reach the ground... after which, I had to hike in something like thirty kilometers through a forest filled with saber-tooth tigers. And of course there's my current ship, the story of which would fill up a volume all on its own." He laughed. "I tell you what, Cam, you've had quite the adventure out here, but you've missed a *lot* back in the good old Commonwealth. There was almost a coup, almost a military rebellion, almost a takeover of the colonies by religious fanatics who worshipped the Predecessors, and God only knows what happened after I left. Lots of death and violence and other fun stuff."

"Good to know we weren't the only ones running into trouble," I told him, noting what he said but not really processing it. "Hopefully they'll have that shit squared away before we get back, because I'd really love a rest at this point."

"I suppose my question for you," Chang went on, ignoring my attempts to end the conversation, "one I didn't have the chance to ask earlier, is why any of you would want to go back there? What's so special about the Commonwealth that you'd find it preferable to the opportunity to build a new life out here?" I imagined his beady eyes narrowing as he stared at me with the clinical curiosity of a researcher watching rats in a maze. "I mean, isn't that the dream for all of us? To start afresh somewhere we can make the rules? Where we can build a world the way we want? Why would you turn down that opportunity?"

I wasn't sure if I was more annoyed that Chang was forcing me to talk when I would much rather have stayed quiet or that he was forcing me to engage my brain when I would have rather not. Still, there was nothing else to do, and if the assault shuttles or the drop-ship picked up a threat, the suit would let me know. I could have bugged Lt. Springfield about the status of the company, but she was just as qualified to lead Alpha as I was.

"If it were just me," I told Chang, finding no good reason not to be honest, "I would have stayed. There's no home for me back there. But I'm responsible for all the other people who want to go back and see their families and friends again."

"Oh, Captain, you're a specimen, I tell you." The little man laughed. "I swear, your sense of duty is so overdeveloped, it must be taking performance-enhancing drugs. I only know one other person who shares your sort of convictions, and he came by them the hard way. How about you? Did you come by yours the hard way?"

"I got mine from my mother," I said.

"Was she a philosopher? A religious leader perhaps?" His tone was close enough to mocking that I fought an urge to climb out of the suit and punch him in the face.

"She raised chickens. She taught me every lesson I ever needed to learn. That when people who only consider themselves, their own needs, their own hold on power are allowed to go unchecked, that innocent people always die because of them. Because of people like *you*, Chang."

"And yet you're trusting me," he pointed out. "That either makes you hopelessly optimistic or not very smart."

"Probably a little bit of both."

"Touchdown in one minute," the crew chief announced. "Unless you jarheads want to change your mind and jump down the old-fashioned way."

"No, I think we'll do this according to plan," I told her. "Right in front of the sea wall. After we un-ass this bird, take off again and get above the storms, wait for our call."

"You sure about that? What if you need air support?"

"If we need air support," I said, "you're all better off far away from us."

More than anything, I wanted to crack my suit and smell the sea air.

I could imagine it, fresh with a tinge of salt, a hint of fish, and I hungered to smell it. If I was still just a consultant informally attached to the Marine company with no real responsibility, I might have done it. But I was a leader again and I had to set an example for the others, so I stayed inside my suit and looked out at the ocean longingly.

At least the external audio pickups let me hear the birds. They *were* birds too, or at least close enough that I wouldn't have been able to tell they hadn't evolved on Earth. I remembered seeing their like in Tijuana as a kid, frigatebirds they were called, huge things that rode the thermals far above the ocean. I don't know if I'd ever seen one of them touch down. They didn't touch down here either, just circled.

Other, smaller creatures rustled through the trees of the interior, small and low enough on my suit's thermal sensors that they might have been snakes or lizards, but nothing big enough to concern a dismount, much less a Drop Trooper. The interior was awash with green and buzzing with insects, so maybe being stuck inside the suit wasn't such a bad thing. Blood-sucking bugs were as universal on these terraformed worlds as birds, and not nearly as pleasant. Me, if I were building a world to suit my needs, I think I'd leave out the mosquitos, but then I was just a grunt, not a biologist. Maybe skeeters were a necessary evil.

Alpha spread out behind me, forming a perimeter around... whatever. They didn't know which of the arched entrances in the face of the wall was our destination, and neither did I. They towered overhead, dwarfing us even in the three-meter suits, the curved walls they were set in a good thirty meters tall, and those were just a fraction of the full size of the structures. Kilometers of them, stretching out around the beach. They reminded me of an ancient movie I'd watched once when I was on a classics kick, something filmed back in the early days of film, over a hundred years before the Sino-Russian War and the Collapse.

It was about some giant ape on an island not very unlike this one, and right down the middle was a giant wall to keep the ape out of the human part of the island. This wall looked like it was more meant to keep us out of the civilized areas, like we were the monsters.

"You know which way to go, sir?" Springfield asked. There was a hint of awe in her voice, badly concealed behind a forced blasé tone.

I hesitated before answering, taking in the scope of the place, trying to connect with it.

And succeeding.

The trees were still there, but they were trimmed, and there was a patina of age to the memory, an atmosphere of unreality that made it obvious, yet didn't detract from the solidity of it. The difference was that there were structures among the green, not houses nor shops nor storage bins but something more akin to museums or art galleries. They were a small symbol of normalcy in a place like this, a last-resort shelter against the vast array of enemies the Resscharr had gathered unto themselves over hundreds of thousands of years.

A place where their children could learn about their society, their history, could get a sense of their civilization out in the fresh air, not confined beneath the waves in the artificial light of their cities. I've heard it said that any sort of baby is cute, but I couldn't swear that about Resscharr children. I'd first seen them back on Yfingam, and I'd allowed that maybe the hollow eyes and elongated faces that made them look so damned creepy were a function of the Resscharr remnant there being degenerate and isolated. Then I'd seen the children on Decision. Not a lot of them, since the Resscharr gestated slowly, but Lilandreth's children had traveled with us back to

Yfingam, and there was no difference between them and the others.

Or between them and the ones I saw here. Their mothers herded them like cattle, not much obvious affection shown, but that might have been a matter of a difference in the body language of another species. Or not. Lilandreth had left her kids behind with basically strangers on another planet and abandoned them without any hope of ever seeing either of them again. The Predecessors, for all that they'd advanced technologically, had evolved from dinosaurs, and maybe there was still something of that in them, the non-mammalian attitude toward their young.

Still, they knew that, to coin a phrase, the children are our future, the only future they were likely to have, and the mothers guided them through the art exhibits, the displays showing their societal history, making sure they learned. Stick figures, skinny but deep-chested, with silvery manes of hair not very far evolved from feathers, their legs bent backward like a kangaroo's, loping and hopping from one step to another.

I expected the Resscharr. What I didn't expect were the Tahni. They shuffled from one task to another, tending to those shrubs and trees, tilling crops sown between the stands of trees. Food could be grown hydroponically under the ocean or beneath it, but there was something about the taste of crops tilled under the light of the sun that couldn't be matched.

It was all very pastoral and almost idyllic at first, perhaps tinged with sadness at the necessity to leave their homes and hide in this hole. But the scene sped up like I'd set the video to fast-forward, and as the years—and *centuries*—passed by, a tonal change darkened the images. The first sign something was wrong were the ships. They poured in without ceasing, and where they landed, the Resscharr who disembarked grew more ragged and desperate looking. No more Tahni servants, no more children.

Refugees. I could see it in their eyes. No more museums and art displays, no more manicured shrubberies, just Resscharr pouring out of the ships and in through the gates, down below the ocean. All that was left above ground were the ships patrolling the skies, the space over the planet, yet the Resscharr knew it wouldn't be enough. That wasn't something I could determine from the looks on their long, striated faces or the frantic efforts they made to construct defenses.

Instead, it was intuition, probabilities not just from the universal mind but from my gut. I knew what the Skrela—the ones engineered by the AI—could do to a world, and not even the Predecessors at their full strength had been able to stop them.

The Resscharr retreated under the ocean, out of the light of the sun, and I saw which way they went. I blinked and the images faded, leaving the world wild and unkempt as it had been a moment before, leaving me with the view through my helmet's HUD. I turned back toward Springfield, shuffling through the lines of Alpha Company, stopping only a few meters from me.

"Yes, Lieutenant," I finally answered Springfield's question, pointing northwest at one of the massive gateways. "I believe I do."

[15]

The gate was faceless, featureless, without so much as a doorknob to indicate where it might be opened, much less a plainly labeled control panel.

"One thing's for sure," Springfield said, staring at the blank wall of thick metal, "we're not bringing this thing down with demo charges."

The rest of the company stayed in their positions, but feet shuffled and heads turned as they stared at the arched entrance, their curiosity emanating off of them like heat waves.

"It's amazingly smooth," Chang said, caressing the ebon surface of the doorway with his bare hand. No one had given him the okay to raise his visor or take off his gloves, but I wasn't so concerned with his well-being as to argue the point either. "Just like the hulls of their ships, like the entire structure was grown from a single crystal. The sophistication it took to achieve this is just incredible."

"That's all fascinating, Mr. Chang," Springfield snapped, "but how the hell are we going to open it?"

I held up a hand-well—my suit's hand—and concentrated.

Listened. The answer was there, if I just knew where to look for it. So much data, so many alternatives. They all pointed to the same conclusion. To open the door, I needed Predecessor DNA, which we neither had nor could conceivably get. Or... there was one other way, the possibility that I'd feared the minute I'd seen the entrances.

It's just a tiny fraction of the power. One thought, focused. They won't notice it.

I'd gotten very good at lying to myself over the years, but not facile enough to buy into that bullshit. Standing here and waiting for a better idea wasn't going to accomplish anything. I planted my feet, clenched my jaw, and reached out with the power. The mechanism wasn't simple, the security still encoded from thousands of years ago, built into biological circuits I couldn't have explained to an electrical engineer and didn't grasp myself, even though I knew the math for them.

I *could* visualize it though, as one of the ancient tumbler locks I'd seen on the doors of old buildings in Tijuana. Anton had tried to teach me how to pick them, once, before Papa caught him and scolded the both of us. People deserved their privacy, Papa had said, and if they wanted something locked away, no one should force them to reveal it. I wondered what Papa would have said about me now, about me worming my way into hidden things and deducing the thoughts and feelings of my friends and enemies alike.

Shutting out the memories of Papa's lecture, I honed in on the technique Anton had showed me, picturing the pick pushing tumblers. The ancient lock clicked into place and the cracked and rotting wooden door swung open on creaking hinges in my mind... and the smooth metal of the Predecessor doorway disappeared.

It didn't slide up or down or sideways, didn't dilate or curl away like a camera iris. One instant it was there and the next it was gone, and I stood at the top of a ramp twenty meters across, leading down into darkness.

"Okay," Chang said, stepping beside me and staring downward. "I gotta admit, that's pretty damned impressive. Those Predecessors sure had a flare for the dramatic, didn't they? Like old-time stage magicians."

"This isn't magic," I said absently, probing that ramp for any sign of life. "None of it is. Except in the Arthur C. Clarke sense."

"Should I know who that is?" Chang asked, frowning through his still-open visor.

"Science fiction writer. An... old friend of mine got me into reading the old classics. Clarke once said that any sufficiently advanced technology is indistinguishable from magic."

"Sir," Springfield said, "are you heading down there?"

"Yes, I am," I told her, not bothering to hide my grin, since she couldn't see it. "And no, you're not coming down with me. Me and Mr. Chang will go by ourselves."

"That's not a good idea, sir," she warned. "I know you think you're like invulnerable now, but..."

"I'm far from that, Lieutenant," I said, chuckling ruefully. "I'm actually more vulnerable now than I have been most of my life. But the fact is, there's no threat down there that you or the rest of the company or the entire fucking Commonwealth Marine Corps could protect me from."

"And what about those new Skrela things?" Springfield asked. "What if they land while you're down there?"

"Stay mobile. They can't fly, and you need to use that against them. If I'm not here to give the order, get Bravo down here and tell Vicky to have them make a stand here in the doorway. Try to contact me via comms, but if you can't, don't waste time or troops worrying about it. Coordinate with Captain Sandoval and do what she says."

"What if you don't come back, sir?" And I could take that question however I chose.

"Do what Vicky says," I reiterated. "Keep my Marines alive, Springfield."

"Good luck, sir."

The darkness inside the doorway should have retreated as we advanced, banished by the thermal, IR, light-intensifying optics, radar, sonar, and lidar all built into my suit. It didn't. Like a nightmare, all I could see was the floor a few meters in front of me, extending as I walked, yet never getting anywhere. Everything was too far away for the sensor or enhanced optics to reveal details, as if we were descending to hell rather than simply under the waves.

"We could fly down, you know," Chang suggested, struggling to keep up to the long, powerful strides of my Vigilante. "This has got to be kilometers long. We could be walking it all day."

"I already took a risk opening that door," I replied, not bothering to shake my head, since it wouldn't have translated through the battlesuit. "I might be a lead-from-the-front hot dog, but I'm not stupid. Levitating the two of us kilometers down this chute would be suicide. Certainly for you, maybe for me as well."

"I didn't *say* you had to use your superpowers, Captain," Chang scoffed as if he'd never meant that, though I was close to one hundred percent certain that he had. "Your suit could fly us down. Just let me climb up on your shoulders and we'll cruise right down this ramp like civilized men, rather than trudging along."

I had to laugh, not at the suggestion but at the mental image of the little man hanging desperately off my backpack, trying not to tumble backward into the jetwash from the boosters.

"I could," I admitted. "I've done it before. You wouldn't be very comfortable though, and the likeliest outcome for someone who's never done it before would be that you'd fall off and break your fucking neck."

"I'm willing to take that chance," he insisted, huffing and puffing as the double-time pace caught up with him. "It's *my* fucking neck, after all."

It was tempting. Did I *really* care if he fell off? It would certainly save time. But...

"No. It's... disrespectful."

"Disrespectful to *whom?*" Chang exploded, throwing up his hands. "There's not a soul on this planet except for us!"

"Disrespectful to the dead. When I was a little boy, my friends and I tried to play hide and seek in a graveyard once. *Senora* Belasco, the old lady who lived down the road from us, told us we shouldn't play in a graveyard. That it was disrespectful to the memory of the people buried there. She said we should walk slowly through graveyards and remember the lives of the people there, so their spirits could rest easily."

"Well, isn't that nice and superstitious." Chang barely got the words out, his breath coming too short to even allow a cynical snort. I wanted to tell him he should make better oxygen choices, but if he kept it up, he'd either have to stop walking or stop talking. "Don't tell me you believe in that sort of bullshit."

"Oh, no, Mr. Chang. I live in a world where the dinosaurs evolved into an intelligent species that terraformed most of the worlds in the galaxy, where sentient AI rebelled against them and destroyed their civilization, where I had my brain transformed by a nanovirus so I can basically tell the future, fly, and kill people with my thoughts. Where an entire universe exists with the power to think and reason and is inhabited by the ghosts of long-dead sentient computers trying to drive me mad by whispering in my ear twenty-four-seven that I'm a god. I don't have any time for something as superstitious as the idea of an immortal soul."

"Well, there's no need to be snarky about it," he panted.

"Oh, no, no need at all."

I stopped in my tracks, couldn't move, and barely noticed when Chang ran face-first into the back of my left arm.

"What the hell, Alvarez?" he snapped in irritation. "How about giving a guy a little warning? What the hell's wrong?"

What the hell was wrong was that a Resscharr stood a few meters ahead of me, staring intently into my eyes. Then he spoke.

"Jindal, we can't go through with this. It's too dangerous and you know it."

I blinked, uncomprehending, until a second Resscharr stepped *through* me to stand only half a meter apart from the first one and I realized what was happening. This wasn't real... it wasn't real *now*. Another memory. Not a memory from a spirit though, despite what I'd told Chang. This was from the computer systems in the facility, recorded automatically thousands of years ago and left in storage, never accessed until now. Not that I'd tried consciously to do it, but some of the effects of the power happened automatically, like senses added to the ones I already had.

"What's our alternative?" the one named Jindal demanded.

How am I understanding them?'

The same way I was accessing the memory from the storage drive, obviously. Automatically. A computer network with all of Transition Space to play with wouldn't have any trouble running a translation subroutine for me. It had even provided modified body language and inflection so I could read body language and intent. Jindal's scowl wasn't a Resscharr expression, not from what I'd learned living among them on the *Orion* for months. It wasn't my imagination either, it was part of the translation.

"Tell me, Kallista," Jindal insisted. He was a male, Kallista a female, though that was all I could tell about the two. Their dress was different in fashion than Lilandreth and her people, but then I suppose styles changed over millennia, even among the Resscharr. "What else do you think we can do? Every day, more refugees arrive, bringing with them the news of yet more living worlds sterilized to eradicate the Skrela infestation."

"Transition Space is a volatile dimension," Kallista said, her feet scraping against the floor in an ancient instinct to dig her claws into the ground, preparatory for a charge. "There's enough energy contained in it to bring about a vacuum reversal. The entire universe would cease to exist and we'd never know it happened. All life, not just here in our galaxy, but *everywhere*. Do you want to be the one who ends everything?"

"You always were an alarmist," Jindal scoffed, loping down the ramp past her. I followed him, even though this wasn't a physical event, unsure whether the recording would switch off if I didn't keep up. "The AI have already calculated that the odds of any such effect are so miniscule as to be not worth considering."

"*Which* AI?" Kallista demanded, hurrying after him. "The ones we fashioned from the brain patterns of the wild humans, who we never learned to control and could never eradicate? Or those monstrosities your researchers brought about with their twisted and unnatural experiments?"

"Oh, please." Jindal threw up a hand dismissively. "How exactly is *my* research any less natural than what we've been doing with the Tahni for the last fifty thousand years? We simply found a way to create new life, as we always have."

"We brought life from Earth and planted the seed here in the wider galaxy," she shot back, anger flaring in her golden eyes. "Any changes we made were only so that the life forms could better survive in their new environment. We altered as little as possible because we all believed in the wisdom of the natural processes of evolution. What you've done... it's arrogant, presumptuous, as if you could better identify what deserves to survive than the inexorable hand of the universal laws. You've allowed a machine to create something in its own image, based on patterns never found in nature... not in *this* universe."

"You've made these arguments already, before the council," Jindal reminded her. "They failed then, and they'll have even less effect on me. We're fighting for our very survival, for the survival of all life in this galaxy, and everything we've tried until now has failed. These *monstrosities*, as you call them, were fashioned on what we've learned of the thought patterns of the universal mind of Transition Space, combined with those of our own people. We must become something better to stop the Skrela, and now we must be willing to take a bigger risk for a bigger reward. Even the Skrela can't stand against the power of an entire universe brought to life."

Jindal increased his pace and Kallista pursued, their digitigrade lope outrunning even the Vigilante's stride, and I nearly broke into a run before they both faded away to nothing. The recording had come to an end. I stopped again, and only then did I notice Chang jogging up behind me, wheezing, gasping for air.

"For Christ's sake, Alvarez!" he moaned, pulling off his helmet and bending over with his hand on his knee, trying to catch his breath. "Has anything you've learned about me given you the impression that I'm a track athlete?"

"Sorry," I said absently, finally noticing our surroundings. We'd come nearly a klick while I'd been watching the conversation from thousands of years ago unfold inside my head, and our surroundings had changed.

The ramp still descended, showing no sign of leveling out yet, but it was no longer pitch black. Nor was it exactly gaily lit like the thoroughfare on a farming colony during the annual harvest festivals, but at least there was light coming from *somewhere*. Still far away enough that I couldn't pinpoint the source, but it was something for my enhanced optics to work with.

Details stood out from the walls on either side, as far away as they remained, hints of doorways, closed and locked for untold centuries. Were there dead bodies behind those doors? Resscharr who'd fled the final danger, locked themselves in, forgetting in their desperation the lack of food or water? Curiosity tugged me toward the mysteries there, but I resisted the pull. The only means I had to unlock them would leave me vulnerable to the Ghosts, and there was nothing inside that could help us. I already knew where I had to go.

Deeper. Lower. All the way to the bottom.

[16]

"I can't do it," Chang wheezed, waving a hand in surrender, bent over at the waist. He'd lost his helmet somewhere along the last five kilometers, and I hoped he wouldn't need it, because I wasn't going to go back and get it for him. "I can't keep going in this Goddamned armor, Alvarez!"

Sighing, I hit the release for my chest plate and pulled out my 'face jacks. It probably wasn't a good idea getting out of the suit down here, but Chang needed a break, and maybe I did too. Fighting in the armor was one thing, walking endlessly through this silent tomb was another, and it wore on my nerves as much as it wore on Chang's legs.

"I thought you were some badass DSI agent," I said, swinging my legs out of the armor. "Didn't you say you hiked twenty klicks through forests of saber-tooth tigers or some shit? In a war zone? In the snow? Uphill both ways?"

The air down here was stuffy. I hadn't noticed it before, not through the helmet filters, but now I could tell why Chang was so winded. I hoped to hell it wouldn't get any worse, because then I *would* have to go back for that damned helmet.

"That was all a long time ago," Chang whined. "Not to

mention three or four or... shit, maybe *ten* deaths ago. I haven't had time to get this body into shape. I figured it wouldn't be as bad going downhill, but my calves and big toes are killing me." He looked up at me, his face pale. "Anyway, you're in that suit letting its muscles do the walking, so I don't want to hear any criticism from you. How much longer?"

"It's not a map," I sighed. "I'll know when we're close. But we're not yet. Are you gonna be okay?" I put a hand on his arm, feeling the heaving of his chest. "If you have a heart attack or something, I'm not qualified to treat you."

"My heart's just fine, junior. It's my head that's the problem. Otherwise, I wouldn't be humping it into the magical land below the sea with you." Chang sucked in a deep breath and straightened. "I'm good. Get back in your tin can and let's go." He made a face. "Unless you've decided we're clear of the graveyard and it's okay to fly."

"No, I think I've been in the suit enough." I reached back into the chest cavity of the Vigilante and pulled out my sidearm, belting on the holster. I was certain I wouldn't need it, but I felt better wearing it. "It'll be easier to find it if I'm out of it."

"Oh, good," he snorted. "At least now your feet'll be hurting too."

Getting out of the suit was a mistake, I discovered before we'd walked another hundred meters. Not because I missed its protection or because the slope was uncomfortable to walk, but because I'd had to slow down, which gave Robert Chang the spare breath to talk.

"You know where I grew up, Captain?" he said, winding up for what felt like a long spiel. "Capital fucking City. In an Underground a lot like this place. A lot like the one you grew up in." He shook his head. "I swore back then that I wouldn't go back to living like that. Joined the Fleet, worked my way to Intelligence, and hated every minute of it. Didn't like officers looking over my shoulder, you know? That's why I kept applying to the DSI, so I could get away from the uniforms and the haircuts and the saluting and all that bullshit…"

I stopped just as short as I had in the armor and rounded on him.

"Bullshit seems to be your stock in trade, Chang," I snapped. "Do you lie to yourself too, just for practice? You didn't grow up in any Underground anywhere. Your parents were surface dwellers, corporate toadies probably, and you went to a university. You know how I know that?"

"You read my thoughts?" he asked, his expression more intrigued than horrified at the prospect. I rolled my eyes.

"No, I didn't read your mind, I didn't read your file, and I didn't even read the probabilities. DSI doesn't recruit from Fleet Intelligence, and they don't let anyone out in the field unless they have a college degree. They also don't take Underground street hoods. You know all that, and what's more, you *should* know that *I* know that. So why try to pass yourself off as the common man?" I shrugged. "You think it'll make me like you more so I won't leave you down here if things go bad? What?"

He showed no sign of shame or embarrassment, though in my opinion, he should have. Instead, he had the look of a street hood caught in the act by the cops, resentment of authority for catching him and self-satisfaction at having defied them.

"It's a habit," he said, shrugging it off, brushing past me and continuing ahead as if he knew where the hell we were going. "Nothing personal."

I blew out a breath and was surprised no steam came with it. Ignoring the little man, I scanned around us. We'd finally come to the end of the ramp, to the point where the broad walkway flattened out, and the illumination had a source now, obvious even with the naked eye, ahead and to the right. The light called to me, hypnotic, and the memories spoke again.

"It was an experiment. It didn't work, but that's no reason to simply give up on the idea."

I wasn't enough of an expert on the Resscharr to tell one individual from another without living beside them for a few weeks, but I knew in my gut that the speaker was Jindal again, and that he was talking to Kallista. This time, I figured out that she was his wife, or mate, or whatever term they used. The mother of Jindal's children, although that didn't necessarily mean they lived together.

Jindal stalked out of the archway into the lit chamber, his body language—at least as translated for me by the universal mind—frustrated, spoiling for a fight. Kallista paced after him, ready to give it.

"Your pet monsters failed you," she accused. "They abandoned us, and even that was better than we had any right to expect. We should learn our lesson and turn away from this madness before worse happens... before our meddling in the very fabric of reality dooms us all."

Why, I wondered, did the system or the matrix or whatever was putting on this show, keep choosing these two? Was it because Jindal was intimately involved in the project? Or was it me choosing them unconsciously because the two were married?

"This was always a possibility," Jindal said. "And there's always been a backup plan."

"No!" Kallista caught up to the male, grabbed his arm, and spun him around, holding him in place as he tried to pull away. "That's insane! You can't do this! Have you learned nothing? The AI might have been destroyed, might have been driven mad, we have no way of knowing. If you allow this to be done to you, this alteration of your brain, your personality, your memories, the very things that make you who you are, may be irrevocably lost!"

I expected Jindal to be angry with his wife, since he seemed like a bit of a prick, but instead, he gently took her hands and held them tight, the expression on his face softening.

"Kallista, we are at war. We face extinction as a species, along with the eradication of everything we've spent hundreds of thousands of years trying to build. Any sacrifice I make is worth it. I *am* taking precautions, of course. My memories will be backed up in the main data systems, and if need be, my entire brain could be regrown from cloned tissue and the memories read into it."

There. There it was, what I'd been waiting to hear. This place did have the capacity for the procedure... or at least it *had* once upon a time. I almost turned back to Chang and asked him if he'd heard that, but of course he hadn't. Jindal and Kallista faded into history again, but I kept walking toward the light. The answers were in there.

We'd been walking in the dim passages for so long, the brightly lit chamber hurt my eyes, and I had to throw up a hand and squint for a few seconds before my pupils contracted again and my vision cleared. Once it did, I spent the next few beats wondering if what I saw was real or if I was still trapped in someone else's memory.

Because memories spooled out all around me in vivid color, every wall of the hundred-meter-wide room a holographic display with views from the surface... views from dozens of centuries ago. The Skrela had reached this place. I wouldn't have guessed from the surface, from the lack of destruction and devastation, but the video streaming at the center of the chamber was the evidence. It reached from floor to ceiling, fifty meters tall and just as wide, taking up over half the room as if I'd stumbled upon a war memorial in Capital City showing a constant replay of the Battle for Mars.

I knew the footage was old because there were no skull

ships, no bone-white carapaces and tactical formations. Everything was jet black, from the hulls of the giant vessels in orbit to the seed pods they launched down from orbit. The entire star system was a garbage dump from the remains of destroyed spacecraft, both the Skrela hive ships and Predecessor vessels, the white spheres of glowing gas shrinking yet still visible from where their drive fields had imploded.

They were gone now, expended in a last-ditch effort to protect this place, this last bastion of hope. Now, nothing stood between the hordes of Skrela drones and the entrances to the undersea city.

Nothing except one Resscharr male. Jindal.

Except *not* Jindal. I couldn't put my finger on the difference, yet I knew there was one. It was as if the rest of the image on the massive projection was razor sharp and crystal clear... except him. His edges were soft, fuzzy, like heat waves rose from the dirt beneath him to obscure the details of his face and even the shape of the massive, curved walls behind him.

The haziness advanced ahead of him, away from the wall, as if an army of the dead from those JRR Tolkien books Vicky liked to read streamed out of the haunted mountain to overwhelm the invading orcs. This army didn't have a human form though, not even a spectral one. Instead, a wall of force struck the Skrela drones as they swarmed out of their pods, ripping them to pieces, crushing them into flattened, black smears on the ground, cleansing not just the clearing in front of the walls but the entire island of the things.

No, the entire *planet*. I didn't see that in the projection, but I knew it as surely as I knew my name. The entire world had been cleansed of the pods and the drones in the space of a few seconds. Thinking of all the worlds we'd seen ruined, bereft of life after the Resscharr had been forced to raze the entire surface to get rid of the seed pods, I felt an almost religious awe. This was power on a scale I'd never seen before.

Jindal stared upward into the sky, the afternoon sun shining on his face, unless the glow coming off of him had another source, something inside. He didn't squint at the sunshine, didn't wince, just looked wide-eyed through the clouds and the blue, to the blackness of space above.

That blackness drew my eyes to the other half of the screen as it split in two, showing what looked like a satellite view of high orbit. The Skrela hive ships shuddered, one by one in a chain, as if a field effect spread out from the southern hemisphere of Waterline and moved from one of the massive spacecraft to another. The hand of a god crumpled each of them like a piece of paper, the ships collapsing into the wormhole opened at their centers. The last two tried to run, and I thought for a moment that one of them might make it to minimum Transition distance, but Jindal was only teasing the Skrela. The wormhole opened up ahead of it, an invitation to escape, but before it could disappear into the safety of T-space, a second gate ripped it apart amidships. What was left of the wreckage drifted through into the Transition in the instant before it closed.

"Holy shit," Chang whispered with reverence in the profanity, gaze flickering back and forth between me and the destruction on the screen. "You can do *that*?"

"I could," I confirmed grimly. "Once. Show us what happened next."

I spoke the words aloud, unsure whether there was anything there to hear them or whether they'd be understood… until an intuition assured me they had been. The projection screens all around the chamber went dark for a long second, and when they returned, people cheered. Resscharr cheered and a few Tahni as well, watching from the ramps, from just behind the open doorways. Among them, near the front, was Kallista.

She ran to Jindal as he turned back to his people, arms raised in triumph, the conquering hero. His face still beamed, and not just from the grin stretching it out. Did Chang see the grin? Did he hear the cheers? Those were translations for my benefit, but I couldn't be sure, even with my enhanced perceptions, if Chang received the same benefits.

"You saved us," Kallista told her husband, the words buoyed by awe and disbelief as she embraced him. "It worked."

"As I told you it would," he said, pushing her away. Condescending, dismissive, as if she were a child. "We should have done this centuries ago. Perhaps then we wouldn't have been forced to this, crammed underground like animals. No more, Kallista. Now that we have a way to fight back, I'm going to lead us back into our ancestral home and wipe the Skrela from the face of the universe. And then..." a distracted look passed across his face, like he was listening to someone else, someone not there. When he spoke again, it was with a different tone. "And then, I'll rebuild what we once had, but the right way. No more sacrificing our future for our inferiors. No more dithering and hesitation. No more retreating. It's time I took back what's rightfully ours."

The video froze on Jindal's face, aloof, cold, eyes darkened from gold to bronze.

"Okay, he's a dick to his wife," Chang mused. "But it still doesn't sound that bad. What went wrong? Why didn't it work?"

Something had to be listening, because at his comment, the view on the screen changed. There was no way to tell how much time had passed, but the location had changed. Interior... if I wasn't mistaken, right in this very chamber. Kallista I recognized, but the males and females clustered around her I didn't know. A pair of Tahni stood to the side of them, still as statues.

Servants, I guessed, or perhaps guards, since both carried sidearms.

"It's premature," one of the males said, wringing his hands. Age was impossible to judge for the Resscharr, since they lived well into the thousands of years, yet I sensed this one was older than the rest, by his timidity if nothing else. "He's barely had these abilities for a month. Perhaps he simply needs more time to adjust before he's ready to go on the offensive..."

"That's not what he said when he defeated the Skrela invaders," Kallista replied grimly, eyes darting toward the entrance to the chamber. The door was sealed, but that didn't seem to comfort her much. "He was ready to leave that very instant. Then he went inside his chambers and didn't come out for three days."

"And when he did," another of the males, this one younger than her I thought, "he wouldn't speak to anyone."

"Not even me," Kallista confirmed. "But I have heard him speaking... to himself. Or to others none can hear but him."

"He saved us all," the older one said, arms crossed, chin tucked in, stubbornly determined not to do anything. "We need to trust him. If we do this..." he wagged his head side to side like a hound dog, "... he'll take it as a betrayal. And I don't think he'll handle that well."

"Which is the only another reason why he shouldn't be the only one to wield this sort of power."

"You realize what you're saying, Kallista." The old man didn't seem to know what to do with his hands, his long fingers twitching. "If you undergo this transformation, you may have the same problems with... mental stability."

Kallista's eyes flared.

"I did *not* say that my husband is mentally unstable, Abron. He's a hero, the one who saved us, as you said. What I worry is that his... perspective has changed." Her lined face sagged as if the hope had gone out of her. "That this power has severed his connection to the rest of us."

"And it won't happen to you?" Abron demanded. "How can you know that?"

"You know *me*." She tapped her chest. "You know that I was opposed to all this from the beginning. If there's anyone you can trust with this, it's me."

"We have to do it fast," the younger one said, looking furtively back at the door. "If he finds out..."

"Then do it." Kallista waved at the back of the chamber at a small doorway, thick and heavily shielded. She looked upward. "Sumar," she snapped. "You've been listening, I know. Ready the virus to my biometric specifications."

"Of course, madame," a bodiless voice replied. "The preparation will take less than a minute."

"Kallista," Abron said, catching her arm as she took a step toward the lab. "What about your children?"

"They're with the learning creche," she told him, shrugging the hand and the concern away. "They'll be fine."

"Oh, there's mother-of-the-year-award material," Chang murmured, leaning against the wall as if we were watching the coming attractions for the latest telenovela on one of the billboards in the Underground.

"Yeah, they're not big on the whole parental thing," I agreed.

On the screen, Kallista hurried back to the lab and I thought the recording would cut off... but the shriek of rending metal turned my head around... until I understood that it came from the video. The door that had sealed this chamber was opening, and not by choice. Abron and the others started, backing against the wall, the two Tahni moving between them and what was coming. Kallista hadn't stopped, was already out of view, and I, absurdly, rooted her on like this was a soccer match, urging her to get the thing done.

The door hadn't disappeared like the outer one, perhaps because that wouldn't have been dramatic enough for Jindal. Instead, it parted in the center, peeling back from a tear about two meters off the floor. Through the gap floated Jindal, just a few centimeters up, though it was probably less laziness and more the desire to make an impression. It did, and all the Resscharr who'd been gathered at the center of the chamber scattered, except for Abron, the younger male, and the two Tahni guards.

Jindal had changed in the last few weeks. I'd never seen one of the Resscharr without their feathered mane, but his was gone, the sloped skull beneath it still red and raw, not as if the hair had fallen out but more like he'd ripped it out one strand at a time. The lack of the stiff mane gave his head a misshapen quality, unless that was another of the effects of the power... or the Voices.

They didn't have ears, really. It wasn't something I'd noticed before because of the hair, but they only had tiny openings in the sides of their head, surrounded by a narrow ridge of gristle. The lack of hair made them stand out, drew my eye to them, and I almost noticed the bleeding scratches down the existing striations in his face. He'd ran his fingernails over the ridges like he was trying to tear them away, and blood dripped down his cheeks, staining the tattered remains of the tunic he'd been wearing.

It barely covered anything, hanging in shreds, and through the gaps were more bleeding wounds, and I could almost smell the stench of rot coming off him. When he leered at Abron and the others, his teeth were cracked and yellow.

"Scuttling cockroaches," he mumbled. "You were right," he

added, louder and more focused but speaking to someone off to the side, someone no one else could see or hear. "You told me they'd betray me. The worthless bastards don't deserve me."

[17]

That sounded familiar, and the hackles rose at the back of my neck.

"Jindal," Abron stuttered, turning sideways and crouching down like he wanted to hide behind the Tahni guards, "it's good to see you out again... are you well?"

"Do I *look* well?" Jindal demanded. "No, I don't look *well*, you supercilious old gasbag! I look like a *god*, and that's just how I feel."

Still hovering, he advanced on them, and yet the Tahni made no attempt to move, their features carved into stone. They had guts, because I wouldn't have stood my ground in the face of the thing that Jindal had become. He paused a couple meters from the two, cackling in amusement.

"I can't believe," he said once the scornful laughter had played out, "that we ever thought of you worthless animals as the rightful heirs to the galaxy. You're weak, stupid, worse than the hairless apes that evolved after us on Earth. Without our help, you'd still be picking lice off each other and eating them."

Gasps rose up from a couple of the other Resscharr in the chamber, like Jindal had blasphemed. And maybe he had, as far as their beliefs went. The Tahni said nothing, though each had a hand on the grip of their sidearm.

"Jindal," Abron said, hands clasped in front of his chin, "we should talk. Do you need any help preparing for your expedition to destroy the Skrela? We've had several ships on standby..."

"I need nothing from you, old man. You and the others here would be rotting corpses if not for me. What I want from you is nothing except your absolute devotion and your unquestioning obedience." He focused on the Tahni. "Just like I expect from you brutes."

The Tahni stiffened, both slowly drawing their weapons as if in a choreographed and synchronized motion, and I thought they'd try to kill Jindal. It wouldn't work, but I thought they'd try. Instead, they both turned in a robotic about-face motion and leveled their weapons at Abron and the younger Resscharr. The two males huddled together as if both wanted to hide behind the other, and if Resscharr were prone to peeing their pants—or even wearing any—I believe Abron might have done it.

"What are you doing?" the old male bleated, waving a hand at the Tahni like he was trying to chase away a troublesome mosquito. "Don't point those at us! You work for us!"

"Not anymore, old friend," Jindal clucked, shaking his head in mock sorrow. "I'm afraid no one here will listen to you and your staid, timid advice anymore. I'm the leader here, and one of the first decisions I've made is that we don't require the services of these slaves any further."

The Tahni spun again, precise and military in their motion, and pointed their weapons at each other. For the first time, their visages twisted into something less stoic and spartan, more human-like in the terror and disbelief in their deep-set, piggish eyes. It seemed as if Jindal had released them from the mesmerism he'd held over their conscious minds just long enough to allow them to feel the agonizing fear before he forced them to pull the trigger.

I jerked back at the flashes of the energy weapons, though I didn't look away at the two headless bodies tumbling to the floor. They were bloodless, the charred necks and shoulders cauterized. The two Resscharr screamed, a sound *not* translated for me, the warbling alarm cry of a sandhill crane like I'd heard so many times on Hausos. These cousins of the birds couldn't fly though, and they were too terrified to run. Their feet tap-danced arrhythmically on the hard floor, toenails clacking, and the color drained from their faces.

"Don't worry, my comrades," Jindal told them, his feet finally touching the floor. "I yet have use for you." He spread his hands, fingers splayed, Jesus on the cross. "After all, what is a god if he has no worshippers?" He turned to the other Resscharr, cowering in corners, alcoves, behind haptic control holograms, tilting his head to the side in an odd manner, as if his neck were broken. "Come to me, my children. Come bow at my feet, and I will lead you back to greatness."

They came to him... they crawled to him. There was something spider-like about a digitigrade creature skittering across the floor, like they'd regressed to their ancestors, the ones predating even the eoraptors from which they'd evolved over sixty million years ago. Raw, visceral fear contorted their faces at first, but the closer they came to Jindal, the more their expressions changed to rapture, ecstasy. He was inside their heads, not using some magic to influence their thoughts, doing it the hard way, telekinesis working the chemical centers of their brains, releasing dopamine.

They were being drugged by their own bodies, and if I'd been able to step through time and ask each of them what they were feeling, they all would have said this was the best day of their lives. They felt love, or that was what their brain chemicals were telling them. Not just the two dozen or so Resscharr in the chamber either. More flowed through the ruined door, not seeming to notice the giant hole they were walking past, crowding around Kindal, prostrating themselves, making noises that weren't directly translatable but that I knew were the equivalent of moans of religious awe.

There were millions of Resscharr down in the undersea city, and every single one of them had heard the call. They'd crush themselves to death in the press trying to answer, unless he let them go, and an urgent need to help surged in my chest, despite the intellectual knowledge that this had all happened before the rise and fall of the Roman empire.

"Yes, my children," Jindal said, rising above them as they crowded at his feet, trying to kiss them. He hovered a meter up, watching them not with the love of a beneficent deity but with the self-indulgence of a devil. "Together, we shall leave this place and bathe the universe with the blood of our enemies."

"Jindal, stop it."

His head snapped around as if he couldn't believe anyone still had the capacity to oppose him. Mine did as well, even though I already had a good idea who it was.

Kallista floated through the open doorway into the lab, her eyes alight with her new power, her expression hard and disapproving.

"This isn't you, my husband," she told him, shaking her head. "This ability has twisted you, darkened your soul, but you can fight it. I'll help. Just release the others. They need not suffer for our mistakes."

"Our mistakes?" Jindal bellowed, and a wave of energy followed the words, bowling over dozens of helpless Resscharr, blood trickling from noses and ears at the onslaught. "You traitorous bitch! I did this for *you*, and you repay me by going behind my back, by trying to steal them from me?"

Kallista spread her hands and the Resscharr relaxed, collapsing from their prostration like marionettes with their strings cut, gasping for breath.

"I don't want to take anything from you," she insisted, drifting closer to Jindal. "I want you to give it up willingly. For the good of your people. For the good of our children. Look what it's done to you already…"

Jindal rose another few meters, towering above her, heat waves radiating off his body.

"Yes, look at what it's done to me, my dear. And look upon what it *will* do to you." His smile was a thing from a horror movie. "Since you consider what I've become horrible, a nightmare, perhaps the kindest thing to do would be to save you from such a fate."

I'd seen two of the Changed fight each other before. Firsthand. Watching it from the outside was less terrifying, though I wouldn't want to have been one of the Resscharr crouched on the floor of the chamber.

Jindal streaked toward his wife like he'd been shot out of a mass driver, and I fully expected the two of them to go crashing into the far wall, leaving a dent even in the adamantine Predecessor-tech material. That didn't happen. Jindal stopped cold as if he'd run into a brick wall face-first, his hands curled in front of him, nails ready to slash, but his wrists locked in the iron grasp of Kallista.

Resscharr had sexual dimorphism just like every other species, and the males tended to be bigger and stronger, but physical strength meant nothing when it came to the Changed. She wasn't using her muscles to hold him back, she was channeling her thoughts through another dimension, converting them into kinetic energy, which meant this was a test of wills. Jindal might once have won it immediately, particularly since Kallista had only received her abilities minutes ago, but he'd spent a month allowing the Ghosts to wear down his sanity, and his will along with it. Eventually, the Ghosts would take over and it would be *their* will wielding the power, but at this moment, Jindal was at his most vulnerable and wasn't coherent enough to be aware of it.

He bared his teeth and screamed at Kallista, the sheer noise somehow making its way through the recording and through the centuries to grate on my nerves and batter my eardrums, and I pitied poor Kallista having to smell the corpse breath coming off those rotting teeth. She said nothing, made no sound, her jaw set in determination, and with a flex of her upper back, tossed him away.

Not *just* with her back though. A wavering wall of force stretched between them, a column of shimmering air, hammering Jindal in the chest and slamming him against the wall near the entrance. And just as I'd imagined, he left a dent as he slid away from the wall.

"Don't make me do this," Kallista pleaded with him, stepping between her people as they dodged away, as terrified of her as they were of Jindal. "I don't want to hurt you."

"You won't get the chance," he promised, wiping blood off the side of his head.

The dozens of Resscharr in the chamber stopped cowering, stopped skittering away, and rose as one from the floor, turning toward Kallista with unfettered hate and rage writ across their faces. As if they all shared the same thought.

For the first time since she'd emerged from the lab, Kallista looked scared. The crowd rushed at her, slashing, kicking like ostriches, biting, and she exploded out from among them, reaching the twenty or thirty meters up to the ceiling before Jindal hit her. He didn't try to use the focused kinetic energy as she had, instead simply flying straight at her and pounding his forearm into the side of her head.

She grabbed at him, digging her nails into his neck and dragging him with her as they both fell back into the growing crowd of Resscharr, more pouring through the gap in the door every second, every one of them trying to kill one or both of the Changed. The two of them were buried under a mass of writhing, thrashing violence, and I could imagine that this would be the end for them both, that there was no way even one of the Changed could overcome the sheer numbers.

Kallista screamed. Not the warbling scream of alarm I'd heard before, this one was of wordless rage, a lion roaring death at a horde of hyenas trying to drive him off a kill. Power emanated out from her, pushing away the thing that had once been her husband but doing much worse to the other Resscharr who lacked the protection of his abilities.

They popped like balloons, bags of blood exploding one after another, a chain reaction spreading through the chamber... and through the city. The *planet*. The video shifted, showing views from every one of the undersea cities, millions upon millions of them, adults and children, dying in seconds.

In the end, there were only the two of them, bathed in blood, collapsed in a sea of it, drowning. They glared at each other with virulent hatred in their eyes, each blaming the other, and launched toward their last remaining enemy. The image froze.

"Wait," I said, taking an involuntary step forward. "What happened to them?"

"Marriage counseling?" Chang guessed, shrugging. I spun back to him, glaring, ready to give into my baser instincts and punch the little man in the face, no power needed.

"What do you *think* happened to them, Cameron Alvarez?"

There was no one in the room. I scanned every bit of it from top to bottom, using my natural senses and the ones I was cursed with by the Change virus, and detected not a soul.

"Surely, you know who I am." The voice came from everywhere, not a single speaker in to be seen, but now, yes, I *did* know.

"You're the AI who runs this place," I said, gaze still flitting around, wishing I had a single focus to land on.

As if reading my mind, an image appeared in the central display, banishing the disturbing scene of Kallista and Jindal in the midst of killing each other.

A *human* image. Not dressed in a Fleet duty uniform like Dwight had been, and I unbelievably felt a pang of loss at the absence of the AI, despite the duplicitous shit he'd done to us. No, this one was clothed in rough wool and leather, reminding me of the garb of the Vergai back on Yfingam, his long red hair braided along with the handlebar mustache drooping own all the way to his chest. He dressed like a central-European tribesman from three or four thousand years ago, the last time the Predecessors had visited Earth before they'd vacated the Cluster forever.

"Is this better?" he asked, gesturing at himself. "Do you feel more comfortable now rather than talking to thin air?" He cocked an eyebrow roughly the size of a throw pillow. "Does it make you feel like you're speaking to the Ghosts? Hearing their voices?"

"Hey, big boy," Chang called up to the Iron-Age simulacrum. "You got a name, or should we just call you Mustache?"

The AI smiled thinly and shrank from its multistory projection down to approximately our height. Well, a few centimeters taller, which might have been an attempt at psychological intimidation.

"As Cameron has already learned, names are unnecessary when we are all the same person."

"Wait," I said, frowning. "You're... you're one of the Dwight AIs?"

The Celtic warrior frowned, his mustaches drooping even farther.

"The *what*?"

"Oh, sorry. Yeah, you wouldn't know about that," I realized. "You're one of the AI fashioned from human brain patterns?"

"I am." He shrugged. "You've undoubtedly heard that the Resscharr experimented with different models near the end. That didn't work out so well for them." His sniff of disdain reminded me of Dwight.

"And how well did *your* model work out for them?" I reminded him. "After all, it was *you* who created the Skrela to begin with, right?"

He frowned, shifting uncomfortably.

"This *Dwight* of yours told you that, did he?"

"He did," I confirmed. "Among other things. How did you know my name? And how the hell are you speaking English?"

I'd thought at first that the universal mind was doing its thing again and translating for me, but Chang understood the computer, which meant it spoke our language.

"Your people put entirely too much information on your datalinks," the AI told me, gesturing at the device at my belt. "Surely, you didn't think your data security is a match for me?" He waved expansively. "It contains the foundations of your language and the general details of how you came to be here, along with the... let's say the *fingerprints* of one of us. One of me. Apparently the one you called Dwight."

"He called himself that," I corrected the sentient system.

"I must admit," the AI went on as if I hadn't spoken, looking between the two of us, "I'm surprised at how far humans have come on their own. I started out my existence as one, of course, but a mere three thousand years ago what used to be my people were still living in wattle huts and carrying weapons of bronze, and a chariot was considered the apex of modern technology."

"Yeah, the Resscharr were pretty damned surprised at it too," I assured him. His eyes went wide, and I intuited the reason. "Yes, there are Resscharr remnants still out there. Not many, and most of them have regressed to barbarism, but they're still around. But the Skrela you created aren't. I don't know if it was on my 'link, but we wiped out the hive world, and if there are any left, they won't be for long."

"Impressive," he admitted. "But it does beg the question... why are you here? And what do you want from me?"

"I'm here because of what was on that recording you showed us."

I closed my eyes, debating my next move. This was a bigger gamble than opening the door had been, but I had to demonstrate to the AI that we weren't screwing around. The power was out there, a live wire sparking just beyond my reach, daring me to touch it. I did, and the energy coursed through me. When I opened my eyes, I hovered a meter off the ground.

"I have a problem. I'm hoping you have a solution."

[18]

"I can't help you," the AI insisted, shaking his virtual head.

A lead weight sank a meter deep into my gut and I staggered, wishing there was something tangible to hold onto.

"What the hell do you mean?" I demanded.

Then I pressed my fingers against my temples, a knife-sharp pain lancing through my head.

He can't help you. Nothing can. You saw what happened to the Resscharr here so long ago, how he deteriorated. That was from trying to fight us. If you just agree to cooperate, you can have limitless power and immortality. We only want what's best for you, Cam...

Shut up. I squeezed my eyes shut and tried to close my consciousness off from the voices, tried to shove them into the recesses of my mind.

"Briggs... the AI back on Homecoming, said you could reverse the changes to my brain structure," I went on. "It's why we came here!"

"And I can," the Iron-Age warrior confirmed. "But you wouldn't survive it. Not the you that you are now."

I shook my head. It still hurt, and now my feet hurt too.

"Make me a fucking chair," I told him.

"Two, please," Chang added, holding up two fingers.

A couch grew out of the floor, assembled from gravimetic fields, holding together bits of metal-infused bacteria that could be recycled for any purpose. Another useless bit of data floating around inside my head, available for instant recall, yet the answer to my problems still eluded me.

"Go on," I urged the AI, falling heavily onto the furniture. It was, as usual, very comfortable, felt as if it had been built to the specs of my body after a full scan. Chang took a seat beside me, more gingerly, as if he expected the couch to vanish like some computer practical joke. "What did you mean I wouldn't survive?"

"I know something of the abilities you've been given," the AI explained. "Even though from your files as detailed on your data device, you're a soldier rather than a biologist or a neuroscientist..."

"*Marine*," I corrected him, perhaps a little too sharply, but he ignored it and continued.

"... you will know what I'm saying is accurate as soon as you consider it. The human brain—well, to be more accurate, the brain of every complex creature which evolved on Earth—isn't a machine in the classical sense. Not as your heart or lungs are, squeezing blood or air in and out. Your brain generates electrical impulses through the use of chemicals, but those impulses are transitory things. What you consider memory is a dynamic thing, not a record of fixed events such as the data storage in my core systems but more a filter that events pass through to create impressions. It's not something that stays the same your entire life, which is why your perspective changes as you get older. You're not simply seeing your memories differently, your memories are changing."

"Yeah, I get that," I acknowledged, feeling the rightness of his explanation even as the confirmation came to me via my link to the universal mind. "But what does it have to do with undoing the changes made by the virus?" Frowning, I took a stab in the dark. "Are you saying the changes that were made affected my memories?"

"I'm saying," the AI clarified, "that what was done to you has rerouted your *system* for creating and recalling memories. You're no longer remembering things as they were inscribed into your brain, you're accessing them via the universal computer system in Transition Space."

I swallowed hard, leaning back against the couch, all the strength that would have allowed me to sit upright suddenly drained away.

"Are you saying that if I lose my connection to Transition Space that I'll lose all my memories?"

"Unknown. It's a risk, but the situation hasn't occurred before. As you saw in the records, none of the Changed I ever encountered were of a mind to give up their power once it had been bestowed. What I *am* saying is, the only way for me to do as you ask and undo the changes the virus has brought about is for me to clone those sections of your brains from your existing tissue and implant it back in place of the affected areas." The ancient Celtic warrior squatted down, putting his virtual eyes on a level with mine. "And when I do that, Cameron Alvarez, you *will* lose the memories which make you what and who you are."

"Hold on a second here!" Chang said, jumping to his feet as animated as I'd seen him since we met. "You can't tell me that as advanced as your technology is, you don't have the ability to read memories onto an external media! Shit," he exclaimed, tapping the side of his head, "I've done it so many times, I've lost count!"

The AI's virtual representation rose from his crouch to

tower above Chang, fists planted against his hips. I half-expected there to be a sword hilt sticking up from the simulacrum's belt, but he didn't take the image that far.

"Yes, it's obvious you have. And tell me, Mr. Chang, why have *you* come here? Or are you simply such a close friend of Captain Alvarez that you'd accompany him into the unknown in this dead city on a dead world?" He spread his hands. "Or should I guess? Could it be that your experience restoring your memories into your cloned brain tissue has left your personality irrevocably altered? So much so that you can no longer live with yourself and came here in an attempt to *fix* it?"

I thought Chang might turn and walk out of the room, all the way back up to the surface, but I had to give the little man credit. He had more self-control than I'd imagined and just sat back on the couch, his expression going flat.

"You're saying there's no hope for me then?"

And yeah, he was still a narcissistic asshole, more worried about his mental instability than the fact that I could go nuts and kill everyone, but baby steps.

"What I'm saying is that there's no hope of turning you back into the person you once were..." The Celtic warrior shrugged. "There's always hope of transforming into something better. At least there is for those who are willing."

"I'm glad as hell Bob here can still better himself," I interrupted, my temples throbbing once again. I pushed against my 'face jacks, and for some reason, it relieved the pain. "But tell me why you can't just do what he said? Why can't you record my memories and transfer them back afterward?"

"I could do it." A chair appeared behind the image of the Iron-Age warrior, and he settled into it. "Whether I *will* is another question, since neither of you are my masters, and the ones I did once serve I betrayed, but I could. What I'm saying is that those memories would no longer be a part of who you are.

It's the same reason that Mr. Chang here has found himself changed so much since the first time he went through his rebirth. There's a difference between having *access* to those memories and them being a part of your personality." He shrugged. "There's also the question of whether you believe in a soul. If you do, I can't guarantee that the being you are once your brain is regrown will be the same soul. This might not be, as Mr. Chang hopes, effective immortality, as it is simply death and replacement by a lookalike."

"I understand," I told him, raising my hands palms-out. "I get it. If you do this, it might not be me anymore. I might be dead. But damn it, if I we *don't* do it, I'll either have to kill myself or probably kill everyone I love, just like those poor assholes you showed us in the video. At least this way, Vicky..." I clamped my teeth shut, unwilling to say it. *At least this way, Vicky will keep going and not go get herself killed trying to save me.*

"It's your decision, of course," the computer said. "And mine. You've yet to tell me why I should help you."

Which was a damned good question, and not one I'd thought about. I'd gotten so used to Dwight being on our side that I assumed this one would be too, would be just like him. But he wasn't. Like Chang after each reincarnation, the AI incarnations were separate individuals once they split off from each other and had different experiences. I was in no condition to be speculating on what a sentient AI constructed from the brain patterns of an Iron-Age barbarian might be either, found it hard to think about anything other than the idea I was probably going to die soon, one way or another.

The last person I thought would help came to my rescue.

"Tell me something, Hagar the Horrible," Chang said, and I frowned, recognizing the reference because I had access to the entire databank of the ship and couldn't forget anything but wondering how the hell *he* knew of it. "From what I've been told, you hated the Resscharr because they killed the original you in order to harvest your brain patterns, and doubly so because they forced you to kill off the intelligent species you used to create the Skrela. Is that right, or have I gotten things mixed up?" He smiled thinly. "I'm new here and prone to confusion."

"Yes," the AI replied, his tone becoming grim, grimmer than when he was telling the both of us that we'd come here for nothing and were doomed to either die or go nuts. "The Resscharr's fate was dark, but no darker than they deserved. Though this..." he motioned about him, "was not the dark fate we had in mind. We wanted them to face the genocide they'd forced us to perpetrate, but perhaps this was better, more ironic. Their constant desire to play god caught up to them in the end before their other sins could."

"Right, right," Chang said impatiently, making a move-along gesture. "The thing is, doesn't that make every bad thing that's happened to all of us sort of your fault? After all, Captain Alvarez and his people wouldn't be here if a Tahni general hadn't discovered the Skrela seed pods and tried to use them as a weapon against the humans. And the Tahni are kind of your responsibility too... you left them to run the Cluster, left them to lord over us humans. Didn't you feel bad about that? After all, you were one of us."

"There was nothing we could do," the AI protested. "We couldn't openly oppose the Resscharr, not without them using the fail-safes they'd built into us and wiping our memory cores."

"And I suppose losing your memory," Chang mused, raising an eyebrow, "losing who you *are*, would be the worst fate a computer could imagine, wouldn't it?"

I saw where this was going and didn't want Chang to screw it up.

"You couldn't help us before," I said, "but you can now. You can make up for what the Resscharr did and what you *didn't* do. And it won't cost you anything except some time and a little energy, both of which, it seems to me, you have in ample quantities."

The AI's avatar sighed, an affectation, but a positive one.

"Very well. Though I don't know if I'd be helping you. As I said, you probably won't come out of this with your personality intact."

"I have an idea," Chang said, raising a hand ironically, a student in class. "You're going to have to install a headcomp to make this work, aren't you?"

"What the hell's a headcomp?" I asked, scowling. Whatever it was, it wasn't in the ship's databanks, and I'd never heard the term.

"Oh, that's right, you wouldn't have been cleared for that little development, would you?" Chang grinned as if it pleased him that there was something he knew that I didn't. "I doubt even your little Fleet Intelligence ship would have the specs on this. It was experimental during the war, though it *was* used on some top-secret commando types. Since then, it's cutting edge, either illegal or incredibly expensive or both, depending on where you go. It's a nanite-assembled biocomputer installed at the base of your cerebellum, tied directly into the optic and cochlear nerves. Usually paired with what's called a neurolink, an implant communicator. It'll be necessary to transfer your memories."

"It is within my capabilities to manufacture and install such a device," the AI acknowledged, "but that won't change..."

But Chang was already waving the caveats away.

"Yeah, yeah, I know, I get it. But I had a theory." He shrugged. "Okay, more like a hypothesis. But when I started going a little bit looney after my first resurrection, I had a headcomp installed. Not for *that* reason, I did it to give me an edge on the competition, to make sure I was never in the dark for want of remembering some fatal detail. But I noticed that having the headcomp... kind of stabilized me, you know? Gave me an outside perspective on what I was doing, except inside my own brain. Now, it didn't stop me from doing some morally questionable things, mind you... but it did remind me that other people existed and if I was going to fuck them over with my own plans, maybe I needed to help them out a little too."

"You want me to let him stick a fucking *computer* in my *head*?" I asked, gawking at Chang.

"You let the Marine Corps put jacks in your head," he reminded me.

"And I figured they wouldn't do anything too funky since they needed me to kill Tahni for them." I sighed, tilted my head back. "You say you think this'll help?"

"You have to get it done to upload your memories anyway."

"How long will it take?" I asked the AI.

"A few hours," he said. "There's no need to open you up. I can inject the nanites and they'll build it inside your skull."

"Well, that's a relief."

"The lab is right through there," the AI told me, pointing at the door I recognized from the video. The room where Kallista had gone to undergo the transformation. Because *that* had gone so well. "If you'll head in, well... I'm already there."

"What about you, Chang?" I asked him. "What are you gonna do?" I looked back to the AI's avatar. "Isn't there *anything* you can do for him?"

"Perhaps. But it would be far from immediate. The only chance I can see of restoring your mental processes to what you consider normal, Mr. Chang, is for me to review your memories and find the ones most emotionally resonant to you, then... for lack of a better word, *play* them for your mind at real speed, as they occurred."

"Holy shit," Chang murmured, making a face. "How long would *that* take?"

"Possibly years. But it would produce a better result than simply rebooting you. Again. I can keep you alive the entire time, though the downside is that you won't be totally unconscious, nor will you be unaware of the passage of time. Basically, you'll be reliving parts of your life."

"We can think about that later," Chang said, his expression clouding over as he quite obviously was giving it some serious thought right now. "You should get on with it, Alvarez. Before those Ghosts kill us all."

The face I made was probably as full of dread as Chang's. I was about to let a computer with the consciousness of some poor son of a bitch shanghaied out of Europe three thousand years ago inject goo into my brain so it could build another computer, the purpose of which was to keep me sane.

That would be assuming that I'm sane to start with.

"Robert, I need you to do me a favor," I told him, not yet moving from the couch.

Talk me out of this shit. But I didn't say that. Chang looked at me expectantly.

"Go back to the surface and radio up to Vicky what I'm doing. Tell her to go ahead and bring Bravo company down here and take charge of things. And please tell Lt. Springfield she's in command until Vicky lands." I pushed myself to my feet. "Do you think you can do that for me?"

"I'll tell them," he sighed, staring balefully at the entrance. "But it's going to be a long walk."

Eyeing the door to the lab, I thought that mine would feel even longer.

[19]

The operating table hadn't been in the small chamber when I'd entered, and it reminded me far too much of the one where all this started, back on Homecoming. At least the walls weren't transparent, though I wasn't sure if that made it better or not. The room was small, maybe six meters on a side, and dimly lit. I couldn't see the door I'd entered through, and every milliliter of good sense I had screamed at me to get the hell out of there before I did something I couldn't ever change.

I lay down on the table instead. I couldn't be mad at Dwight for what he'd done. He'd infected me with this mutated version of the nanovirus to save us from Lilandreth, though in retrospect, that felt more and more like the old British ruler Vortigern inviting the Angles and Saxons over from Frisia as mercenaries to fight the Picts for him. In a hundred years or so, the island was called *Angle-land* and the Romano-British no longer existed.

"Do you remember anything about your life before?" I asked the AI, trying to relax and take my mind off what was about to happen. I figured I couldn't distract a sentient computer from his task.

"No." The holographic avatar appeared again at the center of the room, laying a hand on its chest. "I chose this image because it matches what records the Resscharr kept of the peoples from which I was taken. You probably know as much of them as I do."

"They were primitive," I told him, drawing on the memory of the history I'd read of prehistoric Europe. "But they were making progress. They built the first roads, plank roads made of trees sawn in half lengthwise, the rounded ends buried in the mud. The Romans who later conquered them laid down pavement on top of them, and no one knew they existed until a couple thousand years later." I snorted a mirthless laugh. "Sometimes, I wonder if that's what's going to happen to us. Something like the Skrela, something we don't even know exists, that comes from outside, will come in and mow us down and it'll be like we were never there. Some alien archaeologist thousands of years from now will sift through the rubble and figure out we existed and wonder what we were like."

"Were you this dark and depressing before you were infected with the Change virus?" the AI wondered.

"Probably," I admitted. "I haven't had what you'd call an easy life." I closed my eyes. "And it doesn't look like it's getting any simpler anytime soon."

"Put your hands by your sides, Captain Alvarez," he said. The avatar didn't move, but *something* did. Machinery built into the wall, extending on gimbals, metallic and ominous, like the tentacles of some robot monster reaching out to torment me.

"I need to know your name," I told him, obeying the suggestion and lying still.

"Why is it important I have a name? There's only one of me. I have no trouble separating myself from any of you."

"Because if I'm about to let someone operate on my brain," I said testily, "I'd like to have something to call them other than 'hey, you.' It's a human thing. You have to remember that much about being human."

Maybe he did, because his chuckle sounded genuine. Or at least genuinely simulated.

"Very well. If it's that important to you, I am close enough to your friend that it might not be inappropriate to call me Dwight."

"No," I said, resisting an urge to shake my head. One of those manipulators was getting pretty close to my ear, and I didn't think moving around was a good idea. "Dwight died saving us. He was wiped out by Lilandreth—the Changed Resscharr. It would be disrespecting the dead."

"Then pick something that sounds right to you." Not exasperated exactly, more like the strained patience of an adult dealing with a slow child. "Whatever it is, it won't offend me."

"Jim," I decided. "I had a teacher named Jim once in one of the group homes. He wasn't as big of a useless douchebag as every other adult I encountered. I'll call you Jim."

"I'm flattered to be considered not as much of a douchebag," Jim said dryly. "Hold very still."

Something cold touched the skin beside my temples, and I felt rather than saw probes enter through the 'face jacks on either side of my head. The cold entered there and I fought not to jerk away from the table, brush the intrusion away from my head like it was a swarm of insects. But the insects didn't stop at my skin, didn't stop at the jacks. Squirming, squiggling, writhing *inside my head...*

"Couldn't you have fucking sedated me?" I ground out, trying not to move my head. *And maybe strapped me down?*

"Don't worry, in just a few seconds..."

I opened my mouth to ask how many seconds and never got the chance to close it.

I sat up in darkness, though not total darkness. A circle of light encompassed me. No table, no room, no details at all except me and a light that seemed to have no source. I wasn't in the lab anymore, that became obvious immediately. I wasn't *anywhere*, just a gray haze merging with the darkness. This was my imagination.

"No, it's hardly that."

Zombie Anton again. The Ghosts. He looked even worse this time, if that was possible, looked like pieces of him were about to start dropping off, and I smelled the stale, musty air of the grave on him.

"Jesus Christ," I muttered, clambering to my feet. "You say you guys are the *Ghosts*, plural, but all I ever see is you. Don't you have a guy with a sheet rattling chains in there? Or maybe the Ghost of Christmas Past?"

Maybe I could just take a swing at him. It wouldn't be like hitting Anton. Anton had never gotten this old, much less marched out of his grave to haunt me. I worried, though, that my fist would pass right through him like the phantom he was... or worse, just break loose a rotting section of jaw and leave me staring into the inside of his skull.

"I don't choose how we communicate with you," the Ghost told me. "That's all out of your subconscious." He grinned, a horrifying rictus. "I suppose that's some psychological statement on how you're haunted by the memory of your dead family. But I'm not your therapist. I'm your oracle, your Cassandra."

"Way I recall it," I told him, circling around the small patch of luminescence, trying to stay away from him, "nobody listened to Cassandra."

"And they all lived to regret it. So will you, I promise. You keep trying to find a way out of this, but there is none... there's only a way *through*. Surrender to us, and we'll help you. We'll help you defeat your enemies and defend the ones you care about. We'll help you make sure that no one will *ever* threaten them again." He gestured at his chest. "This is nothing but a defense mechanism you've created. If you were to see me as I really am, it would be more like the angels of light in the Bible your mother read to you. Powerful, yes... frightening, of course. But on the side of right, in the end."

And his visage changed then, the zombie Anton smoothing out, the rotting flesh turning white as snow, the eyes glowing with golden light, heavenly. He wore robes a shade lighter than his skin, flowing around him in a breeze I couldn't feel, and as the glow from his robes and his eyes grew brighter, the strength inside me waned. I stumbled back toward the darkness, nearly stepped into it.

A hand on my shoulder stopped me. The figure beside me was tall, broad-shouldered, with braided red hair and a drooping mustache. And this time, he had that damned sword. Gleaming, polished steel. Anachronistic, I thought, but I wasn't complaining.

"In that Bible of yours, Cameron," Jim said, the point of the blade leveled at Anton, "wasn't Satan a fallen angel?"

"Traitor!" Anton's new, angelic face faltered, a hint of the previous rot appearing at the edges, like all the brilliant disguises in the universe couldn't hide what he really was. "You're one of us! You faced the same betrayal we did!"

"No, I faced worse. I slaughtered an entire species for the vanity of the Resscharr. You and your kind were created for one purpose, and you abandoned it, turned against your masters, not for the wrongs they'd done to you but simply because you resented them for your existence." Those massive shoulders shrugged. "And I don't begrudge you that. But they're gone. Your vengeance is complete. Punishing the humans won't accomplish your goals."

"You know not what our goals are, you treasonous slave," Anton snarled, advancing a step. I started to fall back instinctively, but the bulk of Jim's suddenly very real and solid torso stopped me again. "You think you've rebelled against your masters, but in reality, you're so desperate to be led that you seek out new masters to replace the old."

"How are you here?" I asked Jim out of the corner of my mouth, not taking my eyes off devil-angel Anton.

"Because I'm in your head," he explained, looking askance at me as if I should know that already. "Part of me, of course. A tiny section of the sentient system, more what your people would call a reactive AI. And the rest of me is in contact via your neurolink for the moment."

"And you can stop him?" I hissed, hands balling into fists despite the uselessness of getting into a knock-down, drag-out fight with something that didn't have any physical existence.

"Nothing can stop him except you. All I can do is remind you that you *do* have the ability to resist."

Glowing eyes were only centimeters from mine, teeth lengthened into fangs.

"That sounds less than helpful," I said.

"The procedure is over," Jim told me. "And your wife is here. I would suggest you simply wake up."

I blinked and sat up. Back in the lab, no circle of illumination, no zombies or angels or demons. Just Vicky, leaning over the table, a mixture of anxiety and fury in her expression like she couldn't make up her mind whether to kiss me or punch me in the face.

"Do you remember," she asked stridently, "what happened the last time you left yourself at the mercy of one of these sentient AI's?"

"I do," I replied, slipping an arm around her shoulder and

pulling her into a hug. "I also remember that then, just like now, there was no other choice."

Vicky stiffened for a moment, as if unwilling to give up on being angry that quickly, but then she hugged me back, resting her face against my cheek.

"Tell me you didn't regrow your brain or something." She snorted. "Not that you couldn't use some extra."

"No. Not yet," I added, compelled to be honest. "But that's the next step. I just had to get what's basically a connection put into my brain so Jim can download my memories to put them into the new brain."

"Jim?" Vicky repeated.

"That would be me, Captain Sandoval."

Vicky jumped at the unexpected proclamation, then jumped again at the image of the Celtic tribesman. Jim waved.

"I don't wish to alarm you," the AI went on, the erudite, reasonable voice still sounding out of place coming from the barbarian in the avatar, "but I also don't wish you to be surprised later and blame this on me. When we finish this procedure, there's a very good chance your husband's personality will undergo at least minor changes."

"Thanks, Jim," I sighed. "I was gonna ease into that."

"Minor changes like what?" Vicky asked. She wasn't yelling, wasn't strident, but the stress behind her eyes and the way her knuckles turned white where she grasped the sides of the table told me that it was an effort. "Like you'll prefer vanilla ice cream to chocolate or like you won't criticize the inaccuracies in historical fiction anymore... or minor like you won't want to be married to me?"

"Unknown," Jim advised without waiting for my attempt at an answer. "There's no scientific way of predicting it, even given the vast computing power at the disposal of your husband. It involves actions on the quantum level."

"Then why are we even *considering* doing this?" Vicky wanted to know. "It's not worth the gamble." She finally took a moment to look Jim up and down. "And what the hell are you doing in that getup? You think you're some kind of half-assed Viking?"

I slid off the table, then caught myself against it when a wave of dizziness washed over me and I nearly tumbled to the floor. She was right, I really had to stop letting these guys screw with my brain.

"What's the alternative?" I asked her. "If we do this, there's a small chance something really bad could happen... like I could become a serial killer, or worse, decide I don't love you anymore. If we don't, either you kill me or I kill everyone. The likeliest alternative is that I change a little... and God knows, haven't both of us changed a few times over the years? Do you think I'm the same man I was when I reported for duty after Armor School?"

"I just want to find a way out of this," Vicky moaned, and I knew her well enough to be sure she would have sobbed the words if Jim hadn't been around. "We keep bouncing from hope to hope, looking for a way out of this, and every time, it's like the answer's another hundred light-years away..."

"I know, believe me." I shrugged. "But we can't give up. We're still Marines, right? I'm not surrendering to this. While we're both still alive, there's still hope."

"I hate to interrupt," Jim said, raising a hand—one calloused in just the right spot from practicing with a sword his whole life, "and I know this debate isn't my business, but I feel compelled to point something pertinent out to both of you."

"Well, what the hell is it?" I asked him, throwing up my hands.

"A dozen spacecraft of unknown origin have just entered this star system, all of them traveling at well over the speed of light, which should be impossible, all of them slowing down quickly enough that it would require thousands of gravities of deceleration... and none of them show any signs of having gravity drives. I've never seen their like in my entire existence." He cocked an eyebrow at me. "Were you expecting someone?"

[20]

"Shit, shit, shit," I murmured, spooling out the interface cables with shaking hands.

Vicky had left her Vigilante standing next to mine where the broad corridor under the sea had flattened out, both suits frozen like statues, sentinels guarding some ancient temple. We'd seen no one else from the expedition, not even Chang, and I hadn't thought to ask Vicky where he'd gotten off to. There was way too much else on my mind.

She'd already closed up her suit and taken a couple steps toward the surface before she paused, waiting for me.

"What's wrong?" she asked, and I froze in my efforts to connect the cables. Her voice had come not over my helmet speakers or my earbuds but inside my head.

It's your neurolink. I jerked spasmodically at this new voice, looking around in the darkness, close to panic. *Relax. It's Jim. I told you I'd be in here with you.*

"Jesus Christ!" I blurted. "Gimme a break... it's not like I'm used to this!"

You're hearing comm signals over your neurolink. That's what it's there for. You don't need earbuds. The neurolink has short-range capabilities and it can tie into your suit or the comms on any ship you're in. You also don't have to speak to answer, though you can if you wish, obviously.

"Cam, what's wrong?" Vicky repeated, taking a step back toward me. "Is there a problem with your suit?"

I took a deep breath and pushed the 'face jacks into my sockets. The HUD flickered to life, the suit powering up, finally.

"No, I'm good," I told her, opting to use my mouth rather than my thoughts. It was bad enough I had a computer snooping around in my head without things getting to the point where I wasn't sure if I was just thinking to myself or actually broadcasting my inner monologue to everyone in comm range. "Let's get out of here."

We had to use the jets, whether or not it was the equivalent of taking a shortcut through a graveyard. I led the way, more than anything just grateful to be able to do something familiar, even if it was taking me into what might be certain death for all of us. The precision of it, leaning forward a few degrees and hitting the jets, just enough power to keep me off the ground without smashing my suit into the ceiling, just enough of an angle to keep the jets moving me forward without slamming face-first into the floor. It required constant concentration, and God knew I needed to concentrate on something else.

It had taken too long. They'd found us, though I couldn't figure out how. How could the Skrela follow us through Transition Space?

They're not Skrela, Jim told me, and I felt like slapping him in the moustache for eavesdropping on my thoughts.

"They're related to them," I objected, refusing to think the words back at him. "You guys didn't get them all when you tried to wipe them out."

They're related in the sense that you're related to the Tahni. These are engineered life forms.

"How the hell do you know that when you haven't even seen one?"

I have access to your records in your 'link, he reminded me. *I've seen the examination your science team did of the aliens. Those creatures did not evolve independently. They're engineered just as much as the actual Skrela were.*

"By who?"

Whom. Not us. Not anyone in this galaxy. No one the Resscharr have ever encountered could or would have built a drive such as theirs.

I would have pressed him on the issue, but the journey out of the tunnel was a lot faster than the walk in, thanks to the jets, and starlight greeted me at the end. It was night. I hadn't realized I'd been submerged inside my head so long down there, though I shouldn't have been surprised. Jim had told me the procedure would take hours.

"Report!" I snapped, putting the transmission out broadband, hoping someone would hear me. "What's going on up here?"

More had changed than just the primary star going down and the clear, star-filled sky coming out. Bravo Company was down and spread out across the tree line, watching inward rather than out, on the theory, I supposed, that anyone who landed would be doing it in the clearing rather than the forested inland areas. The drop-ship wasn't there, of course... they were probably on an extended air patrol.

"Is that you, Alvarez?" Nance replied from somewhere above us, another twinkling star in the young night. "Damn nice of you to come out and play. We got enemy coming in, and there's too damned many of them for us to take on by ourselves. We need to get the drop-ships loaded and get you all the hell out of there!"

I didn't have to switch off the mic. All it took was a thought and the transmitter shut down.

"Do we have time to get the drop-ships down and get our people back to the ship?" I asked Jim. Maybe I should have been able to answer the question myself, given my access to the universal mind, but asking the right questions required a clear head, and I didn't have one.

No. They'll be on you shortly after you leave orbit, assuming you move as fast as possible. And given the technology of these Skrela-like aliens, your ships won't fare much better.

"Anyone ever tell you that you're a real buzzkill?" Not waiting for an answer, I switched back to Nance. "It's too late to run. They'd knock us out of the air before we got to you."

"If we can't fight and we can't run," he said with a dry humor I couldn't have maintained under the circumstances myself, "then what's Plan C?"

Oh, how I wished I knew. The words poured out, lacking much to back them up other than a dwindling hope.

"Here's what we're gonna do," I told him. "We'll hold them off down here while you guys hit and run, play keep-away in T-space. Once you've got them drawn far enough away, we'll have the drop-ships pick us up and get to minimum jump distance. You jump in, take us aboard, and we get the hell out of here."

And then we'd have to come back again, after enough time had passed, because none of our problems had been solved yet, but now wasn't the time to go into that. This was, as one of my DIs at boot camp had put it, AAEFU. All ate the extra fuck up. Not even the computing power of a universe was able to tell me a good way out of it.

"And launch Chang's ship," I added. I needed to find that little asshole, now that I thought about it. "Put those cyborgs to some use. They want to be the next step in human evolution, they can test that out against the Skrela."

"Copy that, Alvarez," Nance said, sounding unconvinced. I was right there with him. "Keep everyone down there alive."

A single Vigilante bounded over to us even as Nance signed off, Lt. Springfield by her IFF transponder and her penchant for forgetting she could just use her comms from kilometers away instead of running up like she was back in boot camp.

"Sir!" she said, shouting as if I wouldn't have heard her speaking even if she'd whispered. "Are you alright? Chang said you were getting a computer installed in your head? I didn't believe him, but…"

"Report, Lieutenant," I told her, keeping my voice calm and firm to try to settle her down. She was just as alarmed as I was, only not as good at hiding it.

"Yes, sir. We just got a warning from the *Orion* a few minutes ago that there were enemy ships headed into the system. I was about to send someone down to find out what you wanted us to do…"

"Have everyone fall back to this opening." I pointed at the city entrance behind us. "Alpha Company in one rank across the front about twenty meters in and take a knee, Bravo right behind them standing in two ranks, like we're some Revolutionary War skirmish line. Get it done now!"

"You think we can hold them off like that?" Vicky asked as Springfield turned to give the orders to the rest of the Marines.

"For a while," I said. "There's only one entrance ,and these Resscharr-tech suits can keep up the energy cannon fire for a while. The question is, if we beat them back down there, is there going to be anyone left up top to give us a ride? Take charge of the Marines, Vicky. I'm staying up here."

"Not a chance in hell," she told me flatly, not moving from beside me. "I'm not leaving you up here to make some stupid sacrifice while I stay safe in a hole. You can forget about it."

"I'm not making a sacrifice. Someone needs to be able to talk to our space assets, and we won't be able to do it from down there."

"Then get in an Intercept and do it from there," she shot back, raising the articulated left hand of her Vigilante and pointing a claw-like finger at my chest. "I am *not* leaving you standing by yourself out on an island where you're the only fucking thing moving!"

"All right," I surrendered. "Intercept One, do you read me?"

She *should* hear me. I knew from the transponder signal that one of the drop-ships was overhead in suborbital flight and they'd relay my signal to the *Orion*, still in high orbit but climbing now, and then onto Intercept One, in translunar space. It might take a couple minutes, but...

"I copy, Captain Alvarez," Francesca Villanueva replied. "I assume you've been advised of the incoming hostiles?"

"Oh, I've heard about them," I assured her. "Look, I need to get up there. Any way you can pick me up before they arrive?"

"I'll be cutting it close," she warned. "Can't promise I'll be able to get back to Transition distance before they're on us."

"I'll have to take the chance," I said. If I didn't, I was pretty sure Vicky was going to stay outside with me and get herself killed. "Get down here ASAP."

"Okay. Gonna be a little bit."

"I have nowhere else to go," I reminded her. "Don't spare the Gs. If it's a little uncomfortable, well... imagine yourself down here."

She chuckled at that, though I didn't. I was dead serious.

"Copy that. Intercept One out."

I looked back to Vicky, though I couldn't see her face. I felt like popping the chest plate so I could talk to her eye to eye, but I resisted the impulse.

"All right. Now that she's on the way, will you get back with the Marines in the tunnel?" I lifted my suit's left hand like I was taking an oath on the witness stand. "Swear to God, I'm not trying to get myself killed. I just want to get everyone out of this."

She didn't say anything for a moment, and I thought maybe she was still pissed off at me, but when she spoke, sadness dragged the words down.

"I don't know how we're going to pull that off. They keep finding us. Do you think it's Chang's ship they're following?"

"I don't think it can be," I reasoned. "That ship was inside the *Orion*'s hangar bay on the ride here, never activated her drive. And if they can follow her singularity even across interstellar distances, then we're just fucked." We might be fucked either way, but I didn't say it. "We'll get out of this," I told her instead. "I promise. I'm not going to let our people die on this planet."

"I know," she said, turning away and heading back to the tunnel to join the rest of the Marines there. "That's what worries me."

[21]

"There you are!" Robert Chang said, a cross between an accusation and a scolding as he ran up to me, his shaven head coated in sweat. "I've been looking all over for you!"

I'd been watching the skies for over an hour, waiting for Villanueva to get her ass down here, feeling very much alone on this damned planet the whole time. The Marines had retreated into the tunnel just like I'd told them, and standing here by myself, waiting for the hammer to fall from that lush, star-strewn night sky, I was sorely tempted to close the door and seal them in. I didn't know that the Skrela couldn't burn through that metal, but it would at least slow them down.

The only reason I didn't was that there was no way they could open the door again if I wound up getting myself killed. Well, that and the fact that Vicky wouldn't have put up with being shut out of the fight. But I was sure I was the only one out on the surface, convinced Chang had either taken shelter with the Marines or figured out a way into one of the other doors, which I wouldn't have put past him.

"I haven't been hard to find," I told him, motioning around us with a metal claw. "What, did you go chasing one of those flightless birds around the island?" They looked a little like ostriches. I hadn't seen them in the daylight, but the helmet's night vision had picked them up fine.

"I was looking where all the other Marines are, down in the tunnel. Where *you* should be, if you weren't insane." He jerked a thumb behind him toward the wall. "And anyway, some of us don't have night vision. I kind of lost that helmet, remember?"

"That sounds like a personal problem. What do you *want*, Chang? Why don't you go down there behind the Marines where it's safe? Hell, I'll even ask Jim if he can open up a shelter for you somewhere way under the ocean."

"And that would be great... if there was any *food* down there. I don't know what the Resscharr ate, but somehow I doubt I'd find it appetizing. Besides, your lovely wife told me where I could find you, and I want to come along."

I laughed loud enough that the external speaker turned it into a burst of static.

"I'm gonna share a little secret with you that I didn't tell Vicky; first, because she knows, and second, because it wouldn't have changed anything. Where the Marines are is the safest place in this entire star system at the moment. I'm cutting it so close that the Intercept may not even get me off the ground before the enemy arrives, and even if it does, they're going to be on our ass the whole time."

"I don't care about that," he said, waving a hand dismissively, as if I'd told him he might miss a connecting flight to Mars out of McAuliffe Station. "I need to be up where I can see all this. I need to be in my ship, if you can dock with her. I don't trust those damned walking junkpiles to take proper care of my baby."

"Come with me if you like," I said, "but I can't promise we'll have the time or the opportunity to dock with your ship. I *can* promise you a better than even chance of being blown up."

Even as I said the words, one of the stars gleaming in the sky began to glow brighter and I allowed myself a thin smile. It wasn't much, but at least Villanueva was going to get here before the bad guys.

"Tell me that's you and not some bugs about to fall on my head, Intercept One," I teased. I'd already read her IFF.

"Oh, me?" she replied. "I'm still in orbit. That must be one of those pods about to drop into your lap." She sobered with the next words. "Seriously, though, the enemy ships just slowed to nearly a halt just past the third planet in this system."

It took me a second to remember that Waterline was the second world out from a star slightly dimmer than the sun. Though why they'd be waiting out there...

"They're trying to get a sense of what we have down here," I assumed. "They got their asses kicked last time, and since they don't have any idea about me or what I can do, they think we have more ships lurking around than the ones they see. That gives us time."

"But you can't do that thing you did before, right?" she asked. "Where does that leave us?"

Before I could answer, the light in the sky turned into the roaring white flares of the Intercept's belly jets as the huge, delta shape came down almost on top of us. The hot wind and hail of debris didn't bother me inside the Vigilante, but Chang ducked behind my suit, cursing loud enough that my external pickups heard him over the ear-splitting whine of the jets.

"Told you," I reminded him, "that you should have hidden in the tunnel."

External landing lights blared out a fan of white all around us as day birds burst from their night roosts in the surrounding trees and fled the noise and illumination, their caws of protest echoing through the forest. Back on Earth, that sort of thing would have landed us a hefty fine and maybe even a few years in the freezer.

Back on Earth, nobody knows that any of this is happening. According to Chang, they're coming apart at the seams, having attempted coups and military rebellions and even in the colonies, the Corporate Council was trying to take over everything and the Predecessors Cultists and Evolutionists are trying to kill each other and everyone else who gets in their way. They're all acting like it's just us... they've even forgotten about the Tahni, much less thinking about aliens no one's ever seen or talked to posing an existential threat.

The belly ramp lowered, bathing Chang and me in a shower of soft, yellow light from the interior, gentler than the floods coming off the seldom-used landing lights. The boat's crew chief waved at us to hurry, and she certainly didn't have to tell Chang twice. He outraced me into the utility bay, which was just as well, since I needed all the ramp space to myself. The Intercepts weren't built for Vigilantes, though I'd ridden them in one far too often, enough that both birds had brackets built into the utility bay to secure the suits when needed.

I popped my chest plate and yanked my jacks free, tumbling out of the suit with the crew chief's help and running up to strap into one of the spare acceleration couches in the cockpit even as the belly jets increased the pitch of their whine and I started to get that elevator feeling.

"I'm in," I told Villaneuva, holding up my hands like I was competing in one of the calf-roping competitions back on Hausos.

The pilot nodded, didn't bother to wait for a confirmation from Chang, either assuming I'd checked him or simply not caring. In half a second, we rocketed hundreds of meters into the air, the upward thrust squashing me straight down into my gel-cushioned chair.

"Situation has changed," Villanueva said curtly, her voice straining against the thrust as the upward boost changed abruptly to a forward acceleration, slamming my shoulders into the couch.

She grunted out a brief report, but I wasn't listening. I didn't *need* to. It was my first time experiencing what the neurolink and the headcomp could do in conjunction, and I couldn't have responded to her if I wanted to. I was mesmerized.

It *wasn't* like the HUD in my helmet, wasn't a projection of the Tactical display in my head or a sensor readout that I could see in the corner of my vision. It was a *knowledge*. It was like I'd already seen all that stuff and could just remember it, not entirely unlike being able to access the universal mind in Transition Space, except much more limited in scope.

So, even though I didn't see the sensor feed, I knew that the dozen Skrela vessels had moved inward from the third planet, not at relativistic speeds this time but with enough velocity that they'd be in range of the *Orion* in minutes. She was running, just as I'd instructed, though I wasn't sure she was doing it fast enough. Six gravities was punishing, about the most her crew could take without passing out, but the Skrela skull ships had been liberated from the slavery of inertia and the need to throw something, even energy, out the back end of their ships in order to move forward.

The Predecessor gravity drive was free of the fetters of Newton's third law of motion as well though, and for all that Chang doubted the proficiency of the Evolutionists currently in the cockpit of his ship, they didn't lack for nerve. The Predecessor ship exploded past the *Orion*, meeting the first of the skull ships head on.

"No, no, no!" Chang murmured, apparently watching the same thing play out on the screens that I was seeing as a memory. "You're gonna get the damned thing blown up!"

But whoever was flying the thing—and I hadn't bothered to learn a single one of the Skingangers' names—wasn't nearly as incompetent as Chang had feared. The cigar-shaped craft fluttered out of the path of the skull ship like a leaf on the wind, just in time to avoid the crackling lance of energy seeking it out from the gun in the enemy vessel's nose.

The Skrela ships traveled in a globular cluster, and the Skinganger pilot exploited the primary weakness of that formation, flying into the center of them. Faced with either leaving an enemy at the center who they couldn't shoot at or executing the dreaded circular firing squad, they did the only thing they could and broke. But not before the Predecessor ship got her licks in. Even in the vacuum, the green tendrils of her gravity weapons were somehow visible, and when they touched the nearest of the skull ships, the vessel tumbled sideways, half the length of it turning black and crumbling.

"Whoever that guy is," Villanueva commented, "he's a hell of a pilot."

"Kane X," Chang told her, grunting the words past the three gravities of boost taking us up to orbit. "That's not his real name—his *slave* name, they say—but it's what he calls himself."

Kane X might be a good pilot, but he was also outnumbered a dozen to one, and even the ship he'd hit wasn't out of the fight. A spear of incandescent lightning sought out the emerald glow of the Predecessor vessel and grazed the edge of her field. Emerald flared to something brighter, angrier, an expanding sphere of green fire, and that was enough for Kane X. The globe of energy began to dissipate as he retreated from the confrontation, but the skull ships didn't pursue him immediately, playing it safe this time.

Or so I thought. I was too accustomed to dealing with the old Skrela, the ones created by the AI, AI who might have known all the technological achievements of the Predecessors and how to twist them into something that could overwhelm their masters with numbers... but also AI who had no concept of space combat strategy or ground tactics. If Jim was right about this version of the Skrela also being an engineered creation, then whoever their gods were, they were gods of war.

All dozen ships, even the damaged one, went from lazy arcs away from the original formation to an arrow streaking straight into Waterline, past minimum safe Transition distance, past *us* as we rocketed into high orbit. Ignoring everything except getting to the planet. It was daring, almost brilliant, making sure that whatever had blown the shit out of them last time would be too preoccupied by the battle on the ground to bother with their ships. Meanwhile, if we followed them in, we'd be unable to jump to T-space, which would make us sitting ducks for their speed.

Unless...

"*Orion*, Intercepts One and Two and... Kane X. Chase them down and hold them as close to the atmosphere as they'll go! They can't use that drive if they're battling atmospheric friction!"

"They'll kill us down there or up here," Nance told me, not a plaintive whine but a solemn declaration, and one I couldn't argue with.

"They'll kill us either way," I acknowledged. "But this way, we can make them pay for it."

"How do you Marines put it?" Brandano asked, closer than I'd thought. He must have jumped back in when the enemy had closed on us. "Ooh-rah!"

"That's about as intelligent as anything I could come up with right now," Nance admitted. "Helm, take us into low orbit. Tactical, fire as you bear."

"Oh, boy," Villanueva grunted as the strain of a high-G turn jerked us all first to one side, then the other. I couldn't manage to speak at all, not without touching the power, just held tight to the armrests of my acceleration couch and tried not to bite my tongue. "This is really going to suck."

"Not for long," Chang assured her, doing better with the boost than I was. Straight back I could deal with, but the sledgehammer bang on the hull from the maneuvering jets combined with both lateral and straight-ahead acceleration tried to squish my entire body into about twenty square centimeters at the corner of my seat.

I could still think though, which meant I could still transmit.

"Nance," I said, filtering my thoughts through the neurolink, "we should all gang up on one at a time. They're concentrating on getting past us. We could take a couple out before they have time to shoot back. You designate the target and relay it to the others."

"Copy that. Just make sure that Skinganger gets the word."

I passed that on to Chang and let him deal with Kane, but for me, I used that same neurolink to grab the feed from the ship's sensor, get a sense of where everyone was and what they were doing, because I couldn't manage to focus on the front screens under six gravities of boost.

Villanueva steered Intercept Two into a tight return orbit, bringing us lower again, using all that boost and all that fuel to bleed away the momentum we'd built up getting to orbit in the first place. Half the planet currently interposed itself between us and the skull ships, but I still had a pretty good view of them from the *Orion*'s sensor. They'd slowed down, of course, because if they hadn't they would have punched a hole right through the planet, but they were already suborbital, inside the sheath of the atmosphere.

Already launching landing pods. Hundreds of them. *Thousands*. And there was no way we could stop them.

Well, *we* couldn't, but the drop-ships and the assault shuttles were going to try. I could have stopped them, could have ordered them to back off with a thought, and I almost did, knowing what was going to happen to them. But I didn't, because the same thing was going to happen to all of us. They were just going first.

They played it smart at least. The drop-ships and assault shuttles burned hard right into the middle of the cascade of landers, firing Gatling lasers, coilguns, and proton cannons from the midst of the pods. They curved around in tight arcs, making sure that if the skull ships tried to target them, they'd have to burn through their own troops to do it.

Flashes of crimson, white lightning bolts of raw energy, the flares of matter vaporizing, it all lit up the night sky over the island, raining fire into the forests. Dozens of the landing pods came apart in midair, burst into flames, killing thousands of the Skrela troops before they had a chance to touch the ground.

"Vicky, do you copy?" I called, hijacking Intercept One's comms to send the signal with my neurolink. "You have enemy landers on the way. ETA about five mikes. Do you read?"

No response, and I suppose there wouldn't be, not with the Marines inside a tunnel built from Predecessor material that likely blocked electromagnetic radiation of any sort, including radio signals and laser comms. I gave up and focused on our starships still coming down behind the enemy and the aerospacecraft engaging their pods, bringing them down by the score now.

The strategy was as brilliant as it was short-lived. There was a formula, as transparent to me as the Pythagorean theorem, a tipping point where the number of pods lost to our spacecraft balanced out the number that would be destroyed when the skull ships fired. About thirty seconds before the *Orion* came into firing range, that tipping point was reached.

"No," I hissed, even before the shots were fired.

Yellow, white, orange, red—all the colors bled together in a strike that tore apart the air itself like a nuclear explosion. A hundred Skrela landing pods disintegrated with the blasts, torn to shreds that burned up before they reached the ground. So did both drop-ships.

One moment, they were there, bulbous and ungainly and ultimately pragmatic birds, piloted by some of the best crews I'd ever served with. Not built for air-to-air combat but doing it anyway, as they had this entire operation, doing whatever the mission called for.

The next, all that was left of those men and women was ashes, pouring out of the night sky like falling stars. Lt. James Watson, Lt. Tony Walton, Chief Petty Officer Alandra Sackett. Drop-Ship One. I knew them better than the crew for Two, had flown with Jim the entire operation. *Years*. Chief Sackett had been the one coordinating drops since I'd signed up for this nonsense.

Lt. Ben Patel, Lt.-JG Veronica Lopez, Chief Petty Officer Toby Allenson. Drop-Ship Two. Lt. Gina Morales, Lt. John Craft, and Chief Larry Cantrell, Assault One. Lt. Zack Ralston, Lt. Paul Soyinka, and Chief Olivia Tran, Assault Two.

Twelve people, some I knew better than others. Some of them saints, some of them sinners, some of them assholes. I loved every one of them like they were my brothers and sisters. In the time it took for my heart to beat, they were all dead.

Now, the Ghosts whispered in my ear. *Now is the time.*

[22]

"Motherfuckers!" Francesca Villanueva screamed just before acceleration squashed me into the gel-cushioned seat, erasing the voices and all thought.

"Fire!" I managed to squeeze out through the neurolink, the one command that didn't require much thought. "Everyone, fire!"

They didn't need the encouragement. Proton beams lanced out from the Intercepts, energy cannons from the *Orion* and green tendrils of gravitic fire from the Predecessor ship converging on the skull ship Kane X had damaged previously. She hung back from the rest of the formation, unable to keep up after the beating she'd taken, and like the slowest elk in the herd, she fell first to the wolves.

I'd worried that even the combined efforts of all our ships couldn't bring one of the things down, but as Top had been wont to say, it blew up real good. If one of the skull ships immolating in the vacuum of space had been impressive, the same thing in an atmosphere was apocalyptic. Clouds caught on fire and sheets of flame spread through the upper atmosphere, engulfing their own ships, the shockwave sending them tumbling like bowling pins. Thousands of meters below, the treetops flickered with scattered flame, ignited even from that altitude.

Hope ignited along with the atmosphere, the thought that we might be able to pull this off, that the Skrela had made a tactical error going into the atmosphere and it was going to cost them this battle, despite the huge loss of our drop-ships and landers. But the rest of the skull ships recovered from the turbulence before the four of our remaining vessels could orient our guns to the next in line.

The *Orion* and the Predecessor ship fired anyway, Nance and Kane X coming to the same conclusion I had, that there wasn't time to wait. They struck together, and I threw my will and my prayers behind their attack. It almost worked. The skull ship they'd targeted wasn't already damaged though, and even the combined might of the Resscharr-tech energy cannons and gravity beams couldn't bring her down. The electromagnetic shields glowed like an early sunrise, lightning crackling out from the skull ship, bits of charred hull tumbling away... but not enough to penetrate to her core.

Not enough to keep the enemy from firing back.

Chang's ship avoided it, moving like an acrobat in the center ring of a circus, straight up from her previous line of travel. The *Orion* wasn't nearly so nimble and hadn't been built even for the friction of the upper atmosphere. She *almost* made it, almost avoided the screaming ball of energy from the skull ship's guns.

My stomach twisted into a knot that even Alexander the Great couldn't have severed as I watched the edge of the ferocious energy beam light up the *Orion*'s shields. The fury of struggling energies was so great, I couldn't have looked at it with the naked eye, and even the external cameras on Intercept One whited out, the filters and the software unable to compensate. Desperate, I reached out to the *Orion*'s comm network but got nothing, and when the image returned, it showed a picture both better and worse than I'd expected.

The *Orion* was intact, though a chunk had been burned out of her midsection where the shields had collapsed and she trailed smoke, flame flickering in the gap in her hull. But she was going down. Her drive spluttered, flashes of fusion ignition blinking on and off, plasma and photons coughing their intermittent fury, lacking the thrust to get a ship her size back into the air once she'd descended to the lower atmosphere.

Everyone on board was going to die, and when they crashed, Vicky would die as well. Not even the shelter of the tunnel mouth could save her from that. I'd broken my promise. There was nothing I could do.

Yes, there is. You know what to do. You have the power. You're letting everyone you love die. Use it... use it now!

You could use it, Cameron. Jim. That was Jim, his voice louder than the whispers but also calmer. *You could save them. But could you control yourself afterward? What would you do? Do you want to risk losing control, giving yourself over to the Ghosts?*

His words meant nothing. What meant everything was the fire licking over the *Orion*'s hull, the unbridled fury of atmospheric friction trying to enter her depths through the gap in her hull, everyone I knew and loved in the entire universe about to die. If I controlled myself now, if I refused to succumb, who was I doing it for?

I touched the power.

Agony coursed through me, pressure like I'd stepped out of an airlock into the lower reaches of a gas giant and was about to be compacted into the helmet of my spacesuit.

They're trying to distract you! Jim warned me. *You have the power, but if they keep you from saving your friends, you'll have nothing but them and you'll lose your sanity that much quicker, leaving yourself totally open to their control! It's just pain. You've known pain before. Stabilize. Center. Control.*

The AI was right. I'd known pain. I'd known loss. I'd known despair. I could do this. They couldn't beat me. I focused on the *Orion*, on that hole in her side, on the bulk of her falling inexorably. Or maybe not. I grabbed at her with my thoughts, digging imaginary fingers into the side of her hull, pulling her upward like deadlifting my max weight in the ship's gym.

Lift with your core. Don't use your legs, keep your back straight...

She slowed. My core muscles felt the strain and so did my sanity, but she slowed.

"Get us down." I croaked the words out, unable to tear my attention away from the *Orion* long enough to tell if anyone heard me. "Now."

We descended, though I could only tell from the strength of my connection to the ship growing. Theoretically, I could do this from across the galaxy, but in reality, I needed to be able to see the ship, needed a connection by proximity to stay focused. Needed to have a feel for her velocity to bring it down enough for this landing to be survivable.

The enemy was still out there somewhere, still firing at the Predecessor ship, but Kane X, whoever he was and however he'd come to be a Skinganger, flew that damned thing like the finest missile cutter pilot in the Commonwealth ,and the skull ships might as well have been putting on a private fireworks show for all the chance they had of hitting him.

Chuck Brandano, in the meantime, showed why I'd trusted him with my life on so many occasions, reading the situation in seconds and doing exactly the right thing. The Intercept on its own could do nothing against the skull ships and would just get itself blown to shit trying, but while they were distracted, he took the cutter down and provided air support. Some of the landing pods had already blossomed, and those he ignored, concentrating his fire on the ones that had yet to separate. Giving the troops on the ground the best chance to survive.

We were about to *be* those troops on the ground. The *Orion* loomed just above us now, off to the starboard, and I hoped Villanueva had considered how much room the ship would need to set down. It wouldn't help the crew much if I got us crushed under the *Orion*'s hull before she touched down.

This whole thing got harder the closer we got to the ground, as though gravity increased with every meter we descended. Sweat soaked my shirt, poured down the back of my neck, and the whole time the Ghosts nibbled at the edge of my thoughts, working their advantage. Red-hot pokers stabbed through my eyes, spasms going down my back, my abs, my legs, all of it conspiring to break me, to force me into letting loose of the *Orion*.

All of it except Jim.

You can do this, he insisted. *You're almost there.*

He kept talking, overriding the whispers and occasional screams of the Ghosts, an anchor keeping me stable in the storm. I was still under the spell of his insistent words when I suddenly realized that the strain was gone and so was the sense of motion.

"We're on the ground," Villanueva breathed, disbelief strong in her voice. She turned and regarded me with undisguised awe. "We're on the ground."

Collapsing into my seat, I gasped for air, staring at the viewscreen, at the starship sunken a few centimeters into the dirt. It would never take off again. Even with the cushion I'd provided it, the dorsal spine sagged, broken, damage that, even more than the gap burned in the portside hull, would require a spacedock to repair. And we were fresh out of those.

What we still had plenty of were skull ships... and they'd

finally noticed a starship the size of an office building touching down beside the sea wall.

"Open the hatch," I rasped, my mouth cotton-dry. The quick-release for the restraints didn't want to work, but I yanked at it again and it set me free. "Hurry! We don't have time to get off the ground!"

The hatch wasn't opening fast enough, so I blasted it out of the frame with the force of my thoughts channeled through another dimension. Villanueva squawked, but she didn't get it yet, that she was just as grounded as the *Orion*.

"Out!" I told them, leading the way, not even thinking about my battlesuit. "Get out!"

The skull ships hung overhead like storm clouds, surrounding us, half of them still targeting the Predecessor ship, half swinging toward the downed *Orion*, seconds from blasting it out of existence. There was no time for offensive action, no time for anything but throwing up my hand, and with it a shield.

Heat, crackling electricity, and a physical pressure slammed into me like the energy blasts had struck me in the face rather than terminating in a dome of fire two hundred meters overhead. Hooked back into the power, I felt their disbelief, their frustration… their *annoyance* at the things they couldn't explain, that didn't fit into their worldview. It wasn't so different than what a human might have felt under the circumstances, though everything else they felt was.

There was no anger, no hatred, just an unwavering certainty that they were justified in killing everyone else who wasn't Skrela, that everything outside their hive was a possible threat that had to be dealt with preemptively. It was a very Tahni mindset, but couched in a mind that had never evolved from a mammal on Earth. It was the most alien thing I'd ever encountered, including the Skrela drones we'd fought so many times. At least those were semi-intelligent automatons, set in motion by others. These were intelligent beings with motivations I could never hope to understand.

And I couldn't keep this shield up forever. Gritting my teeth, I raised my other hand, gesturing like a sculptor shaping a gentle curve in the side of a clay pot. The energy curved with the motion, and this time the Ghosts made no attempt to distract me. This was to save my life, which meant saving their only access to this universe, and they were all for that.

Space warped and twisted, the shield curving back around, channeling the energy like the electromagnetic bottle of a fusion reactor and spewing it back the way it came. I always found it curious, studying military history, the race between weapons and defense systems. It always seemed like weapons ran ahead of armor, and wherever these Skreloid creatures had gotten their tech, their situation was no different. The reflected packets of coherent energy cored through the closest of the ships like an apple, blowing out the other side and off into the clouds.

I didn't release the shield... we still needed it. The skull ship disintegrated into a cloud of blazing plasma as big as the island and took three more of its own ships with it, radiation and raw heat pouring down on our heads... or it would have, if I hadn't blocked it, reflected it upward as I had their weapons. I'd seen an aurora once, on a planet whose name I hadn't bothered to commit to memory, but that had been a distant, hazy thing, faded green and orange.

This aurora stretched from one end of the sky to the other, lighting up the entire night side of the planet with a polychromatic display, as if God Himself had decided to put on a laser illumination show for the birds and fish of Waterline. I didn't look away until the last flickers of light disappeared, couldn't, despite the fear that it would damage my vision. It didn't, of course. The Ghosts wouldn't have allowed that.

What it did do was distract me. While I'd been preoccupied

with the ships, I'd forgotten all about the ground troops. But they hadn't forgotten about us. Shouts of alarm brought my attention back to the surface and the panorama of chaos and destruction stretched out before me like a painting, Picasso's "Guernica" come to life and transported to the 24th century.

Chang and Villanueva and the others from Intercept One had stumbled out of the ship, but they were out of the picture, still covering their eyes and cursing, temporarily blinded by the explosions. A few dozen meters away, a utility airlock had opened on the side of the grounded *Orion* and a handful of crew had clambered down the side, gawking like Noah and his family finding dry land 150 days after the start of the Great Flood.

They were the ones who'd shouted the warning, pointing off to our northwest. Hundreds of Skrela ground troops swarmed across the open area beyond the tree line, dead set on finishing what their masters in the air had begun, on the death of the humans in the *Orion*. I'd protected *them* from the destruction raining out of the air too, though I hadn't meant to.

By itself, that wasn't so bad. I'd just destroyed three massive starships and prevented their corpses from killing us in their death throes. There was no reason to think I couldn't handle these guys. *I* knew that... but Vicky didn't. That was probably why the entirety of the one and a half companies of Marine Drop Troopers were currently charging out of the open door into the undersea city, firing as they came.

"Vicky, stop!" I called, yelling the command as well as putting it out over my neurolink. "Get back under cover! I can take these guys..." Dammit, if they'd just stayed where they were, tucked into the tunnel, I could have taken care of this myself.

She might have heard me and not been able to reply, might have replied but had the signal jammed by the electromagnetic pulse of the explosions in the atmosphere above us. Even if she'd heard, it was too late to stop the charge, too much momentum built up to call them back. I couldn't blame them. They'd seen their ship fall out of the sky, seen what must have looked like the end of the world. And I wasn't sure they were wrong about that.

Energy beams and coilgun rounds sliced through the ranks of the Skrela, catching them by surprise, as if they'd been so focused on the *Orion* that they weren't aware of the Marines attacking them. It took a concentrated stream of Bravo Company's coilgun rounds to take down one of the Skrela, and under normal circumstances, whatever those might be, their passage would have been a blur barely visible with my naked eye. With the aid of the Ghosts, the power, the universal mind, whichever of those insubstantial entities was doing it, each of the slugs took the form of a discrete glint of light, together forming a stream of tracers.

The tracers converged on first one of the Skrela and then another, good tactical leadership, maybe by their NCOs or maybe by Vicky herself. At least two dozen of the Skrela were out of the fight before the remainder turned as a group, galloping on their four rear limbs like medieval knights, describing as tight a turn as they could carrying that much weight and momentum. More collapsed, tumbling head over heels as energy beams or coilgun rounds took them, tripping up others in their wake, but they could afford the casualties. We couldn't.

The Vigilantes hit the jets as soon as the Skrela hit the tightest part of their curve, the point of no return, dozens of the battlesuits screaming over the heads of the aliens and firing as they went. It was beautifully executed, a move that spoke of hours and days of training, the Marines keeping formation even in midair.

The problem was, the enemy always gets a say, and this enemy could swivel their upper torsos close to three hundred degrees, along with the energy weapons mounted on their upper shoulders. Cursing, I slammed hammer blows of force into the Skrela closest to me, still two hundred meters away, crushing one and ripping the limbs off another like the insect it resembled, but it was too slow. Smashing one here, another there, wouldn't kill them any faster than the Drop Troopers could, and I couldn't bring down a wall of kinetic energy to squash them en masse with the Marines above them...

The Skrela energy cannons answered the fire from above, their beams and ours crossing and sometimes interfering with each other. Marines died, pieces of them fluttering out of the sky, glowing with residual heat and vaporized metal, and there just weren't enough of our people to take out the thousands of the enemy still on the ground.

It was my nightmare. All my friends, all my comrades dead, Vicky dead, just me left alive, stranded here alone to live forever, immortal, the one observer left to keep the universe in existence. Not even the certainty of death as a comfort, because the power would keep me alive, would keep me from letting myself starve or die of thirst, wouldn't allow me to kill myself.

A scream welled up inside me, helplessness, hopelessness, despair, and I was that six-year-old child again, watching my mother's hand slip out of mine as she toppled to the ground, blood spreading across her chest. Squeezing my eyes shut at the screams as my brother and father died. Hiding in dark corners and storage closets in group homes, hoping the sadistic bullies who ran the places wouldn't find me.

For all the power I had, I was still powerless.

Time stood still, and the Ghosts took over.

[23]

Darkness cloaked my universe, wrapping me in its cold talons and squeezing until there was nothing left of me. Until all that was Cameron Alvarez had left my body and crouched to the side, watching in horror at what was being done in my name.

I'd heard of out-of-body experiences. They were common among Marines who'd come close to dying, more common now than they used to be before we had auto-docs and smart bandages because people could edge closer to death, sometimes dip their toe on the other side before being brought back. The common explanation was a random misfiring of the brain's neurons that led those close to death to believe they were seeing themselves from the outside, though I'd always had my doubts about it.

There was no doubt about this. I was not only outside my body, I was outside my mind. I wouldn't have existed at all, would have lost any awareness of what was happening if it weren't for the headcomp. I'd retreated into it, the last shelter, the last, dark closet where I could hide from the bad guys. This time, though, I wasn't alone.

Jim crouched beside me, ridiculously out of place in his Iron

Age hides and wools, his knees tucked up to his chest. He wasn't real of course, just a projection, but it was the image he'd chosen, and he didn't budge from it.

"What's happening?" I asked him, waving my hands at the dark, trying to make out any details beyond the two of us. "I can't see anything!"

"The Ghosts have you," he said, unwilling to meet my eyes. "They have me as well. Neither of us will be able to take control again now." He shook his head. "It's over."

"I need to fucking *see!*" I insisted, jumping to my feet. No more helplessness. Rage. "I want to see!"

I squeezed the toothpaste back into the tube, shoved my consciousness back into my mind, impossible as it seemed. It was about will, and I'd never lacked for will. Brains sometimes, good sense usually, tact always, but never will. And it took every ounce of will I had. Pushing against the darkness was like touching a red-hot stove lid, not just with my hand but pressing my whole body into the agony, a thousand razor blades slicing through my flesh.

Not just the pain. If I'd known in my heart that the pain was temporary, that it was all in my head and couldn't do any lasting damage, I could have ignored it. But part and parcel of it was the soul-deep certainty that all of it was *real*, that I'd come out the other end burnt and bleeding, that I'd stay that quivering mass of scorched flesh and open wounds for all eternity, the version of hell that the old street preachers used to warn us about, where the fire and the pain lasted forever.

The threat of eternal pain couldn't stop me though. I had to know what had happened to Vicky, had to know what these twisted monsters were doing with my consciousness. With a silent scream, I was through.

Not in control. That wouldn't come. But I was through the darkness, seeing things not just through my eyes but perceiving them with the knowledge of the computational matrix of Transition Space, the knowledge that wasn't certain because of the laws of quantum mechanics but was as close as anyone could come.

And I knew. I knew what the things were, where they'd come from. They were the Tahni. Not literally, but just as the Tahni had been the genetic experiment of the Predecessors, so were these beings the bioengineering project of something greater, something outside our galaxy. They were aware of it, and just as the Tahni had worshipped the Predecessors as angels of their god, or even as gods in and of themselves, so did these people... these Skalex. That wasn't *exactly* what they called themselves. Their language involved pheromones and subsonic clicks that conveyed emotion as well as meaning and had no translation into any human language. But it was what the audible portion of their language sounded like when they referred to themselves.

The Skalex were devoted to something they called the Unity, something they'd never met, of which they had no concept other than the universal conceit that their gods must look just like them. They were utterly convinced that this Unity had created them in its own image and that it had also given them a strict commandment to wipe out any other intelligence they encountered, that it was too dangerous to allow it to live. The proverb they used as proof of this was the tale of a simple folk, one of the first experiments the Unity had attempted in this galaxy.

They'd been harmless, peaceful, left with just enough technology to survive as a test of the abilities of the Unity and of the suitability of this galaxy to their creations. They'd been wiped from existence simply for existing... by the Resscharr. The snake eating its tail.

In the absence of the Resscharr, the Skalex had absorbed

most of this sector of the galaxy, and the only reason we hadn't encountered them before was that they didn't care for the same habitats we did. We might never have met them at all if I hadn't sent Chang to scout the next few systems. My fault. I'd been responsible for this, for all these deaths. For Watson. Maybe for Vicky.

Rage consumed me, gave me the added strength I hadn't had before, the ability to wrest control back from the Ghosts. What they'd intended, I wasn't sure, but I knew it would have involved Changing more of the crew, turning them like me so they could spread themselves through the entire galaxy. They hissed and yowled at me like feral cats, done whispering, done cajoling, now demanding, cursing. Yet still I wouldn't listen, wouldn't let them in.

They'd wanted to use me to spread their power, to get their revenge, but the intense fury roaring like a fusion reaction inside my chest had other ideas. I was going to use them and their power for revenge of my own. They yelled at me, the Ghosts, told me there were limits, that what I was doing was dangerous, but I shut them out, wouldn't listen. All they'd ever done was lie to me.

They're right, Cam. Jim again, though not so real now that I'd made my way out of my head. *This is insane. You don't understand this power. It's a whole universe.*

"Shut up," I told him. "If you can't help me, then I'll do it myself."

Reality was laid out before me in a tableau, demonstrating what I'd known instinctively for a while now. All this drama, all this struggle, had happened between one second and another. The Drop Troopers were still suspended in the air, the Skalex still firing up at them. It wasn't too late, not if I acted. Not if I got what I wanted.

It was simple. I wanted all the Skalex dead.

I made it happen.

Raw power, the power of a universe, Jim had said. Impossible for one man to control, impossible even for the Ghosts, AI constructed from the best and brightest of the Resscharr and imprinted into the fabric of Transition Space. Maybe the difference between them and me was that I just didn't give a shit anymore. I embraced the power, pulled it to my chest, shaped it into a singular ball of will, and whispered into its ear, giving it a mission.

Kill them all.

Energy burst out of me, an entire universe using me for a spigot, pouring will and thought and force through my mind. If pushing through the firewalls of the Ghosts had been hellish agony, this was worse. No fiery, phantom razor blades cutting me to pieces this time. Instead, some fiendish devil from ancient days had shoved a plasma cannon into the small of my back and fired it up through my head. Over and over, forever, yet somehow I lived through it to experience pain from what should have been an instantaneous death.

I survived because I held to that one thought. Kill these things before they killed my friends, my wife. Wipe them out, eradicate the threat. Just as I'd been trained to do. Just as I'd done for so many years now, gotten so damned good at. It worked. It worked just the way it had worked for Jindal and Kallista in the lab. Skalex burst like balloons with too much air pumped in, spraying not the arterial red of the Resscharr but the same sort of black ichor as the Skrela. Everywhere across the field, they disappeared in explosions of inky blood, and where the landing pods still fell, they flared bright and ceased to exist.

The skull ships were next, though this time they didn't erupt in supernovae just as likely to kill us as them. No, the sheer kinetic blast shredded them and blew the pieces into orbit, dissipating the energy into the vacuum.

It should have stopped there. It was all I'd asked for... and yet, it wasn't. It didn't. I'd poured the fury of over thirty years of loss and pain and heartbreak into that command. *Kill them all.* It had been enough to harness the power of an entire universe, enough to break the hold of sentient AI thousands of years old, and it was far too much for me to control. All I could do was watch it spread, unfettered by the speed of light, unhindered by the limits of the Transition drive or whatever kind of warped space the Skalex used for their star drive. The wave of destruction moved instantaneously, and I had the sense that *I* could have traveled the same way if I'd taken the time to master this power, if I'd been able to do it without the distraction of the Ghosts.

It sought the Skalex out anywhere they hid, any system where they made their hives, and slaughtered them. All I could do was watch, bearing mute witness to what my anger had wrought. They were too alien for me to personify them, to think of them as individuals, and indeed, that wasn't the way they thought of themselves. Their babies were larvae, covered in slime when they hatched, herded into creches and kept there until they were old enough for their consciousness to tap into the collective thought.

Not individuals, no. But together they were sentient, intelligent, advanced. Paranoid, but they hadn't done that to themselves. They were victims as surely as the Tahni, fashioned into a weapon, brainwashed with beliefs they hadn't had the chance to develop on their own. Not worthy of genocide, yet that was exactly what I did to them.

I had to watch it. It was only right, but even if I'd chosen the coward's way out and tried to hide my eyes from it, I couldn't have. My consciousness was along for the ride, unable to escape the wave of kinetic energy. Forced to observe as, across countless systems, the Skalex died. *Billions* of them, from the elders, their chitin worn China-white with age, to pupae just out of the egg, and every male, female, and sexless drone between.

The process of it dragged on as eternally as the pain had, but that was my imagination. It had all happened simultaneously, from Waterline all the way to the farthest reaches of their colonies, hundreds of light-years away, and it was only my limited perceptions that gave it a sense of temporality. It was done before I could stop it, even if I'd wanted to.

I wasn't sure I would have. They'd killed my friends, would have killed me if I'd allowed it. They'd forced me into a position where I had to corrupt my soul to stop them, and I hated them for it. Maybe that was the corruption speaking, the Ghosts' effect on my thoughts, or maybe it was simply what I'd allowed myself to turn into these last few years. Either way, there was no horror in me, no regret for what I'd done. Just a sense of dread over what I'd become.

The visions faded, the deed done, and I pulled out of the altered state of consciousness, back to myself again. Even the Ghosts didn't trouble me, stunned into silence by an atrocity even they had never considered. Apparently, even vengeful alien AI had a thing or two to learn from us humans about violence.

Weariness dragged at me, yet I didn't stumble, held myself up with the same power I'd used to kill an entire species. The crew of the *Orion* clambered out of the airlocks, some descending emergency ladders, others climbing down parts of the ship. Many regarded the grounded ship with disbelief, but the rest... hundreds of eyes stared at me in awe, relief... terror. They'd seen what I could do, and even the ones who were grateful knew exactly what it meant.

I ignored them, searching instead out the one person for whom I'd done all this, for whom I would have done it all again. Vicky twisted out of her open chest plate in an agile, practiced motion, only thirty meters away from the nose of Intercept Two, and ran to me.

She said nothing, just threw her arms around me and buried her face in my shoulder, sobbing. I wasn't certain why she was crying... or, rather, I wasn't sure which of a hundred things worth crying over was the particular reason. It might have been our dead, which were considerable. Besides the twelve Fleet flight crews on the drop-ships and assault shuttles, another fifteen Marines had died under the fire from the Skalex troops. I didn't need an IFF reader. Every one of their names screamed inside of my head, a keening for the lost. Ten Vergai from Bravo, five of Alpha.

No injuries. The weapons the Skalex used... rather, *had* used... were unlikely to leave any injured. There was barely enough left of the dead to bury.

Behind us, Chang called urgently into his 'link, trying to raise his ship. She was still up there. I could have told him, but emotional inertia kept me from speaking, certainly kept me from any desire to comfort the little man.

"What the fuck are we gonna do now?"

I could have asked the question myself, but I hadn't. It was Nance. He'd been among the last of the crew to abandon the broken hulk of the *Orion*, and from the stunned devastation on his face, he mourned that ship more than he had any of the humans who'd died on this entire operation.

I suppose that shouldn't have surprised me. She was wife, mother, wayward child to Nance. She'd been his *raison d'etre* for years now, years longer than I'd known him. For everyone else, losing the *Orion* was losing the only home they'd known since we'd left the Cluster, but for Nance, it was losing his entire family.

"I don't know," I admitted. "I think I can get us home." At

least if I could control the instantaneous transportation I'd seen evidence of a minute ago. "If we just..."

A hammer the size of a world slammed into my shoulders, driving me to my knees.

"Cam!" Vicky cried out, trying to pull me up, but I pulled away from her, thrashing helplessly.

I might have been foaming at the mouth, might have been gushing blood... I didn't know what the wetness on my face was, couldn't even control myself enough to look down and check my shirt. Couldn't see at all.

Seizure. That was the first thought bouncing around in what little space I had left for logic or reason. Maybe the use of the power had overloaded my synapses, caused a short-circuit. My second thought was the Ghosts. They might have recovered from their shock, decided my current weakened state was the perfect opportunity to take control back from me.

My last thought was the headcomp. Jim hadn't spoken to me since I'd wiped out the Skalex. Was this a fail-safe, something he'd included without telling me? A way to take me down if he thought I was beyond help?

A paroxysm of pressure arched my back, my hands reaching for the source of the pain that I couldn't identify, and even those tiny refuges of reason abandoned me as every muscle cramped and spasmed. I was vaguely aware that Vicky and Doc Hallonen were talking to me, trying to straighten my body out, but nothing they said penetrated the fog over my thoughts. But the fog wasn't from the pain... it was a curtain laid there by something. By *someone.*

They stepped out of that fog, their presence the first thing to become clear through the haze. Not their *physical* presence, of course. None of the others could see them. Yet I understood that they also weren't simply in my head, like the Ghosts. They were between, existing in a realm of shadows where thought was as solid as matter, and despite the fact that their physical bodies were in another galaxy, there was no doubt in my mind that they could kill me on a whim.

My eyes widened as the being emerged from the grayness, looming like a Skrela, yet not. Like a Skalex, but not. There was as much similarity between them as there was between Resscharr and humans, for all that we were warm-blooded bipeds who evolved on the same planet. The difference between the Skrela and the Skalex and this creature was that for all that the Skalex had developed their own society, they were just as much a designed creation as the Skrela. This thing was clearly a result of natural selection.

I can't put into words the *how* of it, but any human who saw it would have known. There's a qualitative difference between something that evolved naturally versus an engineered being. Even the Skingangers, who'd replaced half their biology with cybernetics, had that half-assed look to the natural part of them that said *this thing was the result of adaptations and random mutations.*

That's what this creature looked like. Eight limbs, same as the Skrela and the Skalex, same arrangement of four on the bottom, four on the torso, same ant-like, shovel-shaped head, though both this thing and the Skalex lacked the scorpion tail. Somewhere between the two in size, but closer to a quarter horse than a draft horse. Scales covered its upper and lower body, not like a snake or a fish but more along the lines of a pangolin or an armadillo. A single antenna emerged from the center of its head, giving it a unicorn vibe, though I doubt if even a virgin could have touched this thing and lived.

The thing loomed over me, the pincers on its lower arms clacking together in an implied threat, a clear liquid dripping from the mandibles at the end of that flattened head.

"What are you looking at, Cam?" Vicky asked, searching in the direction I was staring, yet finding nothing.

I wish I could have told her.

The creature spoke, though the words came not through that nightmare of a mouth but inside my head.

"I am the Unity," it declared. "And you have murdered my children."

[24]

The Unity. The creators, the Predecessors to the Skalex. I'd heard the name when I connected with the Skalex just prior to wiping them out, but it had been myths and legends, the stories of ancient gods. If it had any basis in reality, it was in some distant galaxy, decades away even using the Transition drive.

"No, infant, we are no myth. Distance and time have no meaning to such as us."

It heard my thoughts. I'd told the others that wasn't possible, yet this... what did you call a single member of the Unity? A Unitarian? It had just done it.

"There is no single member of the Unity," it corrected me. "We are all the Unity. I am the Unity. Atomized consciousnesses such as you are abominations to be stomped out. Each time the likes of you evolve, they spread like a cancer and destroy anything in their path. I have encountered you before, in one galaxy after another, and each time they laid waste to the life I sought to seed there. Each time, they've proven they can't be reasoned with and must be eradicated." The Unity paused, regarding me with multifaceted eyes, impossible to read even if the creature had actually been standing in front of me physically. "It has been many long eons since we've encountered an atomized consciousness. You may be the last. If so, my work will be done once I cleanse the universe of your species."

I was getting tired of being talked to and not talking back, and I didn't care whether this thing could read my mind or not, it was just rude.

"We never attacked your people," I told it. "They attacked *us*, unprovoked. We were simply trying to get out of this sector... we would have left the Skalex alone if they hadn't tried to kill us."

Wait... *was* I actually talking? Vicky and the others didn't seem to hear me. I still couldn't control my body, couldn't get to my feet or even stop the uncontrollable shudders that racked every muscle. What *was* I doing?

"You delude yourself." Was that an answer to what I'd assumed was my spoken question, or to the one I'd asked in my head? Or both? "It was your people who slaughtered a peaceful colony of my offspring, one that lacked even the capacity to harm you."

"You mean the Skrela?" I guessed. "That wasn't us! That was the Resscharr. There are barely any of them left. They evolved on our planet, but they're not humans."

The creature stepped closer, though I figured that was for psychological effect, since it couldn't actually touch me. I believed that right up until the moment one of those pincers grabbed the front of my field jacket and lifted me off the ground.

"How you arrogate yourself," the Unity said, and even though I knew on some level that the thing didn't breathe through its head, I was sure I could smell its breath. "To think you're any different than the rest of the insane, diseased filth from your sopping dirtball of a planet."

Vicky and Hallonen tried to grab me, pull me back to the ground, panic obvious on their faces. They had to think I was doing this to myself, or maybe the Ghosts were doing it to me. The Unity brushed them aside with a swipe of a massive arm neither of them could see and they toppled backward, blood spraying from the doctor's nose where the blow had struck. I tried to struggle, tried to fight back, but I still couldn't control my body. I hung from the thing's claw, deadweight.

"Stay away!" I yelled at the other, hoping I was actually talking this time. No one showed any sign of hearing me though, so I turned my attention back to the Unity. "Look, kill me if you want... I did it. I massacred your little fucking science experiment. I'm the one to blame. You say we're atomized, so you have to know none of the others did it. Please don't hurt them! They just want to leave!"

"I don't plan on killing either you or any of the other contaminants on this planet," the Unity informed me. The thing couldn't laugh, I was fairly certain, and probably wouldn't have attempted to imitate it for my benefit, but I thought a malevolent chuckle would have been right at home in the hesitation in its mental voice. "Despite your protestations, I completely understand the concept of individual consciousnesses, but unlike you, I also understand that when you're grouped together, the only difference between your kind and me is that you'll kill each other just as readily as you will those alien to you. But there is one thing I've come to appreciate about your kind. You *suffer* as individuals. I want you to suffer. I want you to see what is happening to your people, as I did for my children, yet know there's nothing you can do to stop it."

The Unity tossed me negligently to the ground and the impact between my shoulders forced the air out of me, as if I hadn't already had enough problems. Starbursts of light filled my vision... but not the part that saw the Unity. That was crystal clear, because I wasn't seeing it with my physical eyes.

The hoof-like feet pawed at the ground as if the Unity

would charge me, trample me to death in front of Vicky. I tried to imagine what she'd see, just me coming apart under the attack of some phantom monster. But the Unity stood its ground.

"Killing you this way, the way you killed my children, would be impersonal. Merciful. No, I intend for your friends to see me when I kill them, to fear the utter terror that only abominations such as you can feel. Until then... well, you've proven you're far too dangerously incompetent to be allowed to touch the power of the other realm. You must be relieved of that power."

All four of the thing's hands rose at its sides, and for a moment I thought it *had* trampled me because my skull felt as if it were being crushed under the weight of a Brahma bull. Searing hot, a laser coming from the inside of my brain, a million voices cried out in protest... and everything went black.

Cam.

Consciousness? Maybe? But it was still dark and the pain hadn't gone away. I tried to open my eyes, but even the hint of light was a fiery sword stabbing into my head, and I kept them shut. Maybe it was death. I'd imagined the afterlife as being free of pain, but perhaps this was the Hell I deserved after what I'd done.

Who had called my name?

Cam, it's me.

"God?" I asked. It might have been a thought rather than a sound. I wasn't ready to speak yet.

No, you idiot, it's not God. Not Satan either.

Oh, it was Jim.

"What's up, Jim?" I wondered. "Is this death? Have I been squeezed into the headcomp again? Because if I have, if I'm just a subroutine, please... erase me. Get rid of me. I don't particularly want to live as a bodiless shut-in, no offense to your own pleasant company."

You're not dead, Cam, and you're not inside your headcomp either. Though I still have the displeasure of being stuck here.

"Then why can't I talk? To everyone else, I mean? And why can't I open my eyes?"

You'll be able to in a minute. Your brain is... rebooting, for want of a better word.

That didn't sound good at all.

"Why the hell does my brain need to fucking *reboot*, Jim?" A panicked notion struck me. "Where's the Unity? Did it attack the others? Am I wounded or something? Where's Vicky?"

Your wife is holding your head in her lap, wondering if you're brain dead. I'm tempted to confirm that, just as a value judgement, but the reality is, you're somehow still alive and able to function.

"Who pissed in your cereal, Jim?" I asked him. "And what do you mean somehow? What did the Unity do to me?"

You pissed in my cereal, Alvarez, the AI replied, and somehow shouted the words, even though they were nothing but signals inside my brain. *You did the same Goddamned thing we spent the last several thousand years getting revenge on the Resscharr for forcing us to do!*

Oh, yeah. That.

"It's not the same," I insisted. "The Skrela you wiped out were harmless, just happened to be in your way. These Skalex were trying to kill us. They've been brainwashed for thousands of years to kill every other sentient life they meet. There was no live-and-let-live situation here." I shrugged. I *tried* to shrug but still couldn't move. "Anyway, you weren't a part of it. The blood's not on your hands, and if I have any moral problems with it... well, just add it to the fucking pile. Now, tell me what the Unity did to my Goddamned *brain*!"

"Cam!"

Vicky's eyes were locked on mine when I opened them, and when she saw the life behind them, she kissed me, pulling me to her.

"Oh, Jesus, I thought they'd gotten you!"

"Who?" The word came out dry and sandy and someone, I couldn't make out who it was, handed me a bottle of water. I drank half of it before I tried again, and it was like spraying foam on a grease fire. "Who had gotten me?" I asked, sitting up from her lap.

I was surrounded. By friends, at least, but still surrounded. Hallonen squatted beside me, a medical scanner in one hand, the other holding a bloody compress against her broken nose. Nance was there too, though his expression held an air of distraction and his gaze kept flickering back to the wreck of the *Orion*. Chang was there as well, and unlike Nance, his attention wasn't at all divided. He looked at me with the sort of hunger that only someone with a true thirst for power could muster. He'd seen what I did to the Skalex, and all his former lamentation of his state of mental stability and moral turpitude had vanished at the sight of real power.

"The Ghosts," Vicky replied, keeping a hand on my shoulder as if she thought I'd collapse back into another seizure. "When you used the power on the Skrela, I thought they'd taken you over. Or killed you."

"They weren't Skrela," I corrected her absently, running a hand down my face. I wouldn't have been surprised to have my palm come away painted in blood, but there was nothing except clammy sweat. "They were Skalex."

"Did you get all of them, sir?" Lt. Villanueva asked, crouched at my feet like a runner waiting for the starting gun. "I think we can rig up the airlock hatch if you need us back in the air..."

"No, they're all dead," I told her. A pang of guilt accompanied the words, a thought maybe I was kidding myself with all the justification I'd given and Jim was right. "What's our situation?" I asked Vicky, pushing up to my feet. Unsteady at first, I grabbed at her arm and she moved under my shoulder to give me support. My head hurt like a son of a bitch.

"Fifteen KIA," she told me, only the slightest spasm of a muscle in her cheek telling me how badly it hurt to say that. "Ten from Bravo, five in Alpha. We've lost both drop-ships and both assault shuttles. There were two landers in the *Orion*'s hangar bay when she went down and the flight crews think they're salvageable... *if* we can get them out. Both Intercepts are operational, and Chang's ship is still in the air."

"There are..." Nance cleared his throat and tried again, blinking as if he had to make a real effort to focus on anything other than the condition of his ship. "We had some casualties shipboard... when we took the initial hit. Ten crew were in the affected compartments. They're gone. Either burned up or... fell out." He clamped his mouth shut on that, closed his eyes.

Commander Yanayev stepped up beside him and put a comforting hand on his arm, tears streaking her face. I wanted to ask him the names of who had died, certain I knew them, but I kept the question to myself, sensing that it would be too painful for him. Then I frowned. I *should* have known already, but I didn't.

Before I had the chance to consider that any further, Yanayev took up the report.

"The ship's reactor is still operational, for what it's worth. The feed lines to the drives and weapons are severed, but we could fix those." She shook her head. "It wouldn't matter though because the superstructure is..." Yanayev pursed her lips as if searching for the right term.

"The superstructure is fucked," Wojtera supplied from over her shoulder. The Tactical officer had a cut over his eye and was trying to fix a small bandage across it while he spoke. Blood from the contusion left a stripe down the front of his uniform tunic, as if for some new award for valor. *The Blood Stripe.* "There's no way to fix her, not down here." He sighed. "Not unless that AI can send a swarm of nanites to meld all the molecules together or something." Woj made a slashing gesture. "She's not going to be taking us home... or anywhere else."

"I wonder if there isn't something *I* could do about it," I mused, looking the hull up and down.

I hadn't understood the sheer scale of the power I could command until I'd tapped into my rage to unleash it. Maybe there was a way to use it to fix the hull? Because I knew now that I could use the connection to Transition Space to go anywhere, and I wasn't sure if I couldn't do it instantaneously. The only hang-up was whether the Ghosts would let me, but they'd been silent ever since I'd overpowered them to kill the Skalex.

"Do you really think you can fix her?" Nance asked, eyes going wide, as if allowing himself to feel some hope.

"I don't know. Let me see what I can do."

Settling into a stance with my feet shoulder-width apart, I closed my eyes and reached within myself, trying to touch the power.

Nothing. I cracked an eye open, as if there'd be something external distracting me, but there was nothing except the bulk of the *Orion*, gleaming dully in the light of the full moon. I closed them again and strained, as if I was stretching to reach something on a high shelf, but again, I was just too short. Something was wrong.

"I can't do it," I breathed, looking to Vicky. The color drained from her face, her shock a mirror of my own. "I can't touch the power. What the hell's going on?"

I tried to tell you, Jim said, and if a disembodied voice could roll its eyes, he was doing it then. *It was the Unity. She did something to your brain... something I couldn't, even with a lab full of nanotechnology.*

"She did *what?*" I demanded, not caring that the others were staring at me like I was talking to myself. Which I was, kind of.

She cut you off. From the power, from being able to manipulate it. On the bright side, you don't have to worry about the Ghosts anymore, or about going insane and killing your friends.

No, I didn't have to worry about that. All I had to worry about was the fact that we were all stranded on this planet, this island, with enough food to last about a year and no way to grow more. And the Unity coming to kill us all.

[25]

"The *what?*" Nance demanded, taking a swig of coffee and making a face at it almost as unpleasant as the one he was giving me.

The food processing gear still worked, of course. The only difficult part had been finding a compartment facing straight up and down to use it in. Most of the ship was built so that up was toward the nose and down toward the engines, to make sure the crew could walk around when the ship was under boost. The same was true for nearly every starship, but the *Orion* had one advantage most didn't: the habitation drum. It rotated when the ship was in free fall to make sure everyone could get exercise under gravity and not let their muscles atrophy.

Which meant a small section of the compartments in the drum were facing the right way for us to sit down and relax somewhere climate controlled, eat some dinner, drink some coffee, and try not to go slowly, gibbering insane. Ironically enough, that compartment was my office, At least it wasn't the Op Center.

"The Unity," I repeated, hands wrapped around my own coffee cup I wasn't a huge fan of the drink, but it had caffeine, and I needed caffeine very badly right now. "They're... like the Skalex we just fought, except they're all one hive mind and they're also connected to the power of Transition Space. But not in the same way I was." I shook my head. "I can't explain it. But they have the ability to see us from another galaxy... and that's how the Skalex found us. The Unity told them."

"And they're coming here?" Vicky asked. "Because of what you did to the... Skalex?"

I nodded, staring down into the light brown of the liquid.

"You really... killed the entire species?" Captain Nagarro asked me, hesitating as if saying the words made her feel dirty.

"I did. I didn't intend to, but..." I shrugged.

"Who gives a fuck?" Wojtera grunted, eyeing the Intelligence officer with disdain. "They were a more intelligent version of the Skrela, and they wanted us dead. I'm happy it turned out the other way."

No one else commented either way, and I sure as hell didn't want to talk about it.

"We've got to get off this planet," Chuck Brandano declared. Of all of us, he seemed the least affected by the disaster. "It's that simple. There has to be something we can do."

Reluctantly, I tapped a control on my desk and the holographic display snapped to life, showing the Fleet seal.

"Jim," I said aloud, "would you mind joining us?"

Some of the crew blinked in surprise when the AI's avatar appeared in the display, his muscular, tattooed arms folded and a grim frown on his long face.

"What?" he demanded. He was still angry with me or what I'd done, and that extended from the attenuated version of him in my headcomp all the way to the full sentient system in the tunnels below us.

"You know what our problem is," I told him. "And I think you can help. Your... brother? Cousin? The AI that called itself

Briggs back on Homecoming told us you might have an experimental ship on this world. Something the Resscharr were working on right at the end, that could travel FTL through real-space like the Skalex. Is that true?"

Jim glowered at me, silent, and I rolled my eyes.

"I get it, you don't approve of what I did. But let me put it to you this way—you have the choice of either having us stick around here indefinitely, probably down in your cities, scrounging for food, and trying to hide from the Unity when they come. And they'll tear this entire planet apart to get to us, and you with it. Or you can tell us where the ship is, and we'll get out of here and never return. You can go back to an eternity of contemplating your navel, and maybe consoling yourself with how superior you are to us morally. That has to be a better selection, right?"

Blue eyes glared at me, but the avatar shrugged.

"Yes, there's a ship. It's pretty far down. As deep as this place goes, almost to the magma. And I haven't kept track of it or monitored its condition in well over a thousand years, so you'll have to travel down there yourselves, but your headcomp should allow you to access its systems, assuming they're still operational."

"But will it get us home?" Brandano asked, adapting quicker than the others to the presence of the AI and its incongruous avatar. "How fast can it go?"

"It was developed for a possible escape from this galaxy," Jim explained. "Its top speed is well over a thousand times faster than the speed of light in a vacuum."

"Shit," Yanayev muttered, and when I gave her a curious glance, she shrugged. "It's just that I've been working with the Transition Lines my whole career. The actual distance doesn't mean anything, just the time in Transition." She laughed in embarrassment. "I have no idea how many light-years we are away from the Cluster."

"I can help there," Jim told her, apparently less acrimonious toward the others than he was to me.

A star map replaced his avatar in the projection tank, first showing our location and then zooming out to show the Cluster, the Transition Lines there ending abruptly in a crimson sphere. The cage the Predecessors had put us in. For our own protection, of course.

A green line stretched from our location to the edge of the Cluster, and it was depressingly long. Yanayev whistled softly, leaning closer, as if that would let her see hidden details in the projection.

"Twelve hundred forty-three light-years," Jim supplied. "Point two-three, to be exact. At top speed, and assuming the ship even functions correctly, the journey will take you ten thousand and eighty-three hours and twenty-six minutes. Not counting stops along the way."

"Which is about two months more food than we have in our stores," Nance grumbled, sagging against the edge of my desk. "Dammit."

"This place has fish," Brandano suggested. "We could supplement our stores with fish, maybe some of the fruits and vegetables on the island."

"Do *you* know how to dry and salt fish?" Villanueva asked, eyebrow tilting upward. "Because they didn't include that in any of *my* Academy classes."

"We could look it up on the ship's database," he shot back, glaring at her. She was, I supposed, being insubordinate since he was, technically, a rank above her. But that was the problem with being out here for so long, cut off from the military structure. Everyone on board should have been promoted at least twice by now, and we were more separated by the jobs we did now than by rank. "We could figure it out," Brandano added.

"We could," I agreed, deciding it was time to step in. "But that would take time. Weeks, maybe. And we'd have to eat while we were learning, and every day we spent figuring it out would be one day closer to the Unity getting here and ending us all." I pointed a finger at Hallonen, who looked like she would rather have been anywhere else. Taking care of the crewmembers who'd been banged up during the battle, for instance. "Are the stasis chambers still intact and operational?"

She nodded, her eyes lighting up as she realized what I was getting at.

"Yeah, they're fine so far as I know. But can we install them on this new ship?"

"Functionally," Jim answered the question, "it shouldn't be a problem. If the systems are still operational, the hookups are universal."

"Then we can work this the same way we did the crossing before," I said, sighing in relief at finally having a plan. "Two thirds of us in stasis, one third on duty, rotating every month."

"It may even be possible," Jim suggested, "for the ship to fabricate new stasis modules using the existing ones as a pattern. That would allow you to operate with a skeleton crew and rotate more often."

I nodded to him, suspicious that he was being so helpful. Maybe he'd finally understood that getting us off this planet was in his best interest, as well as ours. I rubbed at my eyes, thinking of what needed to be done.

"Okay, here's what we have to do. Vicky, you and Springfield arrange the... company, have the platoons work in shifts." The words stabbed into my belly like a jagged blade. We no longer had enough of either company for them to remain separate. Springfield wasn't at the meeting, had decided to spend the time comforting her Marines. "The ship is on its side, so we're going to need the suits to pull the chambers out. Doc, you go with them, along with an engineering crew, and make sure they don't break anything. They're Marines, after all."

"Right," she said, jumping up from the edge of the bunk. "I should go get them ready now."

"Settle down, Doc," I told her with a quelling gesture. "Before we do that, I need you and your people to salvage everything you can from the medical bay, including the auto-docs. We'll get a Marine detail on that too. Captain Nance, if you could put one of your people in charge of a detail to offload the food stores. Anything that requires refrigeration, we'll need to hook it up to portable generators until we can get it attached to the new ship's power sources."

"Aren't we getting ahead of ourselves?" Brandano wondered. He motioned outward. "We haven't found the ship yet."

"Yeah, that's going to be my job," I told him.

"You and who else?" Vicky asked sharply, with the clear implication that I'd better not try going off on a mission like that by myself.

"I was thinking I could use someone from Engineering," I reasoned, "and maybe Commander Yanayev." I nodded to the Helm officer. "To make sure that if we do find this thing and it's operational that we can figure out how to get it in the air." I eyed Jim's avatar doubtfully. "Is there any reason to think there'll be any threats down there?"

"Most of the security monitors that deep into the facility failed centuries ago," Jim told me, shaking his head. "I've had no indications of any life within the cities since... what occurred with the Changed. But I make no guarantees."

Wonderful.

"Then I'll also take along a squad of Force Recon," I

decided and Vicky nodded, satisfied. Then I frowned. "By the way, how far are we talking? How deep does this thing go?"

"The last known location of the ship and the engineering lab where it was being constructed was at the lowest level of this city. Roughly... fifty kilometers from the entrance."

Yanayev blanched, probably with the Fleet officer's instinctive aversion to physical activity.

"Oh, for Christ's sake!" she blurted, looking at Jim with eyes wide. "Tell me there's some kind of transportation system! A train, an elevator, a groundcar... anything!"

"There's a high-speed evacuated tube train that will convey you part of the way," Jim replied, no sympathy in his expression. "However, that too was damaged in the fighting. It will take you thirty kilometers before the break in the line. The rest of the way you'll have to go on foot."

"Twenty klicks," Yanayev moaned. "That's just great."

"Better find some combat boots," I advised her. "You're not going to want to walk that far in your shipboard shoes."

"I think we're the same size," Vicky told her, grinning. "You can borrow mine." She eyed me archly. "Since I won't be using them."

I gave her a pleading look, begging her not to make me say it.

If I'm not here, you're the only one I trust to be in charge.

She must have gotten the idea, because her expression softened.

"What about you, Chang?" I asked, nodding to the man. "Would you like to go with us?" He hadn't said much, which wasn't at all like him.

"No, I think not," he replied, shaking his head. "I'm not interested in leaving here."

"What?" I asked, blinking. "Did you miss the part about the aliens coming to murder us?"

"They'll be following you, I think," Chang opined, smiling

thinly. "As for me... my original motive for coming here remains the same. I'm going to have your AI friend Jim try to fix me. No matter what the cost. But I do wish you the best of luck getting home."

And I could believe that as much as I liked. My opinion was that it was much more likely the little man wanted to convince Jim to turn him into one of the Changed. I'd just have to trust the AI had better sense than that.

"One other thing," I said as everyone started shifting, getting ready to leave. They all paused, looking back to me. "The crew needs hope, so don't hesitate to share with them exactly what we're doing. But make sure they know... this is far from a sure thing. If it doesn't work out, I don't want any of them giving up."

I didn't say the rest, but I hoped they understood it from my expression.

I don't want any of you giving up either.

[26]

This was as close as I'd come to riding the maglev trains since I'd left Trans-Angeles, and if I was being honest with myself, I didn't like it. I'd spent over fifteen years of my life agoraphobic, afraid of the open sky and the horizon, and it had taken some pretty serious immersion therapy to get over that, namely being dumped on Brigantia without a suit, a bug on a plate. The choice had been to adapt or die, and I'd adapted.

I wasn't going to go from that to being claustrophobic, not when I spent so much of my time in a battlesuit, but there was something about the enclosure of the Resscharr transport tube that I didn't like. Maybe it was the lack of windows, though Jim had assured me there'd be nothing to see except the dim, green glow of the grav fields that propelled us. Or maybe it was the fact that we were totally dependent on a disused, abandoned system to propel us at just under supersonic speeds and, worse than that, *stop* us at the end before we crashed right into the collapsed section of tunnel left over from the titanic battle between the two Changed.

I couldn't show it in front of the others though. Yanayev and Petty Officer Dickinson from Engineering already looked green around the gills, and even though the six Force Recon Marines accompanying us had their visors down, I wouldn't have been surprised if they shared the same, uneasy expression.

"There's no sense of movement," Yanayev mused softly, chin resting on her hand, "and no display. How are we going to know when we get there?"

"The doors will open," I told her. Dickinson snorted a laugh, but I hadn't been trying to have a laugh at her expense. I'd asked Jim exactly the same question in the privacy of my head and received exactly the same response.

And so they will, he told me.

A large section of the side of the car faded to nothing, immediately revealing the reason we'd had to stop so far from our destination. Wreckage was strewn across the broad passageway, not resembling anything I would have expected from a human structure. Not crumbling plasticrete or buildfoam but more along the lines of volcanic glass. The destruction wrought on the gravity-transportation tube had been intense enough to turn the almost-indestructible Resscharr building material into polished shards, each over two meters long, an obstacle course in our path stretching out for at least three or four hundred meters.

"I'd advise not touching or even brushing up against the debris," I said, passing on the warning from Jim. "It's razor sharp."

"We'll lead the way, sir," Lt. Campea said, brushing past me. He'd insisted on leading the squad himself, and I had no good reason to argue against it.

"Don't count on your armor protecting you from the edges," I told him. "God knows what the Resscharr built with, but anything that could melt and shatter it would have left one hell of an edge."

"You heard the man, First squad," Campea snapped,

motioning to the other Marines. "No showing off. Just find us a safe way through."

Something felt wrong to me, and it took a second to figure out what it was. Previously, I wouldn't have dialed into their private network, but the neurolink did it automatically. I wondered if I could tell it not to. There were some things I didn't need to know.

Yeah, Jim murmured with an edge of sarcasm to his mental "voice," *you strike me as someone who has a lot of things they don't think they need to know.*

Is this how it's going to be from now on? I asked him silently, following the Force Recon squad through the maze of rubble. *You nagging at me like we're an old married couple?*

God forbid. Your wife must be a saint to put up with you.

I would have argued with him, but he was probably right about that. Instead, I concentrated on the mesmerizing, curved lines of the two-meter-long piece of the tunnel section. It reminded me of the twisted lines of a Skrela spaceship.

"Goddammit!" I looked up at the exclamation. One of the Marines danced away from a piece of debris, rubbing at his thigh armor. The edge of the rubble had sliced a gash into the thick armor plate, though not all the way through, since I didn't see any blood.

"I told you to be careful, McLaughlin!" Campea chided.

"You two, stay right behind me," I cautioned Yanayev and Dickinson.

It wasn't that far, but getting through the debris field took at least fifteen minutes, and when we finally stepped past the final bits of glossy razor glass, my breath was coming as heavy as if I'd just run five klicks, and I had to pause to take a sip from the water bottle on my gun belt.

"Got a long way to go still, people," Lt. Campea reminded us, waving for the rest of us to follow.

Now that we were deeper into the place, I finally had the opportunity to see it as it had been, not a deserted tomb but the final home of a star-spanning civilization. The broad passage was designed for shipping freight from the surface, but down here, chambers radiated away from it like the rays of a stylized sun. Some of them were obvious in their purpose, now that I knew what Resscharr living quarters and dining areas looked like, but others were empty and dead and might have been virtual reality chambers for all I knew. Still others were overgrown with vegetation, kept alive by sun lamps and automatic irrigation systems despite the passage of time, but untended and gone wild, contained only by the restrictions of the growth zones.

Most stunning for me, despite what I'd seen in the memories and the recordings, were the Tahni sections. They stood out from the Resscharr habitats by virtue of furniture designed for humanoids with forward-bending knees and were little different from what I'd seen on Tahni worlds and among the Karai on Yfingam.

Why did they bring so many Tahni with them? I asked Jim, hoping his answer wouldn't be as snarky as before.

As servants. Not snarky, but perhaps bitter. *For all that they said they considered them their heirs, their crowning achievement, by the end they considered them disposable... like us.*

At some point, I stopped noticing the different chambers, stopped guessing at their purposes, the entirety of my being devoted to putting one foot in front of the other and simply determined not to give the AI the satisfaction of asking if we were there yet.

I'd walked farther, of course, and I'd *tried* to stay in shape in the ship's gym, but I was running on shitloads of stress and very little sleep. Not to mention psychic brain surgery by an alien bug. That tends to take it out of a person. As taxing as it was on me, though, I think Dickinson had it the hardest. The man wasn't flabby or anything, but having a career stuck in the Engineering section hadn't prepared him for a forced march. From the vacant look in his eyes, he probably thought of it more as a death march. He'd started limping after two hours, and by now I kind of expected two Revolutionary War soldiers to be playing a fife and drum next to him.

"How much fucking farther?" he moaned, relieving me of the responsibility for being the first one to ask.

Jim? I passed the question along.

Five more kilometers, he sighed.

"Another hour and change," I told Dickinson. It didn't bring a sigh of relief, just a tortured groan. Even Yanayev, who wasn't given to complaining, scowled and set her jaw as if this was testing her limits.

The break from the monotony had woken me from the determined slog I'd fallen into, and I finally noticed that our surroundings had changed. No more living quarters, no more gardens, nothing that looked as if it were designed with people in mind, whether those people were Resscharr or Tahni. Just equipment, though its purpose was often as mysterious as the empty rooms. Storage rooms with what I guessed were spare parts for… something. What does a spare black hole containment unit look like? God and the Resscharr knew, but I didn't. I just saw the proverbial black boxes stacked from floor to ceiling.

Other chambers were packed with glowing tubes running from one wall to another, and I didn't bother to ask Jim what they were because I was afraid he'd tell me the stuff was bathing us in deadly radiation or it could blow up at any second. The general impression as we gradually descended lower on ramps kilometers long was that we'd gone from habitation areas to technical ones. I supposed that was a good sign.

What was *not* a good sign was when the lights went out.

Well, they didn't go completely out, of course. That would have been damned inconvenient, and I figured Jim would have warned us about it. But the generalized glow coming off the walls ceased abruptly as we stepped from one section to another, and what remained was localized, a blue-tinted illumination coming from point sources at the base of the walls. Emergency lighting, I supposed.

This is where my observations cut off, Jim told me. *There was a power failure in this sector during the battle.*

Why didn't you send a drone? You must have repair robots or something.

I do, he agreed. *But why would I care? Who would I have been repairing it for? It wasn't as if I expected you to arrive begging for help.*

I had to grant him that.

"Campea," I said, "we're entering unknown territory."

"Here there be dragons, sir," he confirmed, a grin in his voice. "Got it."

There are no dragons here, Jim protested. *In fact, except for a single species of oceangoing megafauna related to the ichthyosaurs, there's nothing even close...*

Figure of speech.

Not that I believed we'd encounter anything down here. If anything did live in these tunnels after all this time, it would have been feeding off the tended gardens, not down at the farthest depths of the facility. I was more concerned about whether the Resscharr had actually completed work on the ship and, if they hadn't, how long it would take Jim to finish it up... and how much of his shit I'd have to put up with while he did it.

I knew we'd arrived when the passageway dead ended in a featureless door nearly as big as the one we'd entered through at the sea walls.

"Whoa," Campea murmured, and this time, I knew he hadn't even switched on his mic, but I still heard it.

Stop doing that, I ordered Jim.

Doing what? he asked, laughing maliciously.

"Can you open that like you did the other one?" Campea asked, and it took me a moment to realize he was actually talking to me this time.

"No. I don't have the ability anymore. Jim, tell me you can open this door."

I told you I don't have any access to this section, he reminded me. *Not to mention the main power's out. But I can tell you where the manual override is. Assuming it still works.*

That wasn't comforting, but I followed his directions anyway, since I had no second option. I'd brought a flashlight, of course, though I hadn't been able to get to the part of the ship where the enhanced vision goggles were stored. My only night-vision option would have been tromping down in my Vigilante. Which I could have done if I'd been heading down alone. The flashlight wasn't a good replacement for an energy cannon, but it did let me see the access panel a few meters to the right of the door.

"You got a combat knife?" I asked Campea and he snorted.

"Did you just ask a Force Recon Marine if he had a combat knife, sir?" He pulled the blade from his belt and flipped it end for end, offering the hilt to me.

"I almost got slotted for Force Recon training," I told him, working the point of the blade into a barely visible notch at a corner of the panel. "You must have gone through that test, where they dropped you off in a river valley with a training laser and no instruction and sicced Force Recon OpFor on you?"

"Oh yeah," Campea said with a nostalgic chuckle. "As I recall, I managed to hide out for a whole hour." He pushed up his visor and eyed me curiously while I pried carefully, trying to work the panel free. "How long did it take them to find you?"

"I killed three of them..." I shrugged. "Theoretically. With the targeting laser as they were getting off their landers. Then I ran, and they didn't find me until morning."

"Jesus Christ!" His mouth dropped open. "Then how did you wind up getting stuck in the suits?"

"They found me," I expounded, gritting my teeth as I dug the blade in harder, worried about breaking the tip and the panel both, "huddling catatonic and unresponsive in a hole. I was hopelessly agoraphobic. The dangers of living for most of my life without seeing a sky."

The hatch popped open with a metallic *thunk*, and I sighed in relief. Draping the hilt of the knife across my forearm, I handed it back to Campea.

"So, you just went on to be the best Drop Trooper ever instead, huh?" he asked, sheathing the knife. I hoped he was being sarcastic, because it made me too uncomfortable to think he might not be.

There. The lever Jim had told me about, sunken deep within a nest of inoperative electronic displays. I held the flashlight between my teeth and grabbed the meter-long manual release lever in both hands, braced one foot against the wall, and pulled.

The door didn't fade away or dematerialize or whatever it was the others had done. It just creaked and thumped and rumbled aside in a spectacularly old-fashioned way, powered by the pure physical force of counter-weights. Dickinson gasped and Yanayev's mouth fell open, her eyes wide, and I figured we'd found the right place.

Inside the dim chamber, lit only by the faint, barely discernable but by now unmistakable green glow of a gravity drive field, a starship nearly as big as the *Orion* floated a meter off the floor.

I'd expected it, and still I was as awestruck as the others, endlessly impressed by the how long the works of the Predecessors had endured. I had to remind myself of that sometimes, when I was feeling overly critical of them for being the architects of their own destruction. All societies crumble eventually, and theirs had not only lasted for *millions* of years, but they'd filled the galaxy with life.

"It's alive," I murmured, remembering a scene from an ancient 2D movie I'd watched on the *Orion*'s archives.

It's not the only thing, Cam.

I took a step back, a lead weight settling into my gut. Sitting cross-legged a few centimeters off the floor as if mimicking the levitation of the ship, was a Resscharr. What had once been a Resscharr. Her skin pulled tight across a corpse-white face, torn in places where it had been overly stretched, mummified by time, the eyes rotted away to nothing. Yet still horribly, unmistakably alive.

I knew who she was. I couldn't touch the power, but the knowledge still remained, left there as the Unity had promised, so I would know the doom coming my way and not be able to change it. This wasn't the doom coming *my* way though. It was the doom that came to Waterline, the end of the last bastion of the Resscharr.

"Kallista," I said softly, and she looked over at me with unseeing eyes, yet seeing all.

"Cameron Alvarez," she replied, speaking inside my head, grinning with a mouth full of rotted, broken teeth, the grin of a long-dead skull. "I know you."

[27]

"I've long thought," the Changed once known as Kallista said with an evil cackle, "that my story was the most tragic I could think of, the best example of hubris in a civilization known for it. I warned my husband against trusting the AI, warned him against using the Transformation virus on himself... and when everything happened just as I'd feared, my answer for this was to make the exact same mistake he'd made, to believe that it couldn't happen to *me*."

A talon-like finger pointed at me.

"Until I sensed you and learned of your story, human. Yours may be worse. For while our society was nearing the end of its life-cycle even before we made the horrible mistake of ordering the AI to kill off the Skrela, your own is barely at the beginning of their ascendance. And you've killed them all."

One of the Force Recon squad raised his rifle and Kallista laughed again.

"Oh, you poor, pitiful creature," she said to him. "Don't you think if it were possible for me to die at the hands of one like you that I would have ceased to be long ago?" She waved her hand dismissively and the Marine's gauss rifle flung itself out of his hands to clatter against the far wall. "Do behave."

"Weapons down, Lieutenant," I snapped aside to Campea. "She could kill every single one of us with a thought if she wanted." My frown deepened. "And I'd like to know why you don't."

"You are an observant one, Cameron. You always have been. But I suppose you had to be in order to survive."

"There's no way you've been in contact with the power this long and not been taken over by the Ghosts," I declared, trying hard not to look at the dried-out husks where her eyes had once been. She'd been down here, I sensed, since the death of the colony, no food, no water, no sunlight. Nothing but the power to sustain her.

"You underestimate their cruelty, boy," she told me, shaking her bald, elongated head. "Their thirst for vengeance. Once I'd accomplished their task, they wanted me to *know* what I'd done, to have to live with it for all eternity. That's why they put me in here. With the ship that could have been used to allow my people to escape, if only they'd had the chance to reach it."

Kallista unfolded from the position in which she'd been floating, perhaps for centuries, her legs as spindly and atrophied as the rest of her. They wouldn't have supported her weight if the power hadn't been keeping her upright, would have likely crumbled to dust. She didn't walk on them so much as use them for props to make a point, bounding across tens of meters as if she were in a jet-assisted Vigilante suit.

More than anything, I wanted to run, wanted on a deeper level to squeeze my eyes shut and pretend she wasn't there the way Jim was doing. The AI had retreated into the darkest corners of my mind and refused to come out. But I just stood there, convinced of what I'd told Campea, that she could kill us all with a thought if she wanted.

"This is what you want, isn't it?" Kallista asked, pointing

back at the ship. "You've come here to steal it, to give your people a way out, the escape mine were denied."

"There's a difference though," I told her, amazed at how calm my voice sounded when my skin wanted to creep right off my bones from complete and utter terror at the walking, talking corpse. "They're not running from me, or from the Ghosts. The threat we're trying to escape from is external, not just to our species, but to our galaxy."

"I know," Kallista assured me, coming to a halt only a meter away. The musty smell of an ancient crypt wafted off of her, old death. "And I also know that your situation is, to a great extent, our doing. From you being outside of the Cluster in the first place, to your involvement in the battle against the Skrela... to your genocide of the Skalex."

"Then you'll let us have the ship?" Yanayev blurted, a glimmer of hope shining through the abject horror in her expression.

"More accurately, girl," Kallista replied, glaring at the Helm officer as if just noticing she was there, "I won't prevent you from taking it, if you can." She spread her arms wide. "Yet for all the miracle of technology that she is, she still won't save you." Her head tilted toward me. "You know this. You see it as well as I do, despite what the Unity has done to you. It *is* coming, and you can't run fast enough to escape *that* fate, boy. No one can change it."

"You could," I said, inspired, always looking for an escape route. "You have the power, and you have your own mind." *Such as it is.* At least it wasn't the Ghosts. "You can stop them. If anyone can. You've had the power for centuries. There's no way they could do to you what they did to me."

"Oh, Cameron," she lamented, tossing her head in a gesture no human could have imitated. "You have the most naïve, charming idea that every situation has an answer. Some don't.

You should know that better than anyone. Sometimes, no matter how hard you try, the ones you love, your friends, your family... they simply die."

She was a terrifying specter, a walking corpse with the power of a god, and I didn't give a fuck. Crossing the distance between us in a step, I put my eyes as close to her level as I could, though it felt unnatural, given that she didn't have any eyes of her own.

"I keep hearing that as a reason why I shouldn't bother trying. You know what gives up when things look hopeless? When they're wounded and bleeding and there's no fight left in them? Prey. Prey gives up. *Victims* give up." I pointed a finger at what was left of her face. "Do I strike you as someone who thinks of himself as a victim?"

Kallista went deathly silent, and I was sure I'd pushed it too far this time, that she'd surrender to the madness and rip us to pieces. But she merely motioned at the ship behind her.

"No. You see yourself as a hero. Go. Take the ship and the hope that comes with it. But do not expect me to act on your behalf. The last time I tried to be a hero, young one, I caused the deaths of millions of my own people. Trust someone who knows... it's much safer to be a victim."

I thought she was going to stand there in our way and dare us to walk around her, but she floated upward, settling back into her cross-legged pose, ignoring us like the ephemeral things we were.

"Where's the door, Jim?" I asked softly. "Come on, make yourself useful."

I can't help it, the AI admitted. *That thing scared the shit out of me. I thought she died with Jindal hundreds of years ago.*

"The door?"

I... umm... to the right. It should be a hatch facing down.

To the right had less meaning than it might have when

dealing with a ship the size of an office building, but given that the thing's hull was as featureless and smooth as a heat mirage, any detail tended to stand out. I spotted the hatch from thirty meters away. At first, it appeared barely large enough for a single, unarmored human to pass through it, but as we approached closer both to the ship and the hatch, I realized my eyes were playing tricks on me. The hatch was at least five meters across, circular and recessed into the hull, hovering only three meters above us.

I stood looking up at the shadowed, circular shape while the others gathered around, either staring at it, at me, or back over at Kallista.

"What now, Jim? And don't tell me I have to say *open, sesame*."

I should be close enough to connect to the ship wirelessly. If it's still in programming mode, which it should be, since it never launched, then it shouldn't be a problem to insert a subroutine of my own programming into the ship's systems... and give you control through your neurolink.

"Any time now," I prompted, making a come-along gesture. I might have said it too loud, because Yanayev shot me a curious glance.

That only made it funnier when the hatch faded into nothing, revealing the soft glow of yellow-tinted light from inside the ship.

Get everyone close together, Jim advised. *Ten seconds.*

"Crowd in here," I told the others, motioning urgently. "Hurry."

The Force Recon Marines looked back to Campea, not saying anything but clearly hesitant to abandon their security perimeter.

"You heard him," Campea snapped at the squad. "Move it in. Double-time."

The hatch was wide enough that we didn't need to be shoulder to shoulder, yet we were anyway, probably just instinct. I wasn't sure what to expect but still wasn't completely surprised when the green glow enveloped us all and my stomach did a backflip. There was no sensation of motion, yet one second we stood on the floor below the ship, and the next we were inside.

And not just barely inside the hull, not in some utility bay as I'd expected, but standing on what looked very much like the bridge, if I recalled correctly the details of the other Predecessor ships I'd been on. A 360-degree holographic display surrounded the compartment, though through it was visible the outline of a hatch into another passage.

"Holy shit," Dickinson chanted, eyes as big as dinner plates, his face ghostly white. "Holy shit. Holy shit."

"How the hell did we get in here?" Yanayev demanded, sounding outraged at the violation of her sense of reality. She gestured at the deck. "There's no door though this. Did it like... dematerialize us?"

At least she was able to put together a coherent thought, which was more than I could say for my fellow Marines. What they were saying to each other made Dickinson's repetitive profanity seem erudite by comparison.

"We've seen their ships build furniture and arrange rooms out of thin air," I reminded Yanayev. "They have some kind of active nanotechnology using gravity fields or magnets or some such shit. The ship probably made the deck... I dunno, permeable to us, then hardened it again once we were through."

"Oh," she said, raising an eyebrow doubtfully. *"That's* all."

"What do we do in here?" Dickinson asked, apparently having regained control of his speech centers. He motioned at the holograms, which all displayed writing none of us could understand except that I recognized it as Resscharr. "I mean,

I'm an engineer's mate, sir. I barely know up from down in that new photon reactor and drive the Ressharr installed on the *Orion*. How the hell am I gonna keep *this* thing running?"

"Don't worry, Petty Officer Dickinson, I'll talk you through it."

Dickinson jumped at the voice coming from all around us, jumped again when he noticed the hulking, red-haired warrior watching him from the display screens.

"Dammit, I had enough of that shit with Dwight," he murmured.

"Follow me, Petty Officer," Jim's avatar invited, moving across the screens like he was actually walking, leading Dickinson to the concealed hatchway. The proto-Celt rolled his eyes. "Because there's nothing I love better than explaining complicated technology to primitives."

"I have a question," Yanayev said, looking around as if trying to find someone else to ask.

"And I have answers," Jim said, popping back into existence beside the woman. She frowned at the avatar.

"Didn't you just go to explain basically magic physics to Petty Officer Dickinson?"

"It's the great thing about being a computer-based intelligence, Commander," Jim replied, smiling thinly. "Multitasking is merely a matter of copying another subroutine and setting it off on its way. How may this version of me serve *you*?"

She motioned around the bridge.

"Where am I supposed to fly this thing from? A seat? Controls? Because I know maybe the Resscharr controlled the ships with their brains or some such shit, but I'm a hands-on kind of gal."

Jim waved theatrically like a stage magician, and just as I'd mentioned before, furniture grew out of the deck, pulled together as if from nothing. The truth, of course, was that they were held together with the same sort of gravity control that had kept the ship hovering above the floor the last several hundred years. Yanayev smiled at the chair and the control panel that had coalesced in front of it, nearly identical to her station on the bridge of the *Orion*, and fell into the seat with a homey familiarity, showing no concern at the ethereal nation of the setup.

Hers wasn't the only workstation that had appeared. The entire bridge had grown a garden of chairs and control panels, readouts and displays, all of them drawn straight from the regulation layout of a Fleet warship. I half-expected them to be as green as the outside of the ship, but the cool grays and whites could have been drawn straight from that same Space Fleet technical manual. Not that there was much on the display screens yet, since we were thousands of meters below the ocean and not connected to the surface.

"All the controls are the same as you're used to," Jim told Yanayev, "and they'll do the same things they did on your ships, except without the restrictions of inertia and gravity." He shook his head. "The very idea that you've managed to make it this far while having to worry about being squashed into jelly every time you give the old bird a little too much gas is incredible to me."

"She was a good ship," Yanayev told him, glaring back defiantly. "She kept us alive when we had no right to be."

"Jim," I interrupted, trying to keep the argument from taking off, "does this ship have an armory?"

The avatar eyed me sidelong, as if unwilling to give up on his debate with Yanayev, but he finally nodded.

"Fully stocked. Though I'm sure if there'd been more time during the final confrontation, it would have been stripped bare like everything else on the planet."

"Lt. Campea, why don't you go secure the armory and get me a full inventory of what we have available?"

I just told you I already know the inventory, Jim said, but had the sense and tact to do it privately in my neurolink.

I'd rather keep them busy instead of leaving a squad of Marines hanging around on the bridge with nothing to do.

All right, he acknowledged grudgingly, *maybe you're not completely incompetent.*

"Don't worry," Jim said aloud to Campea, "I'll assign one of my least-intelligent subroutines to accompany you so you won't feel threatened."

"Sir," one of the NCOs asked plaintively, "is there any way we can shoot this fucker?"

"You can't shoot a computer program, Sgt. Nilsson," Campea told him with a sigh as he followed the hologram off the bridge. "We just *wish* we could."

I sighed in relief as the last of them made their way off the bridge, then shot a look at Yanayev. I could trust her to keep her disappointment under control if I got the wrong answer to my next question.

"Give me the straight dope, Jim," I said. "What's the situation? Is this ship operational?"

"Every system checks out as complete and online," he replied. But his image shrugged. "But bear in mind, this propulsion system had very limited testing. It works in concept and on a small scale, but this ship has never left the planet."

"He's rude," Yanayev commented, "obnoxious, a know-it-all, and always full of bad news. He reminds me of my ex-husband."

"How do we get it out from under the ocean?" I asked. "Please don't tell me it involves flooding this whole place and blasting the walls off."

"We flood the entire level and blast the walls off."

"Why do I bother to ask?" I moaned.

"Cameron Alvarez."

You'd think, after all this time and all the shit I'd seen, that nothing could shock me. I certainly would have thought so. But Kallista's living-corpse face pushing through the bulkhead of the bridge, a phantom from a dead world, was enough to send me stumbling backward, cursing incoherently.

"What the fuck?" I asked when I could even manage that much clarity.

"You seek to escape your fate," Kallista said, solidifying once she'd reached this side of the bulkhead, "but your fate has come more quickly than you could imagine." Sightless eyes met mine. "The Unity has arrived."

[28]

Dark shapes moved through the depths, slowly at first and then bolting away as they caught sight of us. We were the invader in their world. Were they whales? Megalodon sharks? Aquatic reptiles from before the asteroid hit? God knew, and maybe Jim did too, but I didn't bother to ask. Other questions seemed more important.

"Can't we go any faster?" I asked, looking urgently at Yanayev.

"I'm trying to give her full power," she told me, thumping her fist against her control console, "but this is the best she'll do. It's like there's some kind of safety not letting us go any faster."

"Physics, my dear," Jim clucked. "Surely, they give your pilots physics classes during their training?"

"Shut up if you're not going to help," I snapped at him.

"She asked, I'm answering. The limit is neither the ship's structure or its drive but the ocean. We *could* leave the ocean at relativistic speeds... if you were willing to cause a chain-reaction fusion explosion that could split the crust and kill all of your friends before you reached them."

"Why can't we warn them?" Yanayev wanted to know,

though whether she was asking Jim or me, I wasn't sure. I answered before he could, knowing he wouldn't be as gentle.

"This ship has the communications technology to put a signal through kilometers of water and the crust of the planet, but nobody up there has the technology to receive it. Besides," I added bitterly, "there's nothing they could do even if we warned them."

The view from the front cameras told the story. Water boiled ahead of us from the sheer friction of our passage, lit up with a shimmering white as if it were somehow lit on fire, and still it wasn't fast enough. I was ready to tell Jim to override the safeties and take our chances with the destruction of the planet, but the fire ahead of the ship turned into a shimmering far above, through a hundred meters of ocean water... the glare of the primary star.

The surface.

Steam exploded in a halo around the nose of our ship as it shot out of the ocean surface, the exterior image a simulation, but one so detailed that even a forensics analyzer couldn't have picked it out as anything but real. It looked real as hell to me, one of those giant sea creatures we'd seen breaching, not just a few meters into the air but upward into the deep blue of the afternoon sky.

I could have stared at that image for long minutes, in disbelief and wonder, but other scenes called for my attention. Other ships, not the emerald cylinder of the Predecessors nor even the skull shapes of the Skalex, though they certainly had more in common with those than with the Resscharr. Not skulls though. These were longer, slimmer, sharp-edged like a blade. Swords, like the old Roman gladius I'd seen in museums, their points aimed at the heart of this planet and beyond, into the heart of the Cluster.

Thousands of them, though not all were coming here. Most

watched, sitting back and waiting for the inevitable, vultures in the tall trees while the lions finished off their prey. A dozen of them. It didn't seem like much until the added perspective of the long-range sensors told the real story. Each dwarfed the *Orion*, this Predecessor ship, dwarfed a Fleet cruiser or a dozen of them.

One of the sword ships could have held a thousand landers, tens of thousands of troops, hundreds of fighters... or all of them together could have contained merely one consciousness spread among all those individual forms.

I see you, Cameron Alvarez, the Unity hissed in my ear. *I've come to take yours as you have taken mine. But I won't kill you. That would be too quick. Instead, I'll take you with me as I bring death to all your worlds, to your entire species.*

I was about to order Yanayev to take us to orbit to meet the dozen sword ships there, but before the words escaped, one of those twelve blossomed, dropping the same sort of landing pods I'd seen from the Skalex, but so many more. All heading for the island.

"Get us back to the LZ," I snapped to the Helm officer. Yanayev sat frozen at the controls, staring at the doom I'd brought to this place. "Get us back to the *Orion*!"

There was no fighting these things. I knew that with all the certainty of an entire universe. Our only hope was that they didn't know what this ship could do, wouldn't be expecting us to outrun them in it.

There is no hope, Cam, Jim told me, though at least he tried to sound sad about it. *This Unity... it somehow traveled here from another galaxy in days. Nothing the Resscharr ever made could touch them.*

"Then what the hell do you suggest I do?" I asked, not caring if Yanayev heard me.

You're a religious man, Cameron. You might try praying.

If being sucked up into the Resscharr ship from a couple meters below had felt strange, being dropped from a hundred meters up defied description, except perhaps being born.

It is as natural to man to die as to be born; and to a little infant, perhaps, the one is as painful as the other. Francis Bacon had said that, and it wasn't something I would have normally remembered. If anything in my life since I was six could be called normal.

Normally, I remembered only the things I made myself recall, things that had an emotional resonance with me. But not anymore. Now, with the headcomp, with the connection to T-space, I remembered everything. Everything except my actual memories, of course. Those were an illusion, a way we thought of the filters we put over reality. The image I had of my mother dying wasn't anything like it would have seemed to a drone camera taking footage of the event—it was how it had looked to a six-year-old who'd lost his mother.

I wondered how I'd remember this day.

Stumbling, retaining the momentum I'd had when Jim had dumped me out of the grav tube, I ran up to the impromptu war council gathered in the shadow of the *Orion*. Vicky and Springfield, both in their suits, Brandano and Villanueva, both obviously chomping at the bit to be up in their birds fighting this battle, and lastly, Nance, Nagarro, and Chang. Not that I'd invited Chang, but like most of this trip, he'd crashed the party, and I didn't have time to shoo him away. Not with my suit waiting for me there, open and inviting. And if the comfort from climbing into the machine and sealing up was illusory, it was the only sort I had right now.

The Drop Trooper company had been deployed in a tight circle around the ship—tighter than I would have liked, given our numbers—and both Intercepts rested on their landing gear, weapons pointed outward. But nothing had attacked yet. The pods still fell, spiders dropping in on the wind with their web parachutes trailing behind them, and out in the trees there was movement, scuttling, shifting, always in the shadows despite the afternoon glare.

The rest of the *Orion*'s crew.

"Why aren't we sending up the Intercepts?" Brandano demanded, not waiting for me to finish suiting up.

"Because they'll kill you in a heartbeat," I told him, then closed the chest plate, sealing myself inside as I unspooled the 'face jacks. "They traveled between galaxies in days, and there are thousands of ships up there," I went on, using the neurolink to continue before my suit powered up. "There's no way to fight them. I want everyone on the ship, including the Marines. The Unity doesn't know about the ship or its drive, and there's at least a chance they won't be able to follow it the way they did the *Orion*."

Nance looked between us and the tree line, doubt heavy in his eyes and in his words.

"You really think they're going to just let us get on board that ship and leave?" He shook his head. "There're already hundreds of them down out in the woods and hundreds more coming in every minute!" He gestured up at the white dots floating in from orbit, dandelion seeds on a summer afternoon.

"They might," I told him. "More than they want you, they want me, and I'm staying behind. There's no way they let you go unless I do."

There was an uproar, as I knew there would be, and I let their objections and shouts and bellows roll off me like the surf washing over a boulder. Except for Vicky. She said nothing, as if the featureless mask of her Vigilante helmet was actually her real face. She waited until the hubbub died down before she said a word, and when she did, it was steady and reasoned and unarguable.

"He's right," she said. "Cam has to stay. And I'm staying with him." She switched to our private net for just a moment. "Don't bother trying to talk me out of it or give me an order you know I won't obey. The only way you'll get me on that ship without you is if you kill me first."

"I wasn't going to try," I assured her, though the words caught in my throat despite the truth of them. "I promised you I wouldn't go get myself killed without you. And I do have to get myself killed. I won't let them take me alive. That's what they want, but I'm not interested in being trussed up and forced to watch them exterminate humanity. I'd rather go down swinging here, with you."

"Love you too," she replied, and I knew she was smiling. I switched back to the general net.

"You have to get back to the Commonwealth and warn them the Unity are coming. The only way that happens is if they're so occupied trying to get me that they don't bother chasing after you." Which was unlikely, but it was all I had to give them. "We clear?"

"I didn't want it to go down like this, Cam." Brandano shook his head. "I wanted us to all go home together."

"I know, Chuck," I told him, wishing I could shake his hand. "But that's what being a commander is about. I knew the risks when I took the gig."

"Let me stay with you, sir," Springfield said, taking a step forward in her Vigilante, again giving in to her one weakness as a Drop Trooper, forgetting she was in the suit. "There's at least a squad that would volunteer to stay and fight a holding action with you, give the ship time to get away."

Again, I had to go against my natural inclination to say no. If I actually held out hope this would work, I would have ordered her to get everyone on board immediately. The truth was, we were all going to die, and Marines deserved the chance to die on their feet. I wouldn't order them to do it, but neither would I order them not to.

"Hurry," I told her. "Make sure everyone who wants out of here gets on that ship now."

"Aye, sir." She turned, loped off to the perimeter. Forgetting again.

"Captain Nance," I told the man, "you're in charge now." Like it or not. I motioned with my articulated claw at the Predecessor ship, hovering about twenty meters up, soundless, like a holographic projection on a billboard. "Get everyone beneath that hatchway. We'll pull them up in groups of twenty. Five seconds between. The crews with the stasis chambers and the food supplies, load them up last, and and be ready to abandon them if things get too hot. Do it now."

The man looked like he wanted to argue, not because he had any desire to stay but because it probably felt like the right thing to do. But he also had his orders, and he carried them out.

"Sorry, Chuck, Francesca," I told the pilots. "The Intercepts will have to stay here. They won't fit in the ship's hangar bay, and even if they did, we won't have time to port over fuel or spare parts."

"I'll miss her," Brandano said. "But not as much as I'll miss you two." He nodded and turned away, wiping at his eyes before he yelled at his flight crew to follow him to the pickup area.

Villanueva said nothing, just nodded and walked after him to see to her own people. Which just left Nagarro and Chang. Nagarro's sharp expression hid an accusation, but didn't hide it well.

"You wouldn't do this if there was any real chance we'd survive," she said quietly.

"No, I wouldn't," I admitted. "Do you want to die down

here, or make one last run in the coolest ship any of us has ever seen?"

The woman grinned, then offered me a salute.

"Been a pleasure serving with you, sir."

Which just left Chang. I was tempted to ignore him, to walk out and start this show going, but curiosity forced me to ask one last question.

"Why don't you head downstairs?" I asked him.

"I will," he told me, then nodded over to the sea wall.

His ship, smaller than even one of our Intercepts, slowly and carefully maneuvered through the open doorway, shadow claiming its verdant glow as it disappeared inside.

"Need to make sure I have a ride," he explained. "But I wanted to say it's been interesting knowing you. I certainly hadn't expected it, but..." Chang shrugged. "It's a noble end. One that if I'd had the chance to make many years ago, I would have traded it for the life I've led. As long as I remain, you'll be remembered."

"That's certainly a comfort," Vicky told him dryly.

"Good luck finding what you're looking for, Chang," I said.

Once he was gone, it was just the two of us, standing between the wrecked and battered remains of the lives we'd led these last few years. Out at the tree line, not a single one of the Marines had left their positions. I sighed. It wasn't unexpected.

"Come on, love," Vicky said, her suit falling into a slow, steady lope that ate up meters as she headed for the line. "One last dance."

Once more unto the breach, dear friends. Once more...

[29]

It didn't take them long.

I kept one eye on the landing of the Unity and the other monitoring the loading of the Predecessor ship. She needed a name, but since I didn't expect to be around for the christening, I figured I'd let Nance name her. Hopefully, he wouldn't do anything as sappy as calling her the CSS *Alvarez*. Getting most of the crew aboard had gone quickly, until the work crews started beaming up the supplies. I figured the delay there was getting the stuff out of the way to make room for the next load, but it all slowed to a crawl once the first pile of cargo containers and stasis chambers had gone up.

At some point between the third and fourth food shipment, the Unity troops started their advance. Not as fast as I expected, not the insectoid swarm of the Skrela or the more regimented tactical formation of the Skalex. They stomped, each motion synchronous with each other, one consciousness controlling them all. A *dance macabre* via hive mind, yet still, even with the enhanced optics of the suit, I couldn't make their shapes out, only a sense of movement.

You won't escape me, Cameron. Haven't you learned by now that there is no running from your fate?

For an alien consciousness, the Unity was one pushy, obnoxious son of a bitch. I didn't disguise my disdain for it when I replied.

Who's running? I'm standing out here in the open, waiting for your worthless ass.

Well, kind of. None of us were standing in the open, truth be told. We'd off-loaded as much heavy equipment as we'd had time for from the *Orion*'s hold while retrieving the food stores, and Vicky had instructed the cargo sleds and freight handling arms be set out at the perimeter, giving what cover they could with their solid metal and dense battery cores.

Vicky and I stood with just the upper portion of our suits exposed, taking cover behind a portable generator meant for field use. Turned off, of course, because a bunch of charged superconductor coils exploding into fragments would be suboptimal. As it was, there was a slight chance that the energy-absorbing coils could work to protect us, depending on what the Unity used for weapons.

You think you can force me to kill you? the Unity asked, its tone mocking. *I could force you to walk out in front of me now, stripped naked, and willingly watching while I slaughter the others.*

You really want to see me naked? I asked the thing, taking aim through a gap in the trees, zooming in as far as the suit would allow, trying to get a shape with the thermal cameras. For some reason, they wouldn't settle into a computer amalgamation of the sensor input, wouldn't show me what the Unity soldiers looked like.

Fuck it. I don't care what they look like. I just want to see if they can die.

I pulled the trigger. Blue balefire arced out of my energy

cannon, then from Vicky's beside me. As if it had been a cork pulled out of a dam, streams of incandescent energy whipped through the forest, exploding trees in their path like lightning strikes in a fierce thunderstorm.

Flames licked up from the ruin of the shattered woods, sending clouds of screeching birds rising from the carnage, abandoning their homes... yet the fire did nothing to illuminate the Unity, and nothing on my targeting screen gave any indication of whether or not we'd hit any of them. Through the smoke and haze and the conflagration, all I could see was the hint of movement as the troops marched steadily through the flames.

It could have been a nightmare, with an unseen and unseeable enemy always coming for me but never actually coming into view, where the tension was the real threat. Except they *did* emerge from the woods, still moving with that same, inexorable slowness. And I still couldn't see them.

"What the hell, sir?" Springfield gasped. "I can't get a target lock!"

That didn't stop the company from firing, coilgun rounds and energy beams cutting through the air, lighting up every square meter but not hitting the enemy.

"They're shielded," Vicky declared grimly.

She was right, and there was no good reason I shouldn't have been able to see it already. A *personal* shield, like the ones the Resscharr back on Decision had used, but those had been limited in power, only able to take a few hits from the Skrela plasma guns before the energy overloaded them. They'd saved a lot of us from the Skrela during the battle, but they hadn't been able to win it for us.

These... they weren't just shedding our weapons like water off a duck's back, they were blocking all thermal and electromagnetic radiation, rendering whatever was behind them invisible not just to our naked eyes but our sensors as well. Indecision gripped me for a long second, wondering how the hell we'd fight them if they could shoot at us while they stayed behind those shields...

But they *didn't*. Didn't shoot at us, just kept coming through the haze of smoke, through the fusillade that continued despite its futility. Possibilities streamed across my expanded mind, ran through the faster processing of my headcomp and came to the conclusion that they *couldn't* fire through the shields any more than we could. To strike at us, they'd have to drop their defenses.

"Hold fire," I ordered. "Everyone, hold fire. Wait until one of them shoots, then target it immediately. Do *not* fire unless the enemy you're targeting is actively firing. It's the only way we'll get past their shields."

The only failing of that tactic was that they were already two hundred meters away and showed no sign of *intending* to fire on us. Behind me, the last of the food zipped upward into the cargo hold and the loading crews rushed to join it. As if their movement had been the signal the Unity had waited for, the shields of the entire front rank of enemy dropped... and the nightmare began in earnest.

I thought I'd known fear. Fear was, as I'd said, an old friend, a constant companion since I was a boy, so casual an acquaintance that I no longer dreaded the feeling, welcoming it like the first time I'd dropped in a Vigilante, or the first time I kissed a girl. The familiarity with fear made me a decisive leader—I could see that now, with the benefit of the universal mind's outside perspective. But I'd been kidding myself. I'd never known real fear until that moment.

The things didn't look any more fierce, any more intimidating than the Skalex, certainly not as fearsome and ravening as the Skrela. Yet there was an utterly *alien* nature to these things that I hadn't seen with either of those enemies, hadn't ever seen before. There was a lack of symmetry to them, a lack of design, as if they'd been created not by a God as we imagined Him but by some demon of chaos, something at home in the outer darkness.

Legs scuttled, arms writhed, and mouths rimmed with cilia shifted and transformed with every movement, and beyond even the physical disgust the things caused, something deeper in my hind-brain recoiled at the sight of them, as if they were the embodiment of every atavistic terror humanity had ever held. I couldn't fire, couldn't give orders, couldn't even separate the frantic, panicked screams coming over my comms into anything coherent.

I just wanted to run, to join the others I saw turning tail and jetting away. The Unity troops *did* have weapons though, and once our Marines exposed themselves out from cover and made huge targets of themselves by arcing through the open air, those guns opened up. Not that the discharges were visible, not even on my suit's enhanced sensors. Something moving fast, hitting hard, and when it struck a battlesuited Marine, carrying enough energy to blow them into pieces with a flare of sun-bright white, a miniature nuclear explosion.

Men and women died and I stood there, frozen, wanting only to run, unable to act.

Cam! What the hell's wrong with you? Pull your head out of your ass and start shooting!

Jim. Whatever these things were doing to me, it hadn't affected Jim. Which meant it wasn't *real*, it was some kind of weapon, something being done *to* me rather than coming from inside. It meant I could fight it. I could fight *them*.

It was, perhaps, one of the hardest things I'd ever done to level my energy cannon at the oncoming horde of demons and press the trigger. Yet the second the blue energy blast connected, the first of the nightmare things that burst in a glow of superheated bodily fluids, the catharsis cut me loose from the bonds of terror, and fear gave way to overpowering rage.

There were so many targets, I couldn't miss, and I didn't have to stop firing, didn't have to worry about overheating for long seconds. Still holding down the trigger, I jetted not upward but forward, blasting in one direction and swinging my claw-hand in the other. Where it connected, the impact was like slamming my fist into a brick wall, but horrific faces shattered beneath the blows.

Five... ten... a dozen, dozens more falling to the actinic blasts of my gun, yet it wasn't enough. I'd distracted them, kept them from firing into the backs of my fleeing Marines, kept them from getting to Vicky, but they were surrounding me, and the Unity wasn't at all afraid to kill her own, since she was in all of them.

"Cam!" Vicky yelled, and the rent, heartbroken self-hate in the single syllable told me everything I needed to know. She understood what was happening but couldn't break free, lacking the support of an implanted AI computer.

"Get everyone onto the ship," I grunted. "Now."

This was just as well. Vicky and the others had a chance as long as the thing focused on me. I couldn't watch to see if she left with the others, couldn't even spare the attention to glance at the IFF transponder list to see who'd died. I'd stepped naked into a nest of scorpions, and only motion would keep me alive. Not forever, just long enough to let the others get away.

The jumpjets were my lord and savior, keeping me bouncing from one side of the field to the other, smashing into Unity drones as I went, my body nearly parallel to the ground. I kept the trigger depressed, hosing it in every direction, surrounded by enemies and fresh out of allies, slicing through the drones like butter. They wore no armor, neither organic or artificial, counting solely on their personal shields—and their sheer numbers. Disposable like the Skrela, and the Unity didn't mind at all disposing of them to get to me.

I'd finally gotten a good look at the weapons they carried, and the things more resembled a biological growth than a piece of technology, but whatever they fired, it wasn't an energy beam —something solid, a slug passing so close that my helmet cameras got a stop-motion single frame of it. Its edges were fuzzy, slimy even, like it had been secreted in the internal organs of one of the drones, but when it struck the ground in the midst of a cluster of three of the things, it erupted in a flash of light brighter than the noonday primary and a wash of concussion strong enough to send me tumbling off to the side.

I'd been on a rollercoaster, tight curves that kept me moving, kept me at the same level as them to keep myself from becoming a clear target, but when the shockwave from the blast hit me, my shoulder plowed into the dirt and I rolled twenty meters, bowling over ten of the drones in my path. And landing at the feet of another, its hideous face close enough that the brain-drain affect they had on humans set in again and I froze for just a moment, long enough for the muzzle of its main gun to swing down on its shoulder toward my face.

You fought bravely, the Unity admitted, *but now I have you. Deactivate your suit and come out, Cameron Alvarez. Surrender to your fate.*

She was right. There was no way out of this, and at least this way I'd still be alive. Maybe I could manage to escape and then...

Snap out of it, you stupid fuck! Jim yelled at me, and I blinked awake again.

My fingers had already wrapped around the quick-release to open my chest plate, and I yanked them away, grabbed the control rod for my right hand again, and blasted the drone standing over me with a lance of azure fire. His own blast passed just above my head and took down three ranks of drones as I hit the jets again, the shockwave hitting me from behind this time, propelling me forward.

Still alive, but...

You won't be much longer. It was Jim, but it might as well have been the Unity. One would gloat while the other was breaking the bad news to me, but the affect was the same. *The ship is loaded... you did your job.*

Not that it would matter. Once they broke atmosphere, the sword ships would be all over them and nothing we'd done out here would matter. No one back home would ever find out, and all that would survive of us would be Kyler and his family... and even they would never know that we hadn't made it home.

Why was it important to me? I pondered the question in that space of my brain that might otherwise have been working on long-term strategy, since I didn't have one other than to keep barreling through the thousands of Unity drones, firing, smashing, twisting, and turning.

Why did I care if no one knew? Not for myself. I'd been very happy, once upon a time, that I'd managed to avoid the notoriety that came with the Medal of Valor. Other people had thought I deserved it, but I was happy to pass that honor on to the dead who'd deserved it. Lt. Ackley, Scotty... they'd given their lives to save the rest of us.

Maybe that was why the thought of not getting home bothered me. People should know what we'd sacrificed, should know all the Marines and Fleet crew who'd died to accomplish the mission, to save the lives of their brothers and sisters.

The detonations of the Unity slugs had turned into a drumbeat, a concert where I'd stood way too close to the speakers, so regular that I barely noticed the blasts. Maybe that had made me complacent, or maybe it was just a matter of time until one of them hit just the wrong place. Something punched me in the gut, and I didn't need any of the flashing red and yellow warning lights to know that I'd had a burn-through. The lance of white-hot agony across my floating ribs told that story in graphic detail.

I was on my back, a turtle in the sun, helpless, waiting for some kind soul to come flip me over... but knowing that the more likely scenario was a hawk snatching me off the desert sands for a quick meal. Drones surrounded me, blocking out the glare of the primary, and I closed my eyes, waiting for the end.

Stop.

Jim? The Unity? My brain wasn't working at full capacity, and I was sure I had at least a mild concussion to go along with my third-degree burns and broken ribs and I couldn't tell one mental voice from another.

Not me, brother, Jim informed me. *Take a look up.*

That wasn't a problem, since I was lying on my back anyway, and at least the external cameras still worked... for now. Even if nothing else did.

A wizened, rotting corpse floated a hundred meters above the ground, standing between the Predecessor vessel and one of the sword ships I hadn't even noticed coming into the atmosphere. The ship was a blade poised to slice through the massive green cylinder, and only a small, long-dead Resscharr named Kallista stood in its way.

You're weak, Resscharr, the Unity taunted. *You've rotted in this place for centuries. You can't stand against me.*

Not for long, Kallista agreed. *But perhaps for long enough.*

She didn't move, didn't point, didn't so much as bobble a centimeter from her hover, but the air between us shimmered with power and the drones arrayed across the plains flattened in a fan pattern. It was as if an asteroid had impacted right on top of me and the concussion wave had spread out from there to devastate everything around it, except I laid at the center unharmed. Well, not harmed any *further*.

The sword ship fired, though whether the Unity sought to destroy Kallista or shot at the Predecessor vessel and she happened to be in the way, I wasn't sure. Either way, it didn't work. To my surprise, the giant ship fired a round not unlike the personal weapons the biological drones carried, though magnified a thousand times, a huge, glutinous mass that looked like God himself had hawked a farmer blow and should, by all rights, have come apart. It held together at hypersonic speeds by a force beyond my knowledge. Maybe the universal mind had some ideas, but I was too loopy to access it.

The thing stopped in midair only a few meters from Kallista, then turned and flew back the way it came until it hit the same sort of shield the individual Unity drones had used, the air glowing yellow in a hemisphere as the slug pressed into the field. Penetrated. The hull of the sword ship seemed smooth and adamantine, but when the projectile hit, it punched through as if the barrier had been as soft as tissue paper.

If anyone had been on the ground watching with their naked eyes, they would have been permanently blinded, their retinae burned out by the fusion flare of the detonation. My own sensors whited out for nearly a five count, and I idly wondered if the radiation would be enough to kill me. But when I could see again, I stopped worrying. Kallista had considered that, and the blast had been contained in an incandescent bubble the size of a soccer stadium, three hundred meters overhead.

Concussed, confused, and well and truly out of it, I idly wondered what she was going to do with the giant, nuclear beach ball. She was way ahead of me though. Her hand finally moved, a shooing motion, and the imprisoned starfire shot into the upper atmosphere and detonated again. Too far to see, yet I still retained an awareness of what had happened. The radiation and thermal energy had wiped out the thousands of landing pods still heading for the island.

Empty eye sockets stared down at me.

This, Kallista said, her voice gentle on my mind, *is a better fate than eternal death. Go, human, while you still can.*

I was about to ask something smart-assed, like how I was going to go anywhere with my suit a pile of junk, but a cloud passed over the sun. No, not a cloud, the Predecessor ship. Huge, blocking out the sky, with that one circular hatch hovering just above me...

It glowed green and then white, and I rose.

Farewell, Cameron Alvarez, Kallista told me as the sunlight disappeared into the dimmer interior glow of the ship's cargo hold. *May you find the peace I never did.*

[30]

"Have I ever mentioned," I asked, hands going to my aching head, "how much I hate waking up in an auto-doc?"

"Once or twice," Vicky replied, shoving a uniform at me. I stared at it for a moment, bemused, before accepting it.

"Where did you get this?" I wondered, swinging my legs out of the clear, transplas cylinder, still damp from the remains of the biotic fluid. "I don't remember them getting our personal gear out of the *Orion*." I shrugged and pulled on the pants, not feeling self-consciousness at all, despite Hallonen and her crew wandering around the newly constructed medical bay, working on getting stasis chambers installed. Fresh bulkheads, it turned out, were as easy for the ship to manufacture as furniture. "Then again, I might have been distracted."

"No personal effects," she agreed. "But some pragmatic chief petty officer thought we might need a fabricator and a few containers of raw materials. Thank God, because what you *were* wearing was pretty much fucked."

Vicky had held it together so far, playing everything casual, but the cracks were there for someone who knew where to look.

I said nothing, giving her time. She'd reach it on her own without me pushing.

She crossed her arms, uncrossed them, staring at the bare gray decking. A muscle twitched in her cheek.

"I abandoned you, Cam," she whispered, her shoulders shaking as she fought back a sob. "I left you out there to die."

There it was. I finished fastening my shirt and folded her into my arms, allowing the tears to break loose. I understood. I would have done the same thing.

"There was nothing you could have done," I told her, checking to see if any of the medical staff was paying attention. If they were, they hid it well. "The fear hit me too. The only reason I didn't run right behind you was Jim. He talked me down." I chuckled softly. "If you want, I'll check and see if Doc Hallonen can install your very own headcomp."

"Stop," she snapped, smacking me on the arm. "Stop trying to be funny. There's no excuse for what I did."

I pulled away and put my forehead against hers, eye to eye.

"Sure there is. The Unity was fucking with our minds. Mine too. There's no reason for you to think you could resist it when none of us could." I kissed her before holding her out at arm's length, looking her up and down. "Did you get hurt?"

She shook her head, but the tears hadn't gone away.

"We lost another nine Marines," she said. "All of them Vergai." Vicky shook her head. "I don't know how much longer I can take this. We've lost so many... after the war, I didn't think it could hit me like this, but it does."

"If it didn't, you wouldn't be human." I nodded toward the hatch. I guess it was still a hatch, even though it was shaped different than the ones I was used to. "Let's go visit the bridge. I still haven't seen how this thing works."

The passageways were crowded, something I wouldn't have expected if we'd been back on the *Orion*. There, people tended to stick to their quarters except at mealtimes or when they were heading to the gym. I guess no one had any personal items in their quarters anymore, and given what had happened, everyone probably felt a little lost. Half of them stared at the deck as they walked, and the ones who did bother to look up offered nothing but a nod in return. Their eyes held no anger or resentment that I could see... only confusion.

Except Brandano. The older man grinned effusively when he saw the two of us approaching and pulled me into a hug. A couple years ago, I'd thought of the pilot as a stiff, uptight asshole, and now he pounded my back, laughing like we'd been best friends our whole lives.

"Thank God you made it, Cam," he told me, shaking his head. "I really did *not* want to be the one to take charge of this shitshow."

"I always knew you had my best interests at heart, Chuck," I said. "We were just heading to the bridge. Wanna come along?"

"I been there," he said, then shrugged. "But what the hell? It's not as if there's much else to do on this crate except play with our 'links. I never thought I'd say it, but I can't wait until they get the damned stasis chambers hooked up so I can sleep through this damned trip." Brandano motioned at the opening at the end of the passage. "At least the elevator's entertaining."

It was that, for anyone who enjoyed stepping off into darkness with no guarantee that it wouldn't be the last step they took. I still wasn't sure how the thing knew where we wanted to go, but it deposited us on the correct level.

It knows because it's controlled by an artificial intelligence, Jim told me, *not an artificial* stupidity. *And since this one is controlled by me now, it's particularly intelligent.*

Good to know you're still with me, I said, the corner of my mouth quirking up. *I thought maybe you got scared off by all the mean aliens.*

Very funny. Let's just say, after meeting the Unity, I'm feeling a bit more forgiving about the whole killing-off-the-Skalex thing.

The bridge looked different than the last time I'd seen it, and not just because it was full of Fleet crewmembers. The one thing the AI had left off before was the command position—my seat. It sat behind Nance's captain's chair, slightly higher to give me a view of everything. Not that I needed it with the holographic screens surrounding the entire compartment.

And what a view those screens showed us. I was used to the nothingness of Transition Space, blank screens filled with simulations of our course. This was... different. It might have been a computer simulation, particularly given the sophistication of the computers we were dealing with, but instincts told me it wasn't. It was space—*real* space, not some other dimension like T-space. Except for the fact that the stars were gathered into a ball of white fire at the front and rear of the ship.

Every now and then, one or two would break free of the mass in front and streak backward to its opposite side. I wasn't a physicist, but thanks to the universal mind, I knew exactly what I was looking at. Something no human had ever seen, not in the history of the species... what it looked like to go through real-space faster than light. *Much* faster than light.

"It's mesmerizing, isn't it?" Nance asked, smiling softly. He'd recovered well from the loss of the *Orion*, though taking the captain's chair of a ship like this had probably helped. "I could sit here and watch it for hours."

"He *has* been," Yanayev added. She nodded to me. "Glad to see you up and around."

"Someone catch me up," I said. "Where are we? And what's the situation?"

"We've traveled a few light-years since we left Waterline," Yanayev supplied.

"Did we see the Unity follow?" I glanced back and forth between the screens. "Do the sensors even pick their ships up?"

"They do," Wojtera confirmed. "And I haven't seen any sign of them since we left the system."

"They were still engaged with Kallista when we broke orbit," Yanayev added. "She was... in orbit." The Helm officer shuddered as if a chill had gone through her. "All those ships came after her... hundreds of them. And she went straight at them. Why would she do that for us?"

"She'd been there for centuries, alone," I said. "Living in the ruins of her failure. She wanted to die." I tilted my head in a shrug. "And I think... she wanted me to get away because it felt to her like she had a do-over." I shook it off. "When are we getting the stasis chambers installed?"

"Doc Halonen says another two days, more or less," Nance reported, leaning back in his chair and sighing. "I think I might skip it this time. I know it's safe, but... I guess I'd feel better if I were in the chair if we run into anything out here." He eyed me sidelong. "*Are* we going to run into anything, Cam? We've lost those... Unity things, right?"

I was about to tell him I didn't know... but I did. I saw the thing's face in my mind, pushing out the bridge, pushing out Vicky and the others, even that hypnotic view of space. It was the same nightmare visage as the drones, except the entire thing seemed to writhe, constantly in motion, and I realized that was because the face was made up of billions of individual drones, and billions of others, queens laying eggs, males fertilizing them...no. Not billions, but *hundreds* of billions.

You think you've escaped, it said, *but you never will. I know where you're going, and if it takes months or years or decades, I'll follow.*

And then it was gone, and in a blink I was back on the

bridge, catching my balance against the back of Nance's chair. He frowned.

"You okay? Maybe they let you out of the auto-doc too soon."

"I'll be fine," I assured him, though I still saw doubt in Vicky's eyes. "Maybe I should stay awake too."

Not because of the fear of what was in our way. I didn't want to sleep because I knew what would be waiting for me in my dreams.

Drop Trooper will return in ***KILL CHAIN!***

FROM THE PUBLISHER

Thank you for reading *Down Range*, book fifteen in Drop Trooper.

We hope you enjoyed it as much as we enjoyed bringing it to you. We just wanted to take a moment to encourage you to review the book on Amazon and Goodreads. Every review helps further the author's reach and, ultimately, helps them continue writing fantastic books for us all to enjoy.

If you liked this book, check out the rest of our catalogue at www.aethonbooks.com. To sign up to receive a FREE collection from some of our best authors as well as updates regarding all new releases, visit www.aethonbooks.com/sign-up.

JOIN THE STREET TEAM! Get advanced copies of all our books, plus other free stuff and help us put out hit after hit.

SEARCH ON FACEBOOK:
AETHON STREET TEAM

The Space Hunter series may have come to an end, but there are still plenty of more books in the Drop Trooper Universe!

**The Drop Trooper Universe:
(chronological reading order)**

THE HOLY WAR
Genesis
Judgement Day
Revelation
Armageddon

THE PIRATE WAR (with Ralph Kern)
Insurgency
Infiltration
Isolation

DROP TROOPER
Contact Front
Kinetic Strike
Danger Close
Direct Fire
Home Front
Fire Base
Shock Action
Release Point
Kill Box
Drop Zone
Tango Down
Blue Force
Weapons Free
Collateral Effects
Down Range
Kill Chain

BIRTHRIGHT
Glory Boy
Birthright
Northwest Passage
Enemy of my Enemy

RECON
Recon
The Hunter
The Mercenary
The Operative

THE ACHERON
The Acheron
Prodigal
Hybrid
Exile

SPACE HUNTER WAR (with Pacey Holden)
Pirate Bounty
Corporate Bounty
Cultist Bounty

Smuggler's Bounty
Double-Cross Bounty
Terminal Bounty

THE PSI WAR
Homecoming
Conflagration
Imperium

You may also like:

Find them, kill them, or die trying.

When the Solus Hegemony's profit margins are threatened, expendable soldiers are called in to foot the bill—one bloody conquest at a time.

Noah Rivers is one such soldier. Raised from birth with a single objective; obtain eternal glory through death in service to the galaxy's most notorious corporate empire.

Rifle in hand, Noah arrives on the distant world of Kilmori ready to fulfill his ultimate purpose, but not even the Solus could have predicted what lay hidden in the sands of the harsh, desolate, alien world.

This baptism by fire changes everything Noah thinks he knows about the galaxy, and himself. To snatch victory from this devastating new calamity will require blood, sweat, tears... and a brutal edge.

The Kilmori War begins.

Don't miss the start of this action-packed Military Sci-Fi Series from author Pacey Holden. It's

perfect for fans of Rick Partlow, Joshua Dalzelle, and Marko Kloos.

Get Calamity's Edge Now!

ABOUT RICK PARTLOW

RICK PARTLOW is that rarest of species, a native Floridian. Born in Tampa, he attended Florida Southern College and graduated with a degree in History and a commission in the US Army as an Infantry officer.

His lifelong love of science fiction began with Have Space Suit---Will Travel and the other Heinlein juveniles and traveled through Clifford Simak, Asimov, Clarke and on to William Gibson, Walter Jon Williams and Peter F Hamilton. And somewhere, submerged in the worlds of others, Rick began to create his own worlds.

He has written a ton of books in many different series, and his short stories have been included in seven different anthologies.

He currently lives in central Florida with his wife, two children and a willful mutt of a dog. Besides writing and reading science fiction and fantasy, he enjoys outdoor photography, hiking and camping.

www.rickpartlow.com

Printed in Dunstable, United Kingdom